SILENCED

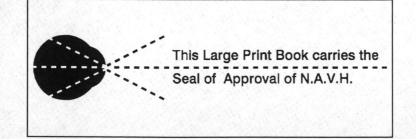

This Large Print Book carries the
Seal of Approval of N.A.V.H.

SILENCED

KIA DUPREE

THORNDIKE PRESS
A part of Gale, Cengage Learning

GALE
CENGAGE Learning·

Detroit • New York • San Francisco • New Haven, Conn • Waterville, Maine • London

GALE
CENGAGE Learning·

Thorndike Press® Large Print African-American.
The text of this Large Print edition is unabridged.
Other aspects of the book may vary from the original edition.
Set in 16 pt. Plantin.

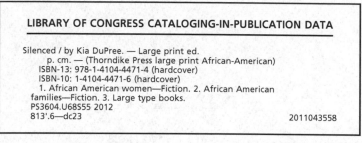
LIBRARY OF CONGRESS CATALOGING-IN-PUBLICATION DATA

Silenced / by Kia DuPree. — Large print ed.
    p. cm. — (Thorndike Press large print African-American)
    ISBN-13: 978-1-4104-4471-4 (hardcover)
    ISBN-10: 1-4104-4471-6 (hardcover)
    1. African American women—Fiction. 2. African American families—Fiction. 3. Large type books.
PS3604.U68S55 2012
813'.6—dc23   2011043558

Published in 2012 by arrangement with Grand Central Publishing, a division of Hachette Book Group, Inc.

Printed in Mexico
1 2 3 4 5 6 7 16 15 14 13 12

Dedicated to my mother,
Cynthia D. Dawkins,
for all the tough choices
you had to make in life.

NOTE TO READERS

I heard the many voices of my old neighbors in my head while I wrote this book: Tiffany Tucker's mother, Ms. Penny (rest in peace), Ms. Linda, Ms. Barbara, Ms. Anne, Ms. Brown, Ms. Lil, Yvette (rest in peace), and Sevette, and all the other women from Jeffrey Terrace on Elvans Road, who watched over me and my brothers and sister when we were growing up in Southeast. I can't forget about all the neighborhoods I lived in that shared similar stories in Washington, D.C., like on Minnesota Avenue, Georgia Avenue, Fairmont Street, Ninth Street, First Street, Abbey Place, and yes, even Sursum Corda. While doing research on this book, I learned that the term *Sursum Corda* is Latin for "Lift Up Your Hearts (to God)." I wondered if I had known that definition when I lived there, would it have mattered as much as it does to me now.

Though many people are happy seeing the

Cordas go down, families are now faced with the sad reality that they must separate or head down a new path. For some families this is good, for others a travesty. Because it's happening all over the country in poor neighborhood after poor neighborhood, I hope these sudden shifts don't leave an everlasting effect on the lives of the people and the families who must leave or the cities that these diverse groups of people are leaving behind. Thank you, D.C., for filling my heart with this story. Whenever I'm away, my heart aches.

Thank you Wilfrance, Sherry, Nikki, Antwan, Jonathan, Omar, Jamar, Grandma Albertha, DeDe, Michelle Joppy, Janai, Darlene Backstrom and Irving (for all your love and support and for saying yes, when everybody else said no), Vickie Jones, Michelle Durham, Dionne (for those last-minute critical feedback points), Aunt Darlene and Aunt Angel Michelle. Aisha, Yani, Kenji, Michael, Timmy, and the rest of the family. Laurie Ligon and Yolonda Body (for helping me keep my sanity and teaching me how to juggle while standing on one leg with one arm behind my back). My teaching colleagues who also happen to be surrogate parents to D.C. children. Thank you,

Mommy and Daddy; my husband, Donnell; and my son Izaiah (who made me type with one hand because I just had to hold him or else). The Duprees, Joppys, Williams, and my Hampton family and friends (you know who you are and what you mean to me).

Extra-special thanks to my editor Karen Thomas and Latoya C. Smith for the brutally frank conversations I needed to get this baby where it needed to be. My agent Victoria Sanders, Benee Knauer, Chris Kepner, Nick Smalls (the ultimate), and the entire Grand Central Publishing team.

And last but not least, rest in peace Jahkema Princess Hansen.

I simply stood still — in the midst of the riot of sound.

— Marguerite Johnson (Maya Angelou),
I Know Why the Caged Bird Sings

PART I

CHAPTER 1
TINKA

I couldn't sleep. Mommy's voice kept growing louder and louder the tighter I closed my eyes. How she think I was goin' sleep as loud as she was talking? I kicked the covers off me, climbed out the bed, and stomped to the kitchen. Mommy had a little glass on the table and a half-empty bottle of Pepsi.

"Hold on," I heard her say. Then she turned to look at me. "What you want?"

"Some water. I'm thirsty."

Her eyes rolled up to the sky, then she plucked cigarette ashes in the ashtray. "Tinka, hurry up fix your water and carry your tail back to bed. Shelia . . . I swear, this child."

I poured a tall glass of water and sipped real slow. Mommy laughed at whatever Ms. Shelia said and then she said, "I know. I know."

I swallowed slower like a fish would and leaned against the sink.

15

"The pay looks real good though, but I just can't tell if they liked me . . . I should hear from them by Friday . . . yeah . . . wait a minute, this little girl think she so goddamn slick! Finish your water and get your butt in the bed. Right. Now."

I took a long gulp, put the cup in the sink, and then ran to my room. Mommy stayed in the kitchen for a long time talking loud, but I ain't really hear nothing she said. I thought I was goin' find out why we was getting put out. Maybe she was goin' talk about why she stopped goin' to work, too. But she didn't. I laid there staring at the clock until I fell asleep.

I woke up again. This time cuz of Mommy's snoring. She only sounded like a lawn mower when she was drinking. Seems like that was all the time now. I threw the hot covers off of me and went to use the bathroom. Marquan was closing the front door so slow it ain't make no noise when I walked down the hallway. He looked shocked when he saw me standing there.

"You still up?" he whispered.

"Where you was at?" I asked. My legs was shaking because I had to pee so bad.

"Don't worry about it. Go back to your room."

16

"I gotta pee."

"Well, do it and go back to sleep," he said with some type of attitude.

I sucked my teeth and ran to the bathroom.

The next morning when we was eating breakfast, Marquan dropped a bunch of dirty crumpled bills on the table, before he opened the refrigerator. Mommy sipped her coffee. "Where the hell this come from?" she asked. Her eyes got smaller and she pinched her face up. Whenever she ain't believe somebody, just like when she asked me if I brushed my teeth before bed, her eyes got like that. A lot of people said me and Mommy looked alike except she was light skin and had light eyes. I couldn't really see it. Mommy told me I looked like my father. I knew we was the same brown color because I seen two pictures of him when they was at some club. He was too far away in the pictures for me to really see his face. Mommy never talked about him and the times I asked, she just said they lost touch. I ain't really know what that mean, but I ain't think Mommy knew what it meant either.

"Oh, so you grown now?" she asked, standing up from the table. Marquan ain't say nothing. He just kept looking in the refrigerator. She got all close to his face, like she could smell his breath.

"You don't have to answer *me* when I ask you questions, Marquan?!" she snapped at him.

"I found it," he said. I knew he ain't care what Mommy thought about it by the way his shoulders went all high up by his neck. My mouth fell open when he walked out the kitchen. Just then Mommy flung her cup of coffee, smashing it against the wall. It happened so fast, me and Taevon jumped. But Marquan stared at Mommy like she was crazy and then he shook his head before he walked out the front door. A brown wet stain dripped to the floor while Mommy rubbed her hands on her pajama pants. I watched her pick the money up without even counting it. When Taevon looked at me, I looked down at my oatmeal. We never seen Mommy so mad at our brother before.

We knew she was worried about a lot of stuff. Our raggedy car was gone. It hardly worked anyway. Mommy couldn't drive it after rainy days, the brakes was bad, and she said it needed some kind of water pump. But at least we had a car. Well, that was before she up and sold it to a man with a nappy beard that lived on Neal Street.

18

Marquan told me and Taevon about the eviction note that was on the door and how Mommy acted like it ain't mean nothing, even though it meant we had to get out. But *go where?* Maybe we could move with Aunt Renee.

Mommy lit up a cigarette and walked to the living room window.

What was happening to us?

Marquan finally came back in the house when Mommy was cornrowing my hair. We was sitting in the living room watching *The Parkers*. Taevon was playing on the floor with a baby turtle he found in our neighbor's backyard. One of the feet looked burned or something. Taevon kept rubbing Vaseline on it, but Mommy said it wasn't goin' to help.

"Keep on," Mommy said when Marquan walked in the room. "You gonna end up just like your father. Locked the hell up!"

"See, Ma, why you gotta say that?" Taevon whined. "You wishing him bad luck."

"Bad luck? Psst." Mommy sucked her teeth and finished the cornrow. "Ain't nobody stupid in this house. People get locked up for the type of stuff your brother out there calling himself doing. What? You selling drugs now, Marquan? You grown now, huh? You can do what you want to? I guess you think you doing something big. When they catch your ass, remember we had this conversation. Marquan's *choosing* to be stupid. Just like his stupid-ass father."

Marquan dropped more dirty bills on the coffee table, then said, "But you still taking the money, ain't you?"

He went to his room and slammed the door.

Mommy yelled, "Slam another goddamn door in my house and see what happen! Sit up, Tinka."

I scooted up and watched her walk to the kitchen. She dug in the bottom cabinet. Taevon got up from his knees and followed Marquan.

"You do your homework yet?" she asked me.

I nodded.

"Good," she said before taking a sip from whatever she pulled out.

Marquan's daddy Mark was in jail in Colorado. Me or Taevon ain't never even meet him before. I think he been locked up ever since Marquan was little. He still sends Mommy letters, but I don't think he never getting out. That's what Taevon told me. Marquan's daddy used to work for some big-time drug dealer named Rayful. Taevon said Rayful was one of the FBI's most wanted or something. He had his whole family working for him, even his mother, and they all got locked up. The way Mommy was bringing up Mark and comparing Marquan, I hoped that wasn't goin' happen to us one day.

When me and Taevon turned the corner on Holbrook Street, we saw a whole bunch of swollen, plastic bags filled with our shoes, coats, and clothes — some still on hangers — sitting on the sidewalk like trash in front of our building. Two big boxes spilling over with more clothes leaned up against our old green chair that Grandma left us before she died. Some bags sat on the worn-out wooden futon Mommy found outside that she made Marquan and Taevon drag in the house late one night. Broken glass from picture frames and dishes was sprinkled around like party specks.

"Man, this some bullshit," Taevon said, as he stood in front of our stuff.

Mommy's mattress — with all the stains and bent springs poking through — was the only bed out there, standing up against a tree. I couldn't help but wonder where the other beds was, especially my princess

21

dresser set. I loved it, even though the whole thing was old. Mommy got it after one of her bosses died, and his daughter told her she could have it if somebody came to pick it up. Two chairs that went with the glass dining room table was still there, but I ain't see no sign of the table or the other two chairs. I heard Talia and Celeste laughing when they walked passed us. My cheeks felt wet, so I wiped my face. Marquan's and Taevon's baby pictures sat on top of a box and a old picture of my daddy hugging Mommy was crumpled up on top of the cracked nightstand. Mommy's GED certificate from Job Corps was upside down on the ground, wet and yellowy, like a dog peed on it. The white puffy insides from my teddy bears was everywhere. My favorite green dress was ripped and wrapped halfway around the fire hydrant. My favorite book, *Danitra Brown Leaves Town,* had a dirty footprint on the front. All of our stuff looked like trash, scattered and picked over.

"Man, come on. Stop crying," Taevon said, snatching my hand.

We walked to the pay phone on Florida Avenue. He tried to call his father Teddy and his grandmother, but got no answer. Then he tried to call Aunt Renee, but she ain't answer either.

22

"Come on, Tinka. Mommy should be back soon," he said. We walked back to our apartment building on Holbrook Street and sat on the steps.

We sat for a little while ignoring people staring at us, the fingers that pointed from across the street, and the cars driving slow, until we saw Marquan riding up on his bike, smoking a cigarette. *When did he start smoking?*

Marquan shook his head like he knew this was gonna happen. "Ma ain't nowhere to be found, is she?"

Taevon shook his head. Marquan shook his head, too. He was real mad.

"Y'all hungry?"

I nodded.

"Here," he said, giving Taevon a ten-dollar bill. "Go get you some chips or something from the store."

We walked down to the corner store on Florida Avenue. By the time we got back to our building, Mommy was there picking through the pile in one of her good suits. She must've had another interview today. She was shaking her head and cursing when we got closer. As soon as she saw us staring at her, she took a deep breath, and then she snapped, "Taevon, watch our stuff and make sure don't nobody take nothing! You hear

23

me? This is *our* stuff, and we ain't giving it away. It all better be here when we get back, you hear me?!"

He nodded, and then she grabbed my hand. We headed to the pay phone on Florida Avenue again. Mommy's hands shook a little when she dialed the numbers. She called Aunt Renee first, then Ms. Shelia, who answered the phone right away. I could tell Mommy felt a whole lot better when she hung up.

"Van on his way to get us," she said aloud.

We waited for Ms. Shelia's boyfriend to come with his company truck. Marquan came over to help us load up, but he was so mad with Mommy about what happened that he ain't ride with us over Ms. Shelia's.

"Oh, you really grown now, huh?" she said, slamming the door. "Don't think this make you a man!"

I watched Marquan ride his bike up the street before we pulled off. Taevon made me turn around in my seat, then I wiped my face and looked out the front window. I ain't know why I was crying. I wanted to be a big girl for Mommy, but I couldn't help the tears that kept falling.

CHAPTER 2
NICOLA

"Thank you so much, girl." I gave Shelia the tightest hug I could without breaking down. My whole life was stuffed in the back of her boyfriend's truck. My whole world flipped upside down. Never in my dreams did I ever think I'd be standing in her doorway, looking for a place to stay.

"What was I supposed to do? Let y'all stay in the street?" Shelia said. "Uh-uh. Girl, get in here and make yourself at home."

As soon as Shelia said it, I felt a weight like no other rise off my shoulders. But what am I gonna do now? She barely got enough space for her five kids, let alone me. How can she squeeze me and mine up in here?

"I see your mind working already, Cola. Chill out. Them boys gon' bring all your stuff in here. My kids can double up. You can sleep in Duane's room. He got his own room since he the oldest. Him and Marquan the same age, fourteen, right?"

I nodded. But how am I gon' put some-body out of their own room just so I can come in and take over?

"Girl, don't you even think about it. I'm the only person who pay rent up in here. Duane gon' be just fine sharing a room with Sammy. And then, let's see, Taevon can sleep in Raynard and Antonio's room. They all about the same age. They should be okay. He's twelve, right?"

I nodded again.

"Tinka might want to sleep in Krystal's room, what you think?"

"That's a good idea, because I need a minute to think. She's such a know-it-all. I need for her not to be asking me a hundred and twelve questions for a change."

Shelia laughed. "I know, and Krystal ain't no different. Let them have each other."

I hope she knew I wasn't gonna be here long. I don't know, maybe if my sister Renee gave me a month to get back on my feet.

"Stop worrying, Cola. Everything gon' be all right."

"Maybe Renee will let us live out Bowie with her, what you think?"

"Renee? Not the same Renee I know. You know and I know that ain't gonna happen."

Shelia was right. Even though I hated to admit it, my own sister ain't have my back when it came to shit like this. And her stuck-up-ass husband Matt ain't going for that, either.

"Girl, just take one day at a time. You ain't gonna be here forever. I know you," she said, smiling.

I hoped she was right.

After Van brought my last bag upstairs, I stared at how much crap we had. Every inch that I had nothing to do with packing was piled in here. We had to leave all the furniture on Holbrook Street. Wasn't nowhere to put it. I shook my head when I looked at the piles of garbage bags. Where was our important papers? I opened the one bag sitting next to me and pulled out shirts still on hangers. I never thought this would be me.

My own son think he don't need me no more. Think he can do better without me. Think he grown enough to make his own decisions, live wherever he wants to, sell drugs or do whatever he call himself doing. After all I done did for that boy. All the sacrifices I made so he could have when his father ain't have no way to make sure he had. I can't believe him.

I rubbed the back of my neck, trying to erase all the tight knots. As pissed as I was with him, I couldn't help wondering where my baby was gonna sleep tonight.

I stayed asleep for a long time. I really ain't want to get up. This wasn't my house, my halls, my steps, or my pictures on the walls. Now I had to slap a smile on my face when wasn't nothing in the world worth smiling about and act like everything was gonna fix itself somehow. But the truth was, I didn't even know where to start. I spent my last unemployment check two weeks ago and been living off of favors and whatever else I could scrape up. Now I had nothing. Not even a pot to piss in, like Ma used to say.

Shelia was burning the mess out of somebody's hair downstairs in the kitchen. That's how she made her ends meet between them weak government checks she always complained about. Van wasn't supposed to be living here either, but he was and his income helped her out, too.

"How you feeling, girl?" she asked when I walked in the kitchen. She was straightening an older lady's kinky gray hair.

"I'm all right."

"This Ms. David. She lives right across the street."

"How you doing?" I asked.

"Good, and you?" she said.

Shelia mouthed the word *nosy* as she combed Ms. David's hair.

I shook my head and looked the other way.

"Mommy, I'm not going to school today?" Tinka asked, walking into the kitchen.

"Not today."

"Tomorrow?" Tinka asked.

"We'll see."

"That child need to be in school," Ms. David cut in.

My neck jerked back. "Excuse me?"

Shelia shook her head, telling me not to bother, but this woman ain't know a thing about me or my life. Who she think she was telling me what to do with my child?

"She don't look sick to me," Ms. David said.

"Ms. David?!" Shelia said.

"What? The child don't look sick. She need to be in school."

With every word that fell out her mouth, my mouth only opened wider. *Who the hell this old lady think she's talking to?* "Don't you tell me about my child! I don't know you and you don't know me. And you better mind your goddamn business before you get to know me!" I shouted.

"Ain't no need for that sorta language. I seen you move in last night. What?" she said, looking me over from head to toe.

29

"Don't look so surprised. Ain't no secrets 'round here. Don't you know where you at?"

I rolled my eyes. Of course, I knew where I was at. "Everybody 'round here as nosy as you?" I snapped.

Ms. David opened her mouth, like I hurt her feelings, but that was just for show. She seemed as cold as ice. I could tell by how she dressed that she ain't have no life. Plaid skirt down to her ankles, a mock turtleneck shirt. I don't care how old she was, she better mind her damn business. Her life was probably hating on everybody else's.

"Tinka, go to Krystal's room. It smell like mothballs in here."

CHAPTER 3
TINKA

My new neighborhood looked funny. It was one long street that wrapped around like the letter U. Tan cement houses smashed up together. Some had signs on the side that said Property of the U.S. Government and Sursum Corda on it. Cars could only go one way around the street. It ain't seem like nobody really drove through without stopping unless they was lost and made a wrong turn off of M Street or something.

Sursum Corda seemed like my old neighborhood in Trinidad sometimes. People never went to sleep at night. The police was there all the time and everybody knew each other. A lot of them was even related. Aunts and cousins lived next door and grandmas lived across the street. The houses had backyards with big sandy dirt patches, and some ain't have no grass at all. Clean clothes dangled from one line to the other. A pissy-smelling alley split the neighborhood up from other houses and towering apartment buildings. People used the alley to cut through Sibley Plaza, Tyler House, and Temple Courts all the time. Taevon seemed to like our new neighborhood. He hung outside with Ms. Shelia's boys almost every night. Mommy ain't even stop him. She seemed like she was in another world. Drinking, chain-smoking, sleeping even when the sun was out, hiding in Duane's room with the door shut.

Ain't no wonder why she ain't seem like she noticed stuff happening all around her, like how late Taevon came in the house at night, or that me and Krystal couldn't stand each other. Mommy acted like she ain't want nobody around her. She got an attitude every time I asked her a question. That's why I ain't tell her I saw a scale and a sealer machine underneath Raynard's bed where Taevon was sleeping when I was looking for lotion. It was just like the kind we saw on *America's Most Wanted,* but I ain't say nothing to nobody about it. I ain't even ask Taevon if he seen it.

Marquan waited outside my school sitting on his bike, looking brand-new. Everything about him seemed clean and fresh. He had a low haircut, new clothes, fresh Jordans, and everything. Him and Taevon was the same light color as Mommy, except Marquan had tiny freckles under his eyes and across his nose, just like the ones I seen in his father's pictures. Taevon looked like Teddy, except he had Mommy's light brown hair. I ain't look nothing like them. Aunt Renee always said I was tall for my age and that I was gonna be tall like my father was, but I wasn't the tallest girl in my class. Sometimes, I felt like I wasn't related to them, because my skin was so different. At least we all had the same short nose. Aunt Renee said my eyes told a story, because they was deep and dark. She said people would kill to have eyes like me, but that's Aunt Renee always blowing stuff up.

I was so happy to see Marquan, I gave him a hug and showed him the star sticker my teacher gave me for getting 100 percent on my spelling test.

"One hundred?!" he asked.

I smiled.

"I'm not surprised. You always reading," he said, smiling. "Keep it up, Tinka Bell."

He gave me back the paper, and then I stuffed it inside my book bag so I could show Mommy later.

"You miss me living with y'all?"

I nodded. "You gonna come stay with us?"

He shook his head. "No, not yet."

"Why not?"

"I just can't right now." He walked beside me while he held his bike.

"Who you stay with?"

"Ced."

"Oh?" I knew him and Ced was friends, but I ain't know he was living with him. I felt jealous. This was the longest we ever been apart in my whole life. "I don't like it over here."

"Things gon' get better soon," he said in a way that made me feel like he wasn't really sure. "Taevon looking out for you, ain't he?"

I nodded.

"Good. How Ma doing?"

"Okay, I think. She let Krystal say whatever she want to me, though. She always trying to start fights."

Marquan twisted his face up. "She do?"

"Mm-hmm."

"Don't take no shit, Tinka. You better hit Krystal if she try to hit you! You hear me?!"

I bit my lip.

"Let me see you make a fist."

I laughed and walked ahead of him, moving fast.

"Let me see, Tinka," he said, pulling my sleeve.

"No!" I said, laughing more.

"I'm not letting you go until you do," he

34

said, laughing and tickling one of my under-arms.

"Okay, okay!" I cracked up, then I squeezed my fingers tight together and curled them into a knot.

"That's right," he said, nodding his head up and down. "And you better not be scared to steal Krystal in her face if she try to hit you. I'm not playing, either."

"Okay," I said, smiling. I missed Marquan so much. He always made me laugh when I felt bad. He gave me some money and his new cell phone number before he walked me to the corner.

"Go 'head. Go straight home. I'ma watch you before I leave."

"Okay, bye," I said, waving. I walked up the street and then looked over my shoulder when I got to the crosswalk. Marquan was still there. I waved bye again and then watched him pedal his bike around the corner.

CHAPTER 4
NICOLA

Shelia got the magic touch. She knew exactly what to do to make me feel brand-new. I *absolutely* loved my hair. The honey-blond color made me feel so much better. It seemed to match my light skin color even more than the natural light brown. Every time I saw my face in the mirror, I felt like the sun was shining in, that's how much I loved it. Taevon kept saying I looked like Biggie's wife, Faith, but I didn't know about all that.

"You ain't gotta look all broke down when you go up there. Forget that," Shelia said, retouching my hair with a few strokes of her big-tooth comb. She was a bit thick, and been self-conscious about her weight ever since I've known her, but she had deep dimples, a near perfect smile, and she always kept her hair hooked up. "You'll be as good as you feel."

Shelia had a way about her that made me

think she knew what she was talking about. I had never filed for public assistance before. Mark took care of me in the beginning, then Teddy for a little while, before I got tired of his cheating, trifling ass and went to Job Corps to get my office skills certificate. I got a job working for the Department of Transportation for a couple years, and then I got a better job working for the Department of Public Works. But this wasn't nothing new for Shelia. She had five kids and three baby fathers, not ne'r one of them took care of their kids, so she needed the help. I guess I could've used food stamps a long time ago, especially after Tinka's father, Cornell, disappeared off the map. Teddy acted like he ain't want nothing to do with Taevon since me and Tinka's father got together. Like it was Taevon's fault that me and Teddy ain't work out. When the truth was, Teddy wanted to charm his way in between every pair of closed legs from Georgia Avenue to the Anacostia River. The minute Teddy found out me and Cornell wasn't together no more, I had to beg his ass to give me a couple dollars every now and then for Taevon.

"Let me grab my bag so we can go."

I nodded and waited in the living room.

My nerves was getting the best of me. My stomach felt tight and knotted up. How embarrassing was it gonna be for me to ask these strange people for help?

A few minutes later, me and Shelia was heading down North Capitol Street to catch the bus to the Department of Human Services Building. The minute we walked in the door, I felt like I ain't belong. It smelled musty, and like disinfectant was mixed with stale air. We was screened by security just to get inside to the room with gray linoleum tiles and two dozen blue chairs filled with people waiting. I stared at faces that looked depressed, worried, and tired. Almost like they expected bad news or like they just heard it. The three small kids playing with toys in the corner was clearly the only people not troubled about being here. I wondered if I looked as concerned as their parents did. Shelia smiled as soon as she sat down.

"Cola, it's not that bad. Give the people what they want, so you can get what you need for your family. It'll only be temporary."

Did she think it would be temporary when she first signed up all those years ago? Hell, I thought it was *only gonna be temporary* when WASA turned off my goddamn water and I had to let my kids use bottled water to wash their faces. As much as I hated it, I borrowed water from my neighbor until Marquan stepped in with that street money I was never supposed to spend. I swear his help was only supposed to be *temporary,* too.

Me and Shelia waited for forty minutes watching Maury Povich before I heard somebody call Nicola Hampton.

"Lisa?" Shelia asked.

"Hey, girl. How you been?" the plump woman said, smiling from ear to ear with a folder in her hand.

"Good," Shelia said, smiling back. I could tell they knew each other real good.

"What you been up to? How the kids doing?"

"They all doing good. Just here with my girlfriend."

"Oh, okay," Lisa said, looking at me. "Nicola Hampton?"

I nodded.

"Come on, y'all follow me."

As soon as we got to her cubicle, she handed me a stack of forms to fill out: food stamps, Medicaid, TANF. She asked for ID, Social Security cards, birth certificates. I felt overwhelmed and like I messed up and now had to beg for forgiveness. It wasn't my fault I lost my job. It wasn't my fault I had three kids who needed to eat and have a roof over their heads. It wasn't my fault none of their fathers turned out to be worth more than a piece of shit. They lied to me and now I had to fill out forms, broadcast my whole life and all my personal business (the form even had the nerve to ask for my bank address and my savings account number, like if there was really money in there I would give it to them or be here in the first damn place) before I could get help to take care of my children. Hell, I used to pay my taxes every year and on time. They owe *me* money.

"Make sure you sign right here," Lisa Turner said. "And I'll go make copies."

"Don't worry," Shelia whispered when Lisa went to the copy machine. "That's Raynard's aunt. She's cool."

I sure hope so. Right now I feel like I broke a law with all these questions. I thought I always made the best decisions for me and my kids. I took a job I couldn't stand because they said I was gonna make more money and get a promotion fast, when instead I ended up getting laid off. Sometimes I got it right. Sometimes I was wrong. I just knew I didn't want to end up stuck in this *temporary* situation forever.

■ ■ ■

"How'd you know I was here?"

"My son called me," Teddy said with that voice that used to make me feel warm all over. "Why you ain't call me is the real question."

I blew out a long breath.

"Stop stressing. I'm on my way around there to get you."

To get me? Who said I wanted to see him? "For what?"

"Stop playing with me, Cola. You always acting like you don't need a nigga. I'm on my way."

It had been a long time since I seen Teddy. He was the first guy I dated after Mark went to jail in 1989 for a life sentence. Mark got me pregnant with Marquan when I was sixteen, but he was too busy doing him that he didn't know the FBI was watching his every little move. They said he killed eight people for Rayful. Mark never denied it to me, either. I blamed myself for loving a man who could actually take the life of somebody else. Obviously, I didn't know him the way I thought I did. Even though he still sent letters to the house, I never wrote him back. I was too scared of him. The first couple of

41

years he called, I barely let Marquan talk to him or write him back. I didn't want my son to know the man who took life for granted. But as the years went on, he wanted to know his father, and I knew it wasn't fair to cut Mark completely out of his life.

Teddy was a refreshing breath of air when I first met him. He laughed a lot and made me feel like it was okay to be weak sometimes. I cried around him, for the disappointment I felt in myself for loving a killer. Teddy picked up the pieces and made me stop feeling sorry for myself. He showed me that it was okay to be happy. And I was for a long time with him, until I realized Teddy made a lot of girls happy. He was gorgeous. Light brown skin, thick dark eyebrows and hair, and he had a smile that made me want to forget every lie I caught him in.

"Why you always want to fight when I see you?" he said, as I climbed in his car. I hated that damn smile.

"Hey, Teddy."

"What you doing in Sursum Cordas now?" he asks in a way that leaves me feeling more pissed about my situation. Everybody knew the Cordas was a black hole.

"Don't wanna talk about it."

"You don't wanna tell me about it?" he

said with those sexy eyebrows raised high.

"Don't you wanna see your son?"

"I'll see him in a minute. I want to see you right now." I could feel his eyes crawling over my body. "Look at you, girl. Still so goddamn sexy. I like your hair like that. That's you right there."

I smirked.

"You hungry?"

"Me *and* my kids hungry."

His smile gleamed, then he put the car in drive. "Cola, Cola, Cola," he sang.

We drove to Hogs on the Hill on the corner of Bladensburg and New York Avenue. Teddy bought some barbeque wings, macaroni and cheese, and greens. I sat in the car reminiscing for a minute about those years I spent hugged up and loving Teddy for loving a woman like me. Our on-again-off-again relationship. Him hurting me one day, then loving me the next. The fact that it was finally over when I met Tinka's father, Cornell, and when I held on to Cornell's promises instead of the ones Teddy was giving me. After Cornell lied about being married and completely vanished, probably to another state, I stopped dating altogether. Who could date after three different men had lied so much? I had had enough. Three kids and three different fathers later, I was only thirty and pretty much homeless. All my crap was stuffed in a room in my best friend's house. My fourteen-year-old son was roaming the streets and giving me money every now and then from doing God knows what. My twelve-year-old son hardly opened his mouth, unless it was about some animal or insect he found in the gutter, and my little girl lived a fantasy life, trying to be characters from books she read. I felt alone and lost. So when Teddy asked me if I wanted to go see R. Kelly in concert at Constitution Hall Friday, it was easy for me to say "Why not?" I needed an excuse to get dressed up.

CHAPTER 5
TINKA

Ms. Shelia's house always seemed too full with people, like it was just gonna burst open and people was gonna fly out the front door and flood the street. It was way too noisy in there, too. Something was always on — the TV, the radio, the washing machine, the dishwasher, the dryer, the vacuum, her blow-dryer. Just loud. Loud with people talking or laughing and cursing. Loud with somebody banging on something, trying to fix it. Loud with footsteps running up and down the stairs. Just too loud. The only time I could be by myself was in the bathroom. I stayed in there as much as I could. Reading, mostly. Books was the only thing I had to myself since I ain't have to worry about stupid Krystal stealing that from me. I saw Ms. Shelia had books, too. Books with black people on the cover. I took one off the shelf with a girl with big gold earrings on the front. She told me not to let Mommy see me reading it, because it was too grown for me even though the title said *Flyy Girl.*

Ms. Shelia's kitchen seemed to be everybody else's favorite place, because somebody was always in it. Sometimes it was Mommy and Ms. Shelia drinking and smoking. Sometimes it was Ms. Shelia perming somebody's hair. Sometimes it was somebody cooking or washing dishes or clothes. Sometimes it was Taevon's daddy, Teddy, and Ms. Shelia's boyfriend, Van, playing cards. If Taevon wasn't outside with Duane, Sammy, Raynard, and Antonio, they was in the room playing PlayStation. I stayed outside by myself sometimes, mostly sitting on the curb, eating sunflower seeds, watching everybody else play. Krystal stayed over her friend's house on the First Street side and sometimes they went across M Street to the basketball court behind Tyler House. She drank cough syrup almost every night and she ain't even have no cold.

"What? You want some?" she asked me with an attitude when she caught me looking at her once.

I shook my head.

"Then why you all up in my damn face? With your nerdy ass," she said, laughing.

I rolled my eyes.

Ms. Shelia's house made me sick. Ever since we been here, Mommy never had time for me like she used to, and she never smiled at me no more. I always saw her smiling at Teddy and whatever stuff Ms. Shelia said. But not at me. I was syced when Aunt Renee said her and Uncle Matt was gonna come get me for a weekend. I couldn't wait to get the heck away from all these people in this crowded house. I ain't understand why we couldn't live with her and Uncle Matt anyway. Mommy said they lived too far and she ain't wanna leave D.C., but why not?

I sat on the curb in front of Ms. Shelia's house coloring on the sidewalk with some chalk I got from my teacher Miss Riley, when a girl I saw in school crossed the street. She stood right in front of me with her long braids. She had pretty dark brown skin just like me and she wore a striped black-and-red shirt.

"You know how to play hopscotch?" she asked.

I shook my head no.

"Want me to show you?"

"Okay."

"Let me see the chalk," she said. I handed her the pink chalk, and then she drew big

47

squares on top of each other, and wrote one big number from zero to ten inside each box.

"My name LaSheika," she said, as she drew.

"I'm Teyona, but everybody call me Tinka."

"You go to Walker-Jones, right?"

"Mm-hmm. I'm in Miss Riley's class."

"Oh, I'm in Miss Brown's. You related to Krystal, ain't you?"

I shook my head and tried not to roll my eyes.

"You don't like her either, do you?" she asked, smiling from ear to ear.

I ain't say nothing.

"You don't have to say it. Y'all never together. Don't feel bad — me and her ain't never been friends. She think she *like that,* but she don't even know who her father is."

I smiled, then I watched LaSheika finish making the boxes. Another girl with corn-rows done up just like hers walked up with a Capri Sun in her hand.

"This my little sister, Laila."

I waved and smiled at her.

Laila said hi and then she sat down beside me. After LaSheika taught me the rules, we played hopscotch until the streetlights came on and her and Laila had to go in the house.

Early the next morning just before school, Ms. Shelia called my name up the stairs. "Somebody at the door for you!" she yelled.

LaSheika and Laila was standing there when I came down the stairs. "You wanna walk with us to school?" LaSheika asked.

I nodded and smiled. "Let me go get my sweater and my book bag." I ran back up the stairs.

When I got to the room, Krystal was stuffing my favorite pink T-shirt in her book bag.

"That's mine!" I yelled.

"What you talking about?" Krystal asked, crossing her arms over her chest.

"My favorite shirt!"

"This ain't your shirt!" she yelled, taking a step toward me.

"I'ma tell!"

"Tell what? This ain't yours!"

I ran up to her, and snatched at the shirt that was sticking out of her bag. Krystal pulled back and before I knew it, the T-shirt was ripping apart like paper.

"You did that on purpose!" I yelled at her.

Krystal laughed.

My hand reached out and smacked her. I couldn't believe I did that. I guess Krystal couldn't either, because she stared at me stunned for three long seconds, then she grabbed my hair and yanked me down to the floor.

"Ahhh," I screamed, trying to peel her fingers off. She wouldn't let go. I tried to reach for something on her to grab — her shirt, her neck, her arm — but her grip only got tighter as she held me down.

"Owww," I screamed louder. All of a sudden, my fingernails scratched her arms and she let go. We ended up rolling back and forth on the floor, punching and kicking each other.

"What in the hell is going on in here?" I could hear Mommy's voice shouting, but I wasn't letting Krystal go. "You two cut it out!"

Mommy broke us up, then Krystal ran out the room while I fixed my clothes and my hair.

"What was y'all fighting for?" Mommy asked.

"She tried to steal my favorite shirt!"

"What I tell you about sharing?"

I couldn't believe Mommy. Taking her side. "But it's my favorite."

"Don't be fighting over no goddamn clothes, Tinka. That's stupid. Now, hurry up and get your butt to school!"

When she walked out the room, a tear crawled down my cheek. I wiped my face, grabbed my book bag, ran down the stairs and out the door. LaSheika and Laila was halfway up the block when I got outside. I skipped up the street to catch up with them.

"You was taking too long," LaSheika said, when I finally caught up.

"Me and Krystal just got into a big fight."

"For real?"

I nodded.

"Who won?" she asked, smiling.

I smiled back, and even though I wasn't sure, I said, "Me!"

"That's my dawg!" she said, wrapping her arm around my shoulders. "I ain't know you was good with the hands!"

I smiled again. *Me either.*

"I been *waiting* for the day to beat her ugly ass up. Guess you beat me to it!"

School went good. Me and Krystal avoided each other at lunchtime. She ain't never even look my way. Maybe I did get the best of her. After school, LaSheika took me to the candy lady who lived in the house on the corner. I couldn't believe how fat she was with her green cotton dress that looked like a sheet. She was sitting on a saggy blue couch in the living room in front of the TV. Her ankles looked like they was gonna explode. All the snacks you could name was sitting on a big table beside her, stacked in boxes and bottles as high as the stairwell behind it.

"Hi, Ms. Carmen," LaSheika said.

"How you doing, Pretty Girl?" she said, smiling.

"Can I have a slice of chocolate cake, some Funions, and some strawberry Now & Laters?"

"Of course you can. Let me get up and cut this cake for you," she said, reaching for the cane beside her. It seemed like it took all Ms. Carmen's might to stand up and walk to the edge of the table. The floor creaked under her heavy footsteps. I watched her slice the cake and wrap it in foil before she told LaSheika it cost $1.75. I bought some barbeque sunflower seeds, a sour pickle, and a strawberry soda with some of the money Marquan gave me, then we left.

"How you think she got that big?" I asked.

"Who knows?" LaSheika said, eating a piece of her cake. "I wonder how she got three children? I don't know who would do the nasty with her big ole butt."

She had a point.

"But she the one all them" — she nodded in the direction of the boys standing on the corner — "get their stuff from."

"What stuff?"

"You know. They stuff," she said, whispering.

I was confused.

LaSheika shook her head and laughed. "You don't know nothing, do you?"

I guess I didn't, because how in the world could that gigantic lady be selling drugs, too?

We was about to walk down the block when a tall dark-skin boy like Marquan's age stopped his bike beside LaSheika. "Let me get a piece."

"Dag, you greedy, Keion!" she said, rolling her eyes.

"Man, whatever, give me a piece!"

"Here." She broke off some cake for him, then he rode off.

"Who was that?" I asked.

"My brother. He get on my nerves sometimes," she said, opening her bag of Funions. "But he always give me money, so I don't care."

"That's how my brother Marquan is. I can't wait until he move around here."

"Where he live?"

"Around my old way."

"Oh . . . where you used to live?"

"Trinidad."

"Trinidad, cop too much bread," she sang a line from a Go Go song Marquan used to

53

blast around the house. "That's not that far away."

But it felt like it to me.

"Look at Ms. David nosy butt. All up in them people business," she said, nodding to the gray-haired lady standing on the steps with a broom in her hand. She looked like she had a permanent curve in her back. I watched Ms. David break her neck to see who was getting into the white Mercedes-Benz in front of her neighbor's house.

"Hi, Ms. David," LaSheika called out, making the old lady jump.

"Good afternoon, young lady. Who this you with?"

"Tinka from 'cross the street."

"Ohhhh. You the one staying with Shelia, right?"

I nodded.

"It's crowded in there, ain't it?" she asked scratching her hair. "I can't see how that woman can afford to have all them kids, plus a grown man who don't wanna work one single job, staying all up in there. And now she got y'all, too. It's a shame."

"Come on, Tinka," LaSheika said, pulling my arm. I looked at the lady over my shoulder and she was still staring at us, shaking her head. "She's so nosy. Her own family don't even like her. That's why they never come around here to see her!" LaSheika said it loud enough for the lady to hear. "Always talking about how she used to be married to some white man, like that mean something or like somebody care. Be careful what you say to her," she warned.

I nodded, then we walked around to the K Street side, where Laila was jumping rope with her friends in the circle parking lot. A sad-looking grocery store with the words *Rich Food* on the top was next to it. A whole bunch of bright-colored signs hung in the window with big sale numbers on them: $2.99 for Ketchup. $1.99 for Idaho Potatoes. $4.99 per Pound of Ground Beef.

"We live right here," LaSheika said, pointing to the house with 199 on it.

"Oh." Their house looked just like all the rest of them. Light brown cement with a chocolate-brown door. No bars on the windows. Dirt in the front yard. Shades where blinds should be.

"Uggh. Why he keep staring at us?" Laila said, rolling her eyes. "Gross!"

I looked up to see who she was talking about. The man looked like Ms. Shelia's boyfriend Van, but I really couldn't tell. He was helping another man fix his car, but every now and then, the man stared over at us. He had the same mustache and beard

55

thing around his mouth and chin that Van did.

"He a pervert, that's why!" LaSheika snapped. "Don't he stay with y'all?"

So that was him. "Sometimes," I mumbled.

"Hmmmm. Better watch your back then, because I heard about him," she said.

My ears perked up. "What you hear?"

"I heard he got locked up for messing with kids before."

"What you mean?"

"For doing the nasty with them," she said, like I was stupid.

But I ain't have to believe everything she said. "How you know that?"

"My mother was talking to her friends about it. They said it happened a long time ago, but once a pervert, always a pervert to me."

I wanted to run home and tell Mommy what LaSheika just said. Maybe she would wanna move out now and go stay with Aunt Renee. Get me and Taevon outta that house as soon as possible. But then again she took up for Krystal way too fast this morning. Like she loved her more than me or something. Ms. Shelia's boyfriend better stay the heck away from me.

Taevon rode up on his bike. His face was dusty as usual. "Look what I found on the way home from school."

"What?"

He opened his hand and a tiny frog blinked his huge eyes at me.

"Ill!" I screamed. "Get that nasty thing away from me!"

He laughed and put it in his shirt pocket before he rode off again.

"Who was that?" LaSheika asked.

"My brother Taevon."

"How old is he?"

"Twelve."

"Oh."

Something told me she liked him, but I ain't know how she could like somebody who seemed to love playing in dirt. Taevon was always digging in the ground, kneeling in grass, or climbing trees for something with four legs. He always talked about how he was gonna take care of animals when he grew up. I stayed outside with my new friends until it got dark. LaSheika caught me up on everybody she thought I needed to know about around here, like Mr. Duncan, the fat maintenance man, and Lanitra, the transvestite who came to see him all the time.

"He look like a gorilla with makeup on," LaSheika said laughing.

I shook my head and half-smiled at her

joke. I could already see LaSheika knew everybody's business. A part of me wondered if I should keep telling her mine. She ain't really tell me much about her own family, but she seemed nice. I ain't wanna go in the house, but Laila came running to tell LaSheika their mother said get inside. When they left, I went in Ms. Shelia's to face the music. I hated Krystal. And by the way Mommy been acting, always up in Teddy's face and ignoring me and Taevon, I was getting real close to hating *her,* too.

Ms. Shelia was in the kitchen braiding Sammy's hair when I walked in the door. "You want something to drink?"

I nodded.

"Good," she said, winking. "Grab me something, too."

I went to the refrigerator and grabbed two grape sodas, then handed her one.

"Sit down for a minute," she said.

I already knew what she wanted to talk about. I tried not to roll my eyes to the back of my head. I sat down across from Sammy and stared at his pain. His eyes was tight and his mouth was closed even tighter. Ms. Shelia was killing him with those braids. I cracked open my soda and took a long swallow.

"Krystal told me this morning y'all was

fighting. That true?"

I took a deep breath and then I nodded.

"Girls shouldn't be fighting. Y'all supposed to be staying pretty. Getting your hair and nails done. Not rolling around fighting. Y'all leave that mess to them boys," she said. She wiped her fingers on her shirt and then opened her soda. "Don't let me find out y'all been fighting again, cuz I'ma half to take my books back from you." She winked and then said, "And I know how much you like them, so be good, Miss Tinka Bell."

I nodded and watched her start another cornrow.

"Owww, Ma!" Sammy yelled, pulling away from her.

I guess Ms. Shelia was cool after all. I loved her books. Some of the people in them reminded me of people I remembered from Trinidad. They talked like them and acted like them, and it was stories from now, and not from back in the slavery days or when black people couldn't sit next to white people. She let me keep them for as long as I wanted, too. Mommy never said nothing about me reading Ms. Shelia's books, because she was too busy in Teddy's face to care.

When I walked upstairs, Mommy told me

I had to tell Krystal sorry before I could do anything else. *Tell her I'm sorry? No way.* I rolled my eyes and crossed my arms over my chest.

"Don't stand there pouting about it. Go do what I said, Teyona!"

I sucked my teeth and stomped out the room. When I got to Krystal's room, she was lying across the bed running her mouth a hundred miles a minute on the phone. She rolled her eyes at me like they hurt when I walked in, and then she went back to running her mouth. I wasn't saying *sorry*. Mommy must be crazy. Krystal was stealing from *me*. Why I had to be the one to apologize?

A week after Easter, Mommy said she found a job taking care of some old people. She had to be the one cleaning up after them, helping them take baths and get dressed, go grocery shopping, get their clothes from out of the cleaners, pick up their medicine, take them to the doctor, and help them pay bills. She seemed happy, even though she used to have an office job before we got put out. I felt like things was about to get better for us.

I called Marquan as soon as Krystal went

outside. I ain't want her all up in my business.

"You all right?" he said.

"Yeah. Mommy got a job. She said we gonna be moving into our own place soon."

"For real? That's what's up."

"You coming with us?"

"I don't know, shawty. We'll see."

"But I want you to come," I said.

I was sad when he acted like he ain't wanna live with us and have things be the way they used to be: him making me pancakes in the morning, Mommy making us dinner, all of us watching a movie with caramel popcorn in the living room. I wanted us to be back like it used to be, before she started drinking all the time and smoking back-to-back cigarettes.

"I don't know. It depends."

"Depends on what?"

"Ma be lunchin' sometimes," he said before mumbling something to somebody wherever he was at. Then he said, "I gotta go, Tink. I'll talk to you later."

He never mentioned moving in with us again. Every time I brought it up, he brushed it off or acted like he ain't hear me.

CHAPTER 6
NICOLA

I had no idea Taevon and Tinka was gonna act totally different from each other after I told them to pack their stuff up because we was moving. Taevon got quiet like he wasn't sure if he wanted to be mad about it or not. Tinka, on the other hand, started clapping and dancing, before she hugged me. The minute I said we was just moving across the street to the empty house next to Ms. David, their reactions flipped. Taevon got excited and Tinka got pissed. But if it wasn't for Shelia's friend Lisa Turner pulling strings and talking to somebody she knew, we would still be on that long-ass waiting list. I heard people be waiting for housing so long, by the time they finally get an apartment, they had given birth to two more kids since they first applied and needed more space. Unlike Taevon and Tinka, I ain't care where we moved to, as long as it was a place of our own.

"Am I gonna have my own room again?" Tinka asked.

"You sure are. I even got one for Marquan . . . if he still don't think he too grown to stay with us."

Tinka couldn't help but smile then.

"Is my father moving in too?" Taevon asked.

I was surprised he asked that. I shook my head. "No."

Taevon didn't ask anything else, and I didn't volunteer any information. I wasn't quite sure how he felt about me and Teddy seeing each other again. They had a decent relationship, I guess.

A week later, me and Tinka mopped the new house from top to bottom, scrubbed out the kitchen cabinets, and killed all the roaches and spiders that seemed like they just kept having babies. Our new house looked just like Shelia's except we had four rooms, two on the second floor and two on the third. I gave Tinka the room across from mine on the second floor. The house wasn't all that big, even though we had three floors and two bathrooms. The hallways was shaped like squares on each floor. I could do a tiny spin and touch the door on my room, Tinka's room, the bathroom, and the closet. A back door led from the kitchen to the empty backyard. There wasn't no grass or trees and no door attached to the brick walls that separated our yard from Ms. David's. Well, there wasn't hardly nothing green in the whole neighborhood. Just dirt not meant for planting, dead tree branches, and beige buildings.

"Oh no, she *not* doing what I think she doing! Hey! Hey you!" I screamed out the kitchen window. A skinny lady with short, matted hair stood up and pulled her skirt down. "Get the hell outta my backyard, you nasty bitch! Pissing in my backyard. What the hell is your problem?!"

That bald-headed heifer turned around and rolled her eyes like I was the one who crossed her, then she took her sweet, precious time strolling out the yard before she cut through the alley.

"I swear to God." I snatched my gloves off so I could light a cigarette.

Taevon was in the living room doing his best impression of Mr. Fix-It. He was trying to put together the big entertainment center Renee and her husband Matt dropped off last night. They wasn't using it no more since Matt had bought them a new one to go with their new big-screen TV a month ago. If it wasn't for Taevon begging the hell out of me, I would've told them hell no when they asked me if I wanted it. Sick and tired of them treating us like we a charity case. All Matt gonna do is write that crap off on his taxes.

There was a knock on our door and Tinka ran to see who it was, since Shelia kept sending Antonio, Sammy, Duane, and Raynard over with stuff she wasn't using no more from her house: curtains, pots, and pans. We was really kinda starting from scratch, so anything she gave us, I knew we could find a way to use it.

When I looked up to see who was at the door, Marquan walked in carrying two big navy blue Nike duffle bags with his friend, whose face I recognized from around Trinidad.

"Hey, Tinka," he said.

"Mommy, it's Marquan!" she screamed, and then gave him a hug.

Taevon ran up and gave him a hug, too. He really did look like Marquan. It seemed like more every day.

"What's up, son?" Marquan said.

"Nothing," Taevon said, smiling. "What's up, Ced?"

Ced just nodded and stayed quiet. I walked out the kitchen, puffing my cigarette. I was a little happy to see him, but he had another thing coming if he thought he was just gonna act like nothing had happened.

"Hey, Ma," he said, squeezing the straps on his bags tight.

"Hey." Something about the way he said Ma made me feel like he needed me still. "So, I guess you ready to listen to me now, right?"

Marquan rolled his eyes and looked at his feet. He looked just like his father with those damn freckles under his eyes.

"Because that's the only way you can stay here. You know that, right?"

His little box-head-looking friend nudged Marquan and looked at him hard like he was his father or something. Marquan looked back, and then he nodded. I didn't know what that was about, but I said, "Good. Your room is upstairs on the third floor."

"Come on. I'll show you," Taevon said. He grabbed one of Marquan's bags and headed up the steps. Marquan knocked fists with Ced and then followed Taevon up the steps.

This Ced looked like he was nineteen or twenty. Too old to be friends with my son. "Marquan been staying with you?"

Ced nodded.

"So you the one been keeping my son in and out of trouble."

He shook his head.

"Hmmm," I said, puffing. "Well, all right. Thank you for bringing my son home, I guess."

"No problem."

I watched the little dude walk out the door and down the steps to his glossy black car, before I threw my cigarette in the yard and closed the door. I felt a breath squeezing past my closed lips. Maybe it was relief.

Tinka wrapped her arms around my waist like she was reading my mind. That girl, I swear. Too grown for her age.

"When we done cleaning, Tinka, let's pop some popcorn and watch that Will Smith movie Ms. Shelia gave me. What's it called again?"

Men in Black," she said, clapping.

"Yeah, that one," I said smiling. "Go tell Marquan and Taevon."

"Okay."

Everything was gonna be like it used to be, I could just tell.

The pictures of me, Mama, and Renee looked perfect on top of the entertainment center. We almost looked like we was happy. Mama had on her favorite blue off-the-shoulder dress, the one Renee got her for her fiftieth birthday, looking like Willona from *Good Times* or somebody. She still managed to look younger than me in that picture. I wiped the frame off again and then went out back to smoke a cigarette.

Huuuhhh. Finally, I was finished unpacking. I sat in one of the plastic chairs I got from Discount Mart and listened to the music coming from somebody's car around the corner. It felt good to be together again. Taevon and Marquan had some friends over, and Tinka was around the corner at her little friend's house. I took a long pull from the Newport and closed my eyes for a couple seconds.

Life was getting better a little bit. I mean, we still had a long way to go. My new job paid me eight dollars less an hour than what I made doing data entry, but at least our rent was only a hundred and thirty-three dollars, and I got two hundred and seventeen dollars a month for food stamps. Of course, it helped, but it wasn't nothing like what I used to have. Yeah, we lived in a house now, but we were still in the damn projects and I'd never make a mistake about that fact.

Every other goddamn night the police blazed through the neighborhood, sirens blaring in the middle of somebody's argument or in the middle of my dreams, just because they felt like it. Sometimes it seemed like nobody worked around here but me anyway. When I got off work, everybody seemed like they just woke up for the day and now they worried about my business and what's going on in my life. That's exactly why I stayed to myself for the most part. I said hello and kept it moving. I didn't need nobody worrying about what goes on in my house.

I couldn't even scratch my butt without Ms. David or Ms. Jackson wondering why it itched. Even Shelia couldn't help asking me every now and then about Teddy. "I can't believe y'all really back together," she kept saying every time I told her he was coming over or whenever we was about to go out. She my girl, though. Been my girl since Mark was around and back when we first went to Job Corps, but she spent so much time in that house that she done forgot how to live. Now my life seemed like it's hers sometimes, the way she be acting.

All at once I heard a loud rumble: "Ma!" and "Ms. Cola!" I turned around just as Marquan, Antonio, and Monte burst through the back door with Taevon limp in their arms.

I jumped up, dropping my cigarette. "Oh my God — what's wrong with him?"

"He can't breathe!" Marquan yelled.

I grabbed Taevon's pale face and pulled him to my chest. He smelled like weed. "Breathe, baby!"

Marquan told 911 what was happening on his cell.

"Breathe, Taevon, breathe!" I shouted.

"He got asthma?!" yelled Taevon's pimple-faced friend Monte.

"Breathe, baby, breathe!" I shouted so loud my throat burned.

"Breathe, Tae!" Antonio echoed.

I felt dizzy. Like all the blood in my body rushed to my head. He wasn't breathing. *What to do next?* I ran through the house, out the front door, and across the street to Shelia's, then banged on the door until somebody opened it.

"Taevon can't breathe. Where Van?!" I begged as soon as I see Shelia.

"Oh my God. He not here, Cola."

I ran back out the house. Scared to death. Blood flooding my brain. *What to do, what to do, what to do?!* My son was dying. I ran up the street and stopped the first person I saw with a car. Mr. Duncan, the maintenance man.

"Please!" was the only word I remembered saying before I heard the ambulance's ear-splitting siren storming down M Street.

■ ■ ■ ■

A few hours later at Washington Hospital Center, Teddy teased Taevon like nothing serious had happened. "I bet that's the last time your little ass gon' smoke, ain't it?" Teddy joked like our son nearly dying was funny. I ain't find a damn thing funny about him suffocating. And Marquan could just go right on ahead and stop looking at me all pitiful. He was the one who gave Taevon that garbage in the first damn place, and Teddy could stop trying to point the finger at me for not knowing Taevon had asthma. How the hell was I supposed to know that if he ain't never had a problem with it before? Teddy talking about I knew *he* had it. No, the hell I didn't. Teddy ain't stay around long enough for me to know that. Between him and Marquan, I don't know who was irking me the most. Maybe Marquan because he ain't have no goddamn business bringing that crap up in my house. Whatever life he was living around Trinidad wasn't welcomed in my house. Period. *Me and him gonna have us a one-on-one. I don't care if he got to go live with his father's mother Gloria or what. If he keep it up, me and him gon' definitely have problems.*

71

■ ■ ■ ■

PART II
THREE YEARS LATER

■ ■ ■ ■

CHAPTER 7
TINKA

The fire hydrant flooded water all through the neighborhood, cooling me and my friends from the ninety-seven-degree heat. Ma told me not to be outside playing in the sun while she was at work, but it was way too hot to stay in the house. The air conditioner broke. The fan blew around hot, stinky air and made my head hurt. Taevon was outside with Antonio, and Monte and I ain't see Marquan all day. Why I had to be the only one stuck in the house? LaSheika's knock on the door, saying, "Why you up in the hot-ass house for?" was all I needed to just say forget it.

First, me and her went to the market to get some freezies, then we met up with Laila and her friend Cookie. Taevon and Monte came up with the idea to turn the fire hydrant on, so Antonio got Van to untwist the lock with his tools. As soon as the ice-cold water shot out, we all ran over desperate to get wet. Clothes on and all. We ain't even care, it was so hot.

Ms. Shelia put a speaker in the window and let WKYS boom Rare Essence's "Overnight Scenario" all over the neighborhood. I could tell old, nosy Ms. David was running her mouth about us to Ms. Jackson.

"Let's get that truck right there!" Taevon pointed at the white Navigator flying down the U toward us.

Antonio, who was slim and taller than the rest of us, had a string-bean can open on both ends that he used to spray us, but as soon as he saw the white Navigator flying our way, he used it to shoot water at the truck. The driver looked like somebody's father trying hard to be young, still wearing cornrows with a hairline that was disappearing. He was rocking an All Dayz sweatsuit and blasting Chuck Brown. His face twisted up, then he blew his horn and yelled, "Get the fuck out the street! Y'all better not get no water in my motherfuckin' truck!" But Antonio kept on drenching it and laughing until the man drove off.

Fifteen minutes later Mr. Duncan's roly-poly self came running outside yelling, "Who the hell turned that water on?!" He was covered in sweat, and huffing and puffing like a bear.

Ain't nobody say nothing. We just stared at how he was breathing all hard and looking from left to right at each of us.

"It's against the law to have that goddamn water running like that! Y'all trying to make me lose my job out here?! Who turned it on?!"

"You ain't nobody daddy, nigga!" Monte yelled.

"Yeah, fuck you!" Antonio snapped. "You fat muthafucka!"

Monte ran up to the hydrant with the can, then aimed the water at Mr. Duncan, and soaked his whole body with a freezing blast. Mr. Duncan looked like a tree being electrocuted. He froze in place and closed his eyes tight. He was pissed.

"You goddamn kids!" His big butt took a few steps like he was about to chase us, but he knew better. I kinda felt bad for him, because he did help my family out a couple times. He was the one who drove all of us to the hospital when Taevon had his first asthma attack a long time ago.

"Don't think I don't know who your mamas is! I know all of you and where you live. Antonio Gorham, 167 First Place! Monte Anderson, 321 First Terrace, and Taevon Hampton, you know I know where the hell *you* live!"

Some of us ran away, but not too far. Laila and Cookie cracked up laughing.

"That's okay. I got something for y'all asses," he said, wobbling across the street like his feet hurt.

"Go fix somebody toilet, you fat mother-fucker!" Monte yelled behind him. If he ain't have all them pimples on his face, he could've been cute.

Taevon jumped back in the water, and then everybody else followed.

"Oh, uh-uh," LaSheika said after she wiped water off her face.

"What?" I said, doing the same thing.

She nodded up the street. Krystal and her two hood-rat friends Mya and Angie was walking toward us wearing bikini tops and tiny coochie-cutter booty shorts, thinking they was all cute. LaSheika rolled her eyes. I couldn't stand Krystal. Before I knew it, those tramps was jumping in *our* water. I was too through and ready to go in the house. I walked back across the street. LaSheika was behind me, but she was so heated she was actually stomping her feet in her sandals.

"Oh no. Why we leaving for? Forget them! I wish one of them *would* say something to me or try to start something!"

"I'm just tired," I said.

LaSheika knew better, but she ain't sweat me. I sat on the sidewalk instead of going in the house. We watched everybody else run in and out of the water. Her brother Keion rode his bike up to us. He was always with Creature and Big Mike on the corner, shooting dice or smoking weed, but he always found a way to check on his sisters. I liked that about him.

"What's up, y'all?"

"Nothing," we both said.

"Y'all hear about what happened early this morning with Lynnda and Teresa?" he asked.

"What now?" LaSheika asked, shaking her head.

"No. What happened?" I asked.

"Teresa stabbed Lynnda slam in her chest. She still in the hospital."

"Damn! You serious, Keion?!" LaSheika said.

"Yep."

"Wow," I said and shook my head. How in the world did two sisters end up pulling a knife on each other?

"See. I don't know why they don't just leave that trifling man alone," LaSheika said. "They just keep having babies by him."

"Back to back," I said.

"His thing must be crucial," LaSheika

79

said, smiling.

I overheard Ma and Ms. Shelia talking about those two sisters and how they kept having babies with the same man, ever since they lived with their mother, Ms. Hooper, across the street. Teresa first got pregnant with twins and moved into her own house in the neighborhood, and her sister Lynnda turned up pregnant a year later. Then Lynnda got pregnant again and moved into her own house on the K Street side. At first, family acted like their kids looked alike because they was cousins, but then the secret came out. They was brothers and sisters, too, and it's been drama ever since. Neither one of them wanted to stop messing with Ramont. He ain't have nothing going on special in his life that I could tell. He ain't have no job, he wasn't pushing a car, and if it wasn't for Teresa or Lynnda, he would be staying with his mama in Golden Rule around the corner on New Jersey Avenue.

One thing kept them fighting over his trifling behind. And Ramont walked around like he knew what it was, too. He was bold. Picking and choosing which one of their houses he was gonna sleep at for the night. He even had the nerve to try to flirt with Ma sometimes, but she wasn't having that.

Straight trifling. The whole neighborhood been up in their business since the beginning like it was a reality show or something.

"Teresa get locked up?" LaSheika asked.

"Naw," Keion said, shaking his head. "Lynnda talking about she ain't know who did it. But I was outside when they first started arguing."

"Heh, right," LaSheika said.

I twisted my lips to the side. "Well, I hope she all right."

"Look at this nigga," Keion said, staring at Delano rolling up in his wheelchair. He used one leg to scoot around everywhere since the day he turned up with one of his fingers missing and a shattered kneecap. I'm not sure exactly what happened, but people said he owed Creature some money.

"Let me get a dollar, Keion," he said with his raspy voice.

"Get the fuck outta here. Nigga, you crazy as shit."

"Oh, I'm not good for a dollar, man?"

Keion dug around in his pocket and gave him whatever change rattled around in it. "I know your beggin' ass getting disability checks."

Delano smiled. "You know my mother be cashing them joints. I don't know what she be doing with the money."

81

"Yeah, right."

"Thanks, man." We watched him scoot away, then Keion said he was gone, too.

A few minutes later, fire truck engines burst down the U, with their loud sirens cursing the music and the sound of my friends playing. Two fire trucks pulled up, stopping right in front of the running hydrant, then three firemen jumped down with supersized wrenches and turned the water off. Everybody got mad, especially Krystal.

"Hahaha. That's what them dumbass chickens get!" LaSheika snapped, rolling her neck around in a circle.

"Naa." I sucked my teeth.

Even though the water was off, the crowd ain't disappear. Everybody hung around trying to fight the boredom, listening to Ms. Shelia's music from the speakers in her downstairs window until the ice cream truck came around with that ridiculous "London Bridge Is Falling Down" song competing with Ms. Shelia's music. LaSheika treated me to a vanilla ice cream cone and she bought one for her sister, too.

I was eating my ice cream on the curb, when a silver car with Virginia tags pulled up behind the ice cream truck.

"Ain't that Marquan?" LaSheika asked,

leaning forward.

I almost dropped my cone when I saw him driving. He was blasting an old Bone Thugs-n-Harmony song.

"Yeah, that *is* him," I said, confused. I stood up and walked over to the car. "Who car is this?"

"Don't worry about it. Move out the way."

"You stole it?"

"Borrowed it."

"From who?"

"Damn. Why you all up in my business?"

Marquan ain't even have a license, let alone a car, so why he acting all surprised that I'm getting in his business?

"Well, can you take me and LaSheika somewhere?" I asked, leaning inside to see what else was in it.

"Nah, not now. I got some shit to do. I'm 'bout to take a shower first, then I gotta go."

"Can I come?"

He looked at me like I was asking too many questions or something, then he shook his head. Taevon ran up and said, "Who car is this?"

Marquan rolled his eyes to the back of his head, then yelled, "Watch out!"

I took a hint and went back to the sidewalk beside LaSheika. Him and Taevon headed inside the house.

"Your brother so sexy."

Uggh. "Which one?"

"Marquan. Look how his chest and arms all muscular, and I love his freckles."

I sucked my teeth. Marquan looked just like the man in those pictures I seen all over his room. His father posed in front of a fence, or kneeling down in the grass or with two or three other men in the same light blue uniforms. "I thought you liked Taevon."

"I do, but Marquan a *man.*"

"He's only seventeen."

"I know. I can look, can't I? Damn, Tinka. You hating."

"He all older than you, LaSheika!"

"So?!" she squealed.

I closed my eyes and rubbed my forehead. Somebody set off some fireworks behind my house. I opened my eyes and saw Chris from school running with some other boys down the street. Monte was driving up the U on a little toy-looking motorbike that sounded like a lawn mower. "You know he got a crush on you, right?"

"Who? Monte?"

She nodded and smiled.

"With all them pimples on his face? No, I don't think so."

"Whatever. You gotta look pass that," she

84

said, laughing.

"How you know he like me?"

"How many times he gon' ride by on that raggedy-ass scooter?"

I hadn't even noticed. I did notice Ms. David watching us. She was still sitting with Ms. Jackson. Every now and then Ms. Jackson went over and tried to do something to those weeds in the yard she wanted so bad to be flowers. A gang of dudes, including two of Ms. Shelia's kids, Sammy and Duane, stood on the corner in front of the candy lady's house. Taevon and Antonio was over there, too, watching some people gambling in the street beside the Navigator. Ms. Carmen looked out of her upstairs window, checking out everything. It was so funny how she was the real person running this block. Telling Creature what to do on the low. A head nod here or a wink there. Sometimes people came in the front door and went out her back door. Who knows all that she did in that house. She just never came outside. Way too big to.

"I think I'm about to go inside," I said, standing up.

"What's wrong with you?"

"My head hurting."

"Oh. You coming back out?"

"Maybe later. When it's cooler out here."

"Oh, okay. Don't be in there reading and whatnot. With your nerdy ass," she said, laughing. "I know how you do."

"Whatever," I said, smiling. If she know how I do, then why she think I'ma switch it up for her.

"See you later." She stood up and went back across the street where her sister was jumping double Dutch.

When I got in the house, I looked out the window to finish watching everybody. Monte rode around again on his scooter. He looked up at my house, but he didn't stop. Maybe LaSheika was right. I still felt gross and sticky, so I went to take a shower. I was surprised Marquan was still in the house by the time I got out. Music boomed from his speakers, and the house smelled like skunk. Ma would kill him if she knew he was smoking weed in here. She always faked getting mad with him, but she gave up on my brothers a long time ago. As long as they kept the front room clean, she ain't never get too pissed with them. Not the way she should have. Too busy up Teddy's butt.

I changed into a tank top and some shorts, then I stayed in my room watching TV for a while, before I opened up the book Ms. Shelia bought me for my birthday. I read until I fell asleep.

I felt like I was only sleeping like ten minutes when Taevon woke me up, shaking my shoulder hard and screaming something I ain't understand. My room was dark, but I could've sworn I just went to sleep. Taevon shook my shoulder hard again.

"What?" I sat up and wiped my face with my hands.

"I said, the police locking up Marquan!" he yelled.

"What?!" My eyes popped open.

"They locking him up, Tinka! Right now! Outside!"

I jumped up and ran down the stairs behind Taevon. The house was dark and empty. Ma must've still been at work. Blue and red lights lit up the neighborhood. In front of our house: four police cars, three undercover cars with bright lights flashing in the back windows, people standing behind police, Marquan in the back of a police car with his head down.

"Marquan!" I yelled at the window, crying.

"Where your parents at?" the police asked me.

I wiped my face and looked for Taevon. Ms. Shelia came from out of nowhere and wrapped her arms around me.

87

"Is this your daughter?" the police asked her.

"It's my goddaughter," she lied.

He nodded and then Ms. Shelia took me across the street. "We gonna call your mother at work."

I wiped away tears and looked over my shoulder at all the people, some in uniform, some in suits with badges around their necks. It was just too much. I couldn't believe what was happening. I wished I could blink and it would all just go away.

CHAPTER 8
NICOLA

I told that boy to stay the fuck out of trouble. My hands wouldn't stop shaking no matter how hard I tried. I squeezed the empty box of Newports. "Babe, you gon' run up to the store and get me some more jacks?" I said, but my voice sounded hoarse even to me, so I knew I sounded crazy.

"Yeah, I got you. Whatever you need, Cola, I got you," Teddy said, getting up with his keys. "Ride with me, Van."

Van stood up. "You need something, Shelia?"

"Bring us something to drink, too," Shelia said.

As soon as the door closed, the tears poured out. "Look at how they left my house," I whispered. "No respect whatsoever."

Them bastards had combed over everything looking for evidence, before they left with two brown paper bags. The house still looked a mess. "I feel so goddamn violated. Like I did something wrong! Done went through every single drawer and closet in here. Look at how the hell they left it!"

"But, Cola . . . they said he might've been involved in a shooting," Shelia said. "Two people died."

My heart swelled up all of a sudden, my chest so tight now I couldn't breathe. "Not my son," I whispered.

I heard Shelia calling my name when I closed my eyes.

Renee and Matt was sitting in the living room when I opened my eyes. Shelia gave me a glass of water when all I really wanted was a drink from Teddy. Matt kept talking about some lawyer he knew who could help. Renee looked at me with her condescending eyes and said she was going to check on Tinka. Who was she to act like she could be a better mother than me? She ain't have no kids, and she couldn't have none if she wanted to. I could read her mind and she looked like she was dying to tell me what was on it — how I should've never got pregnant by Mark in the first place or how I screwed my whole life up when I dropped out of high school. I wished that bitch would.

And she didn't. Her and her egghead husband left just before the ten o'clock news came on. Teddy, Shelia, and Van watched it with me. They knew how scared I was. The damn police ain't tell me nothing. Just flashed a warrant in my face and told me what the hell they was going to do. Yelling something about *this government property anyway.* My heart jumped when the news people said there was a double homicide in Ivy City. Marquan's little hangout in Trinidad wasn't too far from there.

It was still dark outside when I woke Taevon and Tinka up the next morning. I looked at the clock and it was a little after six. Teddy left at five for work. I didn't get much sleep. All I kept thinking was how Marquan slept. Did he sleep? Did he get dinner last night? Did he really have something to do with two people getting shot and killed?

I put on my best suit, the cream-and-black one with the black collar and pockets I used to wear to my interviews with my double-strand pearl necklace and earrings. I had to call out from work to go to court today. My boss wasn't too happy to hear that, and they ain't care much about the fact that my son was in jail. Guess I shouldn't have men-

91

tioned that part. I smashed out my cigarette and swallowed the last sips of coffee.

A few minutes later, we walked out the door. It was drizzling. Me and Tinka huddled under my little umbrella and cut through the back of the house to get to K Street. We headed toward North Capitol Street.

"Ma, let's catch the train," Taevon begged. Rain dripped from the tips of his shoulder-length hazelnut dreadlocks. He wiped water from his face.

"It costs too damn much. Plus it's rush hour."

We passed Gonzaga College Prep on the right, where all the senators sent their sons to learn how to rule the world like them one day. I stared at the neatly cut dark green field behind the school where they played lacrosse and soccer. Neither one of my sons could've ever gone there, even though we lived right across the street. Three white women jogged around the track like they ain't have a care in the world, with their long ponytails bouncing behind them. We lived close to the Capitol Building and Union Station. Life was so different once you crossed K Street. All kinds of government buildings was right here, like the Board of Education and the Office of Vital

Records. K Street ran all the way through Northwest and Northeast. Major buildings was on that street with a lot of companies, government buildings, nonprofits, banks, and law firms.

I lit a cigarette and puffed while we waited for the X2 at the corner of North Capitol and H Street. Taevon played with a worm he picked up by Gonzaga and tried teasing Tinka with it. I guess that's how he chose to deal with what was really on his mind. I stared at the puddle and the soft drips that bounced off of it. I wondered what Marquan was doing right now. Did he eat breakfast this morning? Did he have to use the bathroom in front of everybody? Was my son getting picked on? Did somebody try to rape him? Did he have anything to do with the Ivy City murders? I tried to shake that thought away, but it was hard to. I wished Teddy was here. He'd know how to make me feel stronger.

When we got to the courthouse, a long line trickled outside. People huddled close with their umbrellas while they waited to get inside through the metal detectors. After we finally got in, I found out the courtroom for Marquan's pretrial. Room 122. Renee was waiting in the hallway with a white man dressed in a gray suit. She had the nerve to walk up and give me a hug.

"Hi," I said, trying not to roll my eyes. At least she came.

"This is Shawn Clemmons, a junior attorney with Klein, Westin, and Gholston."

"Nice to meet you, Ms. Hampton. Can I talk to you privately?" he said.

I nodded and followed him down the hall.

"So I had a chance to talk to your son briefly. He's doing okay. We're going to see what we can do," Mr. Clemmons said.

I folded my arms in front of me and waited for the rest of his words. Marquan was being charged with driving a stolen car, but because the car was identified by a witness as the same car fleeing the scene after a double-homicide shooting around Ivy City, Marquan might be charged with two counts of first-degree murder, too.

First-degree murder? His words hit me like a ton of bricks. I tried to balance myself and face each sentence head-on, but my hands locked tighter around the strap of my handbag. Mr. Clemmons's lips went into a straight line that told me he ain't know what might happen next.

Moments later inside the courtroom, it was already crowded. Three young girls sat in different corners of the room hushing their children. Somebody sat in the second row wearing a FedEx uniform, and another sat in the center wearing a post office one. A lady in the front with a short brown wig signaled for us to walk up to her.

"Who're you here to see?" she asked.

"Marquan Hampton," I said.

"What's your relationship?" the woman asked.

"He's my son," I said, confused.

The woman scribbled some words down on paper. "And what about you?" she asked Renee.

"I'm Marquan's aunt, Renee Hampton-Straus."

As soon as we sat down, I leaned over and asked Renee if she knew why the lady asked all of that.

"I think it's because the judge wants to know who took time out of their busy day to see about someone they have to make a decision about. I guess it shows if the person has any support," she whispered back. "Maybe they can tell if you're always in and out of trouble."

"Don't seem fair to me. What if I didn't call out? People do have to work."

"Yeah, but you wasn't gonna miss this."

She was right. My baby just made a mistake. Wrong place. Wrong time.

The judge was a round, yellow woman

with long, straight hair and too much bright makeup. As soon as she sat down, the muscular men wearing guns and dark clothes brought in a stream of black men chained together, looking like a bunch of slaves. Everybody's head was down and they all looked tired and like they was starving. I kept seeing some of them turning around to look out at us in the audience — some looked embarrassed, some shy, some pissed — but I guess they wanted to see if anybody was here for them. Where was Marquan? Every time the court doors opened, a man with dreads wearing a gray hoodie looked back to see if it was a person there for him. It was the saddest thing.

We waited two and a half hours before the judge announced the court was breaking until one o'clock for lunch. I was heated. My baby was back there waiting for these people to eat. Did he eat? I got up and stormed out. Taevon and Tinka followed behind me. Renee offered to treat the kids to Subway sandwiches across the street, but I couldn't think about eating. I lit a cigarette.

When we walked back inside, the police brought Marquan out chained up with another stream of black faces. He looked miserable when he saw us, like he been up all night. I blinked back tears. When they finally called his name, and the prosecutor read his charges, Mr. Clemmons spoke up. The lawyers and the judge went back and forth talking about things I didn't understand until I saw them taking Marquan back to the room where they brought him from. He ain't even get to say hi or bye to me.

"What's going on?" I asked, confused.

Mr. Clemmons signaled for us to go in the hallway.

"His next court date is September thirteenth. They've decided to take him to trial for the stolen car. Apparently, they don't have enough to connect him to the double homicide. Maybe their witness can't place him there. We'll see."

"Thank God, that's it," I said. "I don't know what I'd do with myself if it was more."

"Well, let's just be cautious. The prosecution is in the early stages of their case," the lawyer said. "But for now, try not to worry. He's a juvenile, plus this is just the first offense for him — that might work in his favor."

I felt a chill rise up my neck. He said *first offense* like he knew there was gonna be more one day or something. My child ain't capable of killing nobody. But obviously Mr.

Clemmons ain't care one way or the other. I forced my lips to move. "So what does this mean?" I asked.

"Honey," Renee reached out for my shoulder, then she said, "Marquan is going to Oak Hill until he goes to trial."

The trial was almost two months away. And now Marquan was gonna be stuck at a juvenile detention center all the way out Laurel, Maryland.

"Nicola, are you going to write his father to let him know what's going on?" Renee asked a few moments later, when we was waiting for her cab in front of the court building. She was meeting Matt back at Andrews Air Force Base.

"No." I fished around in my purse for my lighter. "Whenever he calls again, I'll let him know. I can't even *think* about what my son is going through, let alone wanna *write* about it. How do I write something like this?"

Renee nodded, but I could care less about what she thought. That was her problem. She always had a damn opinion and wanna help.

"I guess I can understand. Just know that everything will be okay," she said.

"Mm-hmm," I said before I lit up my

cigarette. "I appreciate you and Matt getting this lawyer for us, but I don't know if you can imagine how I'm feeling right now. Trust me . . . I just don't know what's going on with my son."

Renee shook her head.

"He act like every single bad thing that happens to us is my fault somehow. I can't tell that boy nothing. And now he doing God-knows-what out Trinidad. Stealing cars is one thing, but a double homicide?! No."

Renee fanned her thin fingers in the air to get rid of my smoke. "Well, Nicola, try not to get too stressed out about it. You still got Taevon and Teyona to take care of — and they need to see you being strong."

I smirked before I took another puff.

"There's my car service right there," she said, pointing. "Call me when you get home, sis. Come on, you two. Give Auntie a hug."

Tinka and Taevon hugged her, and waved bye as the black car pulled off.

I shook my head. "What does she know? Her life ain't nothing like mine. She always had it easy. Come on y'all, let's go."

I tossed my cigarette to the ground, and led the way back to the Cordas. At least it had finally stopped raining and the sun was coming out.

CHAPTER 9
TINKA

On September 13, the judge asked Marquan if he wanted to say something before she sentenced him. He shook his head, then looked back at all of us. Ma squeezed her shirt, right over her heart. The judge said, "Twenty-four months and one day," like she was saying what time of day it was, then she scribbled on some papers and said, "Next case."

"That's some bullshit," Taevon said under his breath.

Ma shook her head so much I thought she was hoping it was gonna help erase the memory of this day.

Afterward, Mr. Clemmons said that Marquan probably would've got more time if he wasn't about to be eighteen. I wanted to throw up. There wasn't nothing we could do about it. Marquan was gonna have to do time. Keion told LaSheika he heard one of the people who got killed that day was a

100

boy named Terry from Ivy City who went to Dunbar. Whenever I thought about Marquan having something to do with it — a shiver slithered down my back.

When we got home, Teddy showed up in his uniform, looking like he needed a bath bad. Black smut and sweat was all over his face.

"That boy gonna be done doing that time before you know it, baby," I overheard him saying to Ma. "Two years ain't nothing."

She looked like she wanted to cry. I watched Teddy pour her some Rémy Martin in a glass, then rub her back while she stared at the refrigerator. I went upstairs to sleep off the nightmare.

Later, loud groans woke me up. I opened my eyes and looked at the clock beside my bed. I heard the groaning again. Ma was in the bathroom coughing up her lungs in the toilet. *Where the heck was Teddy?*

I climbed out the bed and stood in the bathroom doorway. "You all right, Ma?" I asked, crossing my arms.

She looked up at me with red eyes and nodded. "Go back to bed, Tinka. You and your brother taking y'all asses to school in the morning. Don't think you slick, little girl!"

I shook my head and walked back to my

room. See, this is why I can't get no sleep in this house. And she expects me to get straight As, too? Yeah, right.

Teddy stayed the next night and the night after that. Then one morning he was in the bathroom taking forever shaving or picking boogers or whatever the heck he was doing when I needed to be getting ready for school. He took so long that I ended up taking a shower upstairs in Taevon and Marquan's filthy bathroom. Taevon seemed to love the fact that his father was around more. Nothing I complained to him about seemed to be a problem with him. I felt like I was by myself.

"What the fuck is all these damn roaches about?" Teddy asked Saturday when he dug around the kitchen cabinets. "We gotta do better than this. This shit don't make no motherfuckin' sense."

I almost swallowed my tongue when I heard him say *we. Was this fool moving in?*

"What we having for dinner? I know we having a Sunday dinner up in here," he said on Sunday.

"Who the fuck keep leaving all this nasty toothpaste in the sink?" he asked on Monday. "And I'm sick of seeing all these disgusting hair strands in here, too!"

As soon as he left for work, I went in Ma's room.

"Is he moving in or what?" I asked. "He keep talking all this *we* stuff."

"Stay in a child's place, Tinka," Ma snapped.

She ain't seem like she was getting ready for work again. She was laid up in bed, twisted in the sheets, with a pillow over her face, blocking the sun from her eyes. I sucked my teeth and went back across the hall to get ready for school, then I went outside and waited for LaSheika.

"What's wrong with you? It's way too early for an attitude," she said in her cute black Citizens and light purple tank top with silver-and-black sparkling designs. "You ain't even see Ms. Basque's grouchy face yet."

True. I had a love-hate relationship with my English class and especially my teacher, Ms. Basque. English was my favorite subject, but who wanted to read Edgar Allan Poe, John Steinbeck, F. Scott Fitzgerald, and William Shakespeare? Their books seemed like another language to me, not English, especially with all that *Ye* and *Thou* crap. One time Ms. Basque let us read a book called *Native Son* by a man named Richard Wright, but what about those books

Ms. Shelia got me reading hard? *B-More Careful, The Coldest Winter Ever,* or *Street Dreams.* Ms. Basque don't want us to read any of them. She makes me sick with her stuck-up self. I think she takes all the fun out of stories. Keep asking us what we think about it and whatnot. What she mean what we think about it? It just is.

Plus all she ever do is talk about how handsome her husband is, pass pictures around of her house in Bethesda, and brag about how she supposed to be one of the best teachers in D.C. She was on *20/20* before, talking about how she "believes students are only as gifted as they believe themselves to be." Woo, woo, woo. I can just throw up.

"You have no F-ing idea how much I'm sick of this dude. I can't take it!"

"Who?"

"Taevon's father."

"Oh."

"If Marquan was here . . . man . . ." But I couldn't even finish my sentence. I have no idea what he would've done. He spent so much time out of the house, he probably wouldn't have even cared.

Later that night, Teddy bought over two big old bags of clothes from his mother's house like this was a permanent situation. Taevon was syced, but I wasn't. I only dealt with his father because I had to. Teddy walked around the house like he been living here all along. Sometimes he was even in his drawers, scratching his balls on the couch, then taking his trifling dirty hand to touch sandwich meat and bread in the refrigerator. He plucked my nerves, every single one. Complaining and acting like I was in his way, whenever he walked in the kitchen or the living room.

At the same time it seemed like the more I couldn't stand him, the more Taevon loved him. They played John Madden on Taevon's PSP almost every night after Teddy got home from work. Teddy even took Taevon shopping like he was bringing home straight As or something. One day, when I came home, Taevon was sitting outside on the steps with a cocoa-brown pit bull puppy in his lap, talking about his dad bought it for him. And Ma allowed all of this. I couldn't believe she was really gonna let a pit bull run all up and through this house. She ain't even say nothing when Taevon said he was naming the dog Hitler. *Hitler? For real though?* I heard what that man did to all them Jews and my social studies teacher let us watch some of that movie *Schindler's List.*

Ma seemed like she was in a trance these days, but at least she had finally started going back to work. Her supervisor was calling every day, leaving messages on the voice mail. I'm surprised they ain't fire her already.

When November rolled around, Ced from Trinidad made a surprise visit. I was leaning against my fence talking to LaSheika when he pulled up in his big black car with shiny rims and dark tint.

"What's up, Li'l Sis. Your mother home?"

I nodded and then watched him park his car.

"Hold on LaSheika. I'll be back out," I said, and then walked Ced in the house. "Ma! Ced's here to see you!"

I could hear her moving around upstairs, then she came down with her robe tied tight and a cigarette in her hand.

"How you doing, Ms. Hampton?" he said.

"What you want? You already got my son locked up. What else you want? My other son?"

Ced looked down and flipped his keys back and forth. "I figured you might need this," he said, digging in his pocket. He tried to hand my mother a wad of money the size of a wallet.

106

Mommy looked at it like it was poison, and then she said, "Get the hell outta my house!"

"I don't mean no harm, Ms. Hampton. I just thought —"

"Get out! Out, I said!"

Ced nodded, turned around, and walked back out the door. I followed him outside and watched him get in the car.

"Li'l Sis?" he called after he rolled his window down.

"Huh?" I said.

"Come here."

I walked over.

"Here, put this up for me," he said, handing me the money. "Your mama saying she don't want it now, but she will. Keep it for her. It's gonna be some rainy days before she know it."

I bit my bottom lip and squeezed the money until my fingers felt a little wet.

"You hear from Marquan?" he asked.

"A few times."

"How he doing?"

"He doing okay, I guess. He don't say much on the phone. We might go up there before Thanksgiving to see him."

"Oh, that's good. Tell him I said what's up. Okay?"

I nodded again. Ced pulled off up the U.

"What the heck is going on?" LaSheika asked. Her eyes was bigger than I ever seen them.

I just shook my head and stuffed the money in my pocket. "Nothing."

"You *wellin',*" LaSheika said, eyeing my pocket.

Two days before Thanksgiving we went to see Marquan at Oak Hill. The place seemed and felt cold. He looked like he lost some weight. There was dark rings under his eyes, and his hair was growing into a little bush. Marquan may have said all of forty words the whole time we was there. When Ma asked him how he was doing, all he said was, "Fine."

But that was *so* not the case by the way he looked.

"You eating in there?" she asked.

"Sometimes," he said.

"You sleeping?" she asked.

"Not really."

"Boy," Ma said. "You need to sleep. I know it's hard, but you need your sleep, Marquan."

He stared at her, but didn't say nothing. Taevon tried next.

"You get in any fights?"

Marquan shook his head, but it seemed

like he was lying.

"You see anybody you know up here?" Taevon asked.

"A couple people from Dunbar," Marquan said.

That was the most words he said together at once.

"You miss us?" I asked.

"Yeah, I do," he said.

I smiled.

"You should write me, Tinka. Maybe send me some of those books you like reading. It'll make time go by faster."

I smiled again. I knew just the book to give him — Ms. Basque made us read it. *Manchild in the Promised Land.*

Thanksgiving over Aunt Renee's was weird with Teddy at the table. I never noticed before, but he ate with his mouth wide open and he had the nerve to suck his fingers in between bites.

"It's good, hunh?" Uncle Matt said, looking like he wanted to punch Teddy with all that slurping noise he kept making.

"It's all right," Teddy said. "Could use a little more salt. Lawry's. Something."

Aunt Renee pushed away from the table and went in the kitchen. I got up and followed her before Ma caught me rolling my eyes. Teddy was so gross for somebody who wanted to nitpick over toothpaste in the sink.

"Good. I'm glad someone decided to help me with the dishes," she said while wiping her hands on a dish towel.

"Anything to get away from him." I scraped off a plate in the trash can.

"I take it you don't approve of Teddy moving in." She dished some of the leftover food into plastic containers.

I shook my head.

"I guess I can understand that. You've never had a man living in the same house with you before now. It probably feels a little strange. You'll get used to it."

I hoped I ain't never have to get used to it.

Both of us was quiet for a little while cleaning up. Aunt Renee and Ma looked alike a little bit, except Auntie's skin was much darker, a few shades lighter than my color. She rinsed dishes off in the sink and then she passed them to me to stack in the dishwasher.

"Auntie?" I said. "How come you and Uncle Matt ain't never have no kids?"

She took a deep breath and a long look at the empty cake pan in her hands. "Well, it's really not too late. We just haven't been so lucky."

I never thought she wanted children. She was always at the gym or shopping. One of the extra bedrooms upstairs was filled with junk she bought off of TV and on the Internet. There was brand-new stuff still in boxes, like the big wooden picture frame that was really a jewelry box, and the foldaway shoe box holder. She had two different kinds of pedicure foot massagers. Two walls was covered with huge plastic closets, filled with clothes that still had tags on them. The other extra bedroom had all these different glass dolphins, butterflies, and unicorns she collected. The room looked like some kind of museum to me. Uncle Matt had an office on the first floor. Whenever me and Taevon spent the night, we slept in their big basement where they had the big-screen TV, the best DVD collection I ever seen, and even a little kitchen. Sometimes I wished that I could live with them. I wouldn't have to worry about nothing. I bet she'd buy me whatever I wanted, and we'd go places out of town all the time.

Her and Uncle Matt was always on vacation somewhere — the Bahamas, Aruba, Las Vegas, Trinidad . . . so I knew they would take me too. And then I thought about the two Talking Elmo dolls that was still in boxes on top of a plastic closet. Maybe Auntie *was* pregnant before. Why else would she have them?

We went back to being quiet while we finished cleaning the kitchen. After Teddy finished eating his peach cobbler, he stood up, stretched like he just woke up from a yearlong nap, and then he told Ma he was ready to go. I knew he was gonna want Ma to make him a plate to take home, even after all that crap he was saying about the food. When she was done, we all said our good-byes, piled into his gold Camry, and headed down Route 50 back to D.C. Teddy made me so sick. Twisting that toothpick back and forth in his mouth only made it worse.

LaSheika left a voice message for me to call her when I got home, so I called her back.

"You should ask your mother if you can spend the night over here tonight," she said.

"Why? It's all late."

"Tomorrow Black Friday, silly."

"What?"

"Tinka . . . Black Friday?!"

She knew I ain't have no money.

"We getting up real early so we can catch them sales out Pentagon City. You in?"

Why would I wanna go watch her and her

family shopping, buying this and that, while I was all broke? LaSheika's gear had went from average to excellent. I noticed on the first day of school that she was wearing some real Trues and some of the new Jordans. But of course everybody wears their best the first week. No, LaSheika stayed fresh two straight weeks after that. She had four new pairs of tennis shoes, plus like five different pairs of cute boots. I couldn't keep up with all her new stuff. Plus, I felt like a bum beside her, with the hand-me-downs Ma got me from the church around the corner. I mean I had one new pair of shoes, and a week's worth of summer clothes Ma got on sale. But it was about to be fall, and I was gonna have to dig in my trunk for the same stuff I was wearing at Walker-Jones last fall. When I asked LaSheika what the heck was going on with her wardrobe, she said, "My brother got it for me."

I felt so jealous and thought about Marquan.

"You know I ain't got no money LaSheika," I said.

"Yes, you do. Stop lying. I know you still got that money that dude gave you for your mother. You better use it and stop being stupid."

I never said I was a good liar. I had put

the money Ced gave me in a sock in my drawer. I was doing just what he said, and saving it for when Ma might really need it for something. Ain't nobody know I had it but LaSheika. Taevon would've tried to spend it on something stupid like some special dog food for Hitler. Or probably some Jordans or weed. Maybe I *could* get away with spending it.

"You can hide the clothes at my house."

I was tired of looking like a loser standing next to her everywhere we went. Me in my corny off-brand-looking Nikes Ma got from AJWright while LaSheika had on her cute colorful wrestling shoes that came up her legs. I went to beg Ma to let me stay the night. I knew she wasn't gonna care one way or the other. She had already cracked open her Rémy and it wasn't gonna be long before she got twisted.

CHAPTER 10
NICOLA

"I got something for you," Teddy said, walking into the bedroom smiling like a ten-year-old who snuck money out of his grandmother's purse.

"What?" I lifted my head up from the pillow. Ever since I got home from work, I been laying down. Teddy kept trying to tell me I was depressed. He was probably right. Sometimes I felt like my head was slowly separating into four tiny different parts and spinning all around in every direction. I hated leaving the bed. I felt safe on my island of pillows, buried under blankets.

He opened his hand and showed me a red Baggie stuffed with weed.

"Teddy? Come on now."

"What?" he said, lighting up the dark room with his smile. "Cola, stop playing. You know this shit gon' make you relax. It ain't no big deal."

"You know the last time I smoked?" I said,

holding my head up off the bed with my fist.

"Before Tinka was born. I know, I know, I know," he said, shaking his head and rolling up a joint just like he ain't hear a damn word I said.

"So why am I gonna start now if you know that? Don't light that shit up in here."

"I'ma grown-ass man, Cola. Don't start tripping and shit."

This nigga. I rolled my eyes and pulled the blanket over my head. I didn't feel like arguing with him. The minute I heard the lighter flick, and the smell of paper burning and the strong weed scent, I squeezed my eyes tight. I couldn't believe his ass was gonna ignore what I just said. The longer he smoked and the more the room filled up with the heavy odor, the more I wanted to smoke it. I yanked the blanket down and looked at Teddy.

He smiled. "You want some, don't you?"

I rolled my eyes and reached for it.

"Ah, ah, ah. Not until you say please," he teased.

"Stop playing, Teddy. Give it here."

He leaned over and kissed my forehead. "Anything for my baby."

It didn't take long for me to get high, since it's been so long. I sat back and watched

TV. Before long I heard my voice, but I had forgot that I wasn't planning to talk to him for the rest of the night. "You know what that lady I work for had the nerve to say to me about Marquan?"

"What?"

"That bitch said it's my fault Marquan did what he did. Can you believe that?"

"What! How she gonna blame you for what *he* did? She sound stupid. She got that ahh . . . that ahh . . . whatchucallit disease . . . Alzheimer's?"

I shook my head. "Talking about the problem starts in the home. 'If only he had a better home environment, your son wouldn't be in jail.' Like she fucking know me."

"See, that's exactly why I don't like you working with them stuck-up-ass old people. If she knew anything, she'd know you already beating yourself up about that shit."

I felt a tear sliding down my cheek. I wiped it away and took the blunt from him. "I'm like this close to quitting. I can see her judging me every time I come in there."

"Why you tell her anyway?"

I shook my head. "Being stupid, too, I guess."

"That bitch live on Sixteenth Street with all them other old gold coast niggas holding

117

on to a dollar and a dream."

I took another hit. Teddy didn't understand. He ain't know how hard it's been for me raising three kids, without anybody here helping me for all these years. Sometimes when you see a kind face or you know a person praying for you, it's easy for you to tell them what you going through.

"Quit if you want to, baby. You know I'll take care of you."

Nigga, please. You just now getting back in the picture. I smoked until I felt sleepy and the room felt too big for me, then I pulled the blanket over my head and closed my eyes.

The next day at work, I tried to clean without thinking about what Eileen Wheeler thought about me or my kids. She was a retired vice superintendent of D.C. public schools who was dealing with kidney failure. She slept mostly, read the other part of her time, but when she wasn't doing either one of those things, she was telling me what she thought about today's kids, especially the ones who ain't have no fathers around. She ain't care about what I thought either. She just wanted to hear herself talk, seemed like to me. From what I could tell, Eileen Wheeler's own kids ain't give a shit about her. They never came to see her, and just because they helped pay for the nurse and me, to help clean and take care of her, she thought they did care about her. Eileen actually taught me a lot, but I'm guessing it wasn't what she thought I would learn. That no matter how important you think you are in this world, if your family don't give a damn, then you ain't nobody really.

Teddy told me he was taking me out tonight and that he had a surprise for me. Thank God. I needed to go out bad. I hoped he would take me somewhere to dance. Maybe the Crossroads or Zanzibar. Anything to take my mind away from everything. After Shelia retouched my hair real quick, I put on a black sleeveless dress that hugged my body the way it was supposed to, a wide cheetah-print belt that highlighted my hair, and some cute leather knee-length boots Teddy bought me.

"Damn, girl!" Teddy said as soon as he saw me. He always made me feel like I was the sexiest woman he ever saw, which was just fine with me.

He took me to my favorite restaurant, Phillips on the waterfront. I can't believe he still remembered after all this time. It was real nice. When the waiter came, I ordered the shrimp and spinach pasta, and he got crabs.

"You surprised, ain't you?"

I nodded.

"See, Cola, you can still enjoy yourself," Teddy said.

"What you mean?"

"I'm saying it's okay for you to still enjoy life. Shit might not always be the way you want it, but at least it ain't over. You might as well enjoy it."

I raised one eyebrow and pressed my lips together. That was easy to say. The only stress he had in his life was what was happening to me. Of course he wanted me to stop stressing. I was messing up his plans.

CHAPTER 11
TINKA

It was so much colder now than when I first left the house for school. A chill raced down my back. I hurried up and fastened my coat. Ms. Basque had just made me so mad about not knowing all my prepositions by heart or for thinking I was "too cute to study," as she said it, that I just walked out altogether. Forget it. It was like she be waiting for a chance to jump down my throat, no matter how hard I try. The part I hated the most was she teach my favorite subject and I felt like she be trying to stress me sometimes, to see how much I could take before I break. But why it gotta be that serious?

I walked across Rhode Island Avenue and headed toward Ninth Street, up to the Giant Food grocery store, then I cut through Kennedy Park, then down O Street toward Dunbar — the high school Marquan used to go to and where Taevon's supposed to be at. I walked down New Jersey Avenue and across New York where two homeless dudes was trying to catch people at the traffic light. One stood in the middle dancing and holding a sign that said, Hungry. The other was trying to sell cheap socks and gloves he got from the Florida Avenue Market. He had his filthy hands touching everything. I don't know who was stupid enough to buy from him, but some people was doing just that.

I turned down M Street. Taevon stood on the corner of First with Hitler. He never went to school no more. Might as well consider him a dropout now. Wasn't nothing Ma could say. At least Marquan went to high school, even though he ain't never finish. Taevon showed up when he wanted to, just to see his friends or to try and holler at some girls. Teddy told him, all Taevon had to do was get his GED later and he could work with him doing plumbing. I thought that was stupid.

"What you doing home?" Taevon asked, trying his best not to let Hitler jump all over me. He slobbered buckets on the ground. *Gross.*

"What *you* doing home?" I kept walking past him.

"Yeah, all right. Smart-ass," he said, trying to hold his sagging pants up with one hand and gripping Hitler's chain with the other.

"Oh. Teddy in the house?" I asked over my shoulder.

He shook his head before he threw a treat at Hitler. I headed down the block.

"What's up, Tinka?" Monte said, riding his bike up beside me.

"Nothing."

"What you 'bout to do? You home all early."

"Nothing."

He smiled like he wanted to say something, but then he didn't. "You hungry?" he asked.

I squinted my eyes, not sure why he cared. He ain't have no money. "Why?"

"Man, yes or no?"

"A little bit, I guess."

"All right. I'll be back. You going in the house?"

I nodded, still confused. LaSheika must have ESP or something.

I threw my book bag on the floor, then I looked at the caller ID. Nothing. I went to the living room and turned on the TV. Nothing was on but *Judge Mathis.* I watched it until I heard a knock at the door. Monte stood there with a plastic bag.

"Hey," I said.

123

"Hey, got you some breakfast," he said, trying to walk in the door.

"Boy, I can't let you in here!"

"What? Why not? Look," he said, opening the foam carton. "I got you some eggs, home fries, bacon, and toast. Smell good, don't it?"

It did smell good. The only thing I ate today was a strawberry Pop Tart. "How I'm gon' let you in here? Nicola Hampton would kill me."

"What?! Your mother *like* me. Your whole family cool with me. You faking. Girl, it's starting to get cold. Me and the food." He raised his shoulders up to his ears and rocked side to side like he was trying to keep warm.

He *was* Taevon's friend. I knew where he lived. As long as he was gone before anybody came, I guess it was okay. I stepped back and let him in the door. We sat on the couch eating and watching *Real World.*

"Thank you, Monte. It's real good."

"You welcome."

We was quiet for a long time, then I said, "What made you buy me some food?"

"Why it gotta be a reason? I can't just wanna be nice?"

"But why you being all nice?"

He smiled. "I'm just a nice dude."

"Yeah, okay." I still ain't know what to think of Monte. He ain't try nothing. He just sat watching TV with me. We watched *Divorce Court* and then some reruns of *Fresh Prince.* We laughed and joked, then he was like, "I gotta bounce."

I walked him to the door and said bye.

"See you later," he said before he lit a Black & Mild up and walked out the door. I watched him walk up the street where Creature and the rest of his friends was standing. I couldn't wait to see LaSheika so I could tell her what happened and she could help me figure out what it all meant. As soon as I closed the door and went in the living room to throw away our plates, I heard the front door open up. Teddy walked in. I didn't know if he saw Monte leaving or not. He ain't say nothing but, "What you doing home so early?" when he saw me.

I told him the same lie I told security at my school. My stomach was hurting and it was that time of the month. He left me alone, even though he had a strange look in his eyes. If he ain't say nothing, I sure wasn't goin' say nothing. He ain't my father anyway. He ain't got no right to say nothing.

When I went to my room, I took out a sheet of paper and wrote the first lines of a letter I promised Marquan a long time ago.

Dear Marquan,
  I hope you're doing good in there. Everybody miss you. I'm okay, I guess. School all right. I could be doing better, but I can't stand one of my teachers. Ma getting on my nerves around here. You know how she can be. Plus, did anybody tell you yet that Teddy moved in? I know he Taevon's father, but I can't stand him. I wish you was here. I feel like I'm by myself whenever you not around. Anyway, I hope you taking care of yourself. This place ain't never the same without you. Call me when you get a chance.

Love,
Your favorite little Sis

CHAPTER 12
NICOLA

The snow was trickling so lightly, I didn't think it was gonna stick like the weather people said it was. This old, ugly, nasty neighborhood needed to be covered up in something clean, though. Just like three days ago, that little boy in that wheelchair got hit by a car with temporary tags that came speeding down M Street. Taevon said his name was Delano. Said his wheelchair went flying through the air and that it was the scariest thing he ever saw in his life because Delano was all broken up with one of his legs twisted the opposite way from his body. I couldn't get that picture out of my head.

The person driving the old white Caprice didn't even stop. The car made a left on North Capitol Street and disappeared. No news coverage. No search team. Nothing. I'm pretty sure if Delano was in a whiter part of the city, it would've been blown up all out of proportion. The whole damn city would've been on lock so them cops could find who the hell did it. The boy's mother couldn't even afford a real funeral. Some little girl with braids came around with the boy's picture on a can, taking up a collection. I gave them fifteen dollars, but Ms. David told Shelia Ms. Carmen paid for everything. That fat lady was something else. I knew damn well she ain't make all that money selling no goddamn candy from her house. Giving money and gifts away almost every holiday. I heard she was giving away twenty turkeys for Christmas. She paid for the Labor Day cookout and she gave away ten pair of Jordans to all the kids who was starting their first day of kindergarten the next day.

I was staring at the tiny snowflakes melting on my window and at two of Lynnda and Ramont's kids trying to scrape up enough snow to make one snowball. Ms. Jackson rushed to put up the rest of her Christmas lights before the snow really started coming down. She always waited until the last possible minute to put her decorations up every year. It was like a game watching her.

The phone rang. Oak Hill Youth Detention Center popped up on the caller ID. Marquan hardly ever called. I snatched the phone up. "Hello?"

"Merry Christmas, Ma," Marquan said.

"Hey, Quan. How you doing? You eating and sleeping and everything?"

"Uh-huh. Tinka there?"

My feelings was hurt. "Dag, you don't wanna talk to me?"

"Ummm . . . yeah. I just got her letter and wanted to see if she was okay."

"What you talking about? *Okay* about what?"

"Oh . . . nah." He hesitated. "Just checking on her."

"Oh? Hold on . . . Tinka!" I shouted.

I waited for her to come inside because I wanted to hear this conversation. She stood in the doorway looking confused. I showed her the phone. She walked over and sat on the bed.

"Hello? . . . Hey Marquan! . . . Yeah . . . No . . . Yeah . . . I don't know . . . Yeah."

She wasn't saying nothing, for real. Talking slick.

As soon as she hung up, I said, "What's wrong with you?"

"Nothing," she said, looking awkward.

"What y'all was talking about?"

"Nothing. He just asked me if I was ready for Christmas. If I got him something, stuff like that."

129

"Yeah right, Tinka."

"Huh?" she asked, giving me that stupid smirk she always do. The kind where she's thinking I'm crazy or that I just woke up out of a coma yesterday.

"Don't play dumb with me, little girl!"

"Ma, I don't know what you talking about. I swear."

"Just go."

Tinka rolled her eyes and stomped out the room.

Two more seconds and I would've snatched off her damn face. I was tired of looking at her. The older she got, the more she and me was getting like oil and water. Tinka always had a damn attitude about something. She liked to act like she was quiet, but I knew her and that little fast-ass girl around the corner wasn't as innocent as they liked to act in front of me. She better not be into nothing she ain't got no business in. The problem with Tinka is the only person who she really listens to is Renee. That shit gets on my nerves. I let her spend time with her aunt only to get her out of this fucked-up neighborhood as much as possible. Plus, she's the only girl, so I don't want her up in here all the time with the boys and their nappy-headed friends. Girls get pregnant and then stuck. And I ain't

130

want that for her. Renee could show her shit I couldn't, and I wanted Tinka to be better than me. She'll never understand it that way, if I told her. I try to *show* her that I'm stuck every chance I get so she can want more out of life. Three damn babies and three baby fathers will find your ass stuck with a shitty-ass job and living in the fucking projects. She too damn smart for that.

The phone rang again. It was Shelia this time.

"The DJ said he'd do it for a hundred. Me and Van can do fifty."

I thought for a second. Yeah, I definitely still needed to have my New Year's party. "Okay, go head. Me and Teddy'll pay the other half."

"Good. Talk to you later."

On New Year's Eve I got up early to cook dinner. Something about this time of year really made me want to start fresh. New Year's just gave me hope, I guess. That things could get better with time. New Year's was better than Christmas to me. Everybody seemed like they was taking a big deep breath everywhere I went. People got to wipe the slate clean and leave the past in the past. It was like turning a light switch on in a dark room or like that burst of energy meant to push me in that last stretch of a race. That's why I invited some of my old coworkers over, a couple of people from the neighborhood that I actually liked, like LaSheika's mother, Tracy; Janice up the block, who caught the same bus I did to work; and then some people Shelia wanted to come because she did their hair. Maybe we could all be renewed and our good energy could rub off on each other.

I had already soaked the black-eyed peas overnight, and the spicy barbeque ribs in the oven had been marinating in a Ziploc bag for two days. The candied yams with marshmallows was simmering, and the greens was in a big pot on the stove. Tinka had helped me make my special cornbread with honey. This year I got her a cute bookcase from IKEA that I made Teddy put together and a cute gray sweater from Macy's. Taevon got a doghouse for Hitler (so he could stop sleeping in here), but that little boy had the nerve to say somebody might try and steal that big vicious scary thing. Teddy agreed with him, even though he helped me get the damn house in the first place. I swear, the two of them something else sometimes. Hitler still running through the house leaving slob on everything. I bet his big ass gon' be in the doghouse tonight.

Renee wasn't coming by for the New Year's party. That wasn't a shock. They never came. But she tried to say her and Matt still had jet leg from their trip to St. Croix. Whatever the fuck. She got an excuse every year for why she can't come. They ain't like coming around here. Period. I could hear her nauseating voice complaining already. *It's terrible in this neighborhood. When do people sleep around here? The city need to tear this raggedy place down.*

Hell, she think I love it around here or something? This neighborhood is what it is and it serves its purpose. She just ain't like no decision I ever made. Probably never will.

I had just got out of the shower and was just about to put my clothes on when Teddy trapped me in the room. He had just finished smoking a whiteboy, and he locked the bedroom door.

"Boy, what you doing? I got people on the way over here!" I said, trying to move around him to get my earrings.

"We got time," he said, smiling. "You smell all good and shit."

"Teddy? Quit playing. I gotta get dressed now."

"Come're, Cola," he said, before he just

133

straight ripped my panties off until they popped with his fingers.

"See what you did?"

He forced me to lay down across the bed, so he could lick in between my legs. He ate me the way he used to do, back before them bitches started calling my house and waiting outside for him to get off work when Taevon was just a baby. He took his time to see how my body curled to his touch. Looking up every now and then to check my facial expressions. Loving every desperate sound my voice made. He could definitely still handle his business and he knew it. He made my body feel young again, and Lord knows I needed it.

CHAPTER 13
TINKA

At first I was gonna spend the night over LaSheika's, but she begged me to stay home so she could come over. Ma said it was cool as long as we stayed upstairs. Her mother, Ms. Tracy, was coming over anyway, so it wasn't like we could get too out of control. Ms. Shelia and Van was coming over and Taevon was staying the night over with Antonio and the rest of them. Some other people from the neighborhood, like Ms. Janice up the street and her sister Niecey, was coming by. Lynnda and Teresa said they might come over, too. If Ramont showed up, that would be too much drama, but I couldn't wait to see. Maybe Leon, the man who drove the Navigator that Ms. Tracy been checking out, might show up too. Oooh. I was gonna be watching people like a hawk.

Ma sent me and Taevon to the store to get some snacks, six bottles of Pepsi, ginger ale soda, and five bags of pretzels while she finished cleaning up and putting up decorations everywhere. She made Taevon put Hitler in his new doghouse in the backyard so he wouldn't scare the heck out of nobody. At ten o'clock, Ma turned the stereo up loud when she heard Mary J. Blige's voice seeping out the speakers.

"I'm searching for a real love." Ma sang an old-school song. She had on a tight black stretch jean skirt and a light black-and-white striped sweater that showed off her shoulders.

"Someone to set my heart free. Real love!" Teddy added, dancing up behind her. I rolled my eyes when he kissed her.

When LaSheika and Ms. Tracy knocked on the door, I was so happy. Five more minutes and throw-up was gonna fly out my mouth watching them doing their old-school moves. Taevon left to go over Ms. Shelia's. All of her boys was gonna be there, probably drinking and smoking weed like usual. Taevon thought he was so slick.

"Hey, LaSheika. Hi, Ms. Tracy. I like your outfit."

"Thank you, girl. It took two hours to squeeze in these pants," she said, laughing. Her scar, from all those days of fighting like her daughter, danced high on her cheek.

"I picked it out," LaSheika said.

"I hope we not too early?" Ms. Tracy said as she looked around at the empty house.

"No, not at all," Ma said, walking up. "Go 'head and make yourself a drink."

Me and LaSheika went upstairs. She couldn't wait to tell me about some boy named Carlos she been talking to who go to Dunbar.

"I think I'ma let him hit," she said, smiling.

My eyes flashed open. She was a virgin just like me — well, at least that's what she said, but I couldn't tell no more. Not since she been hanging with Melissa. This boy was in high school. Why was she even looking his way?

"For real?"

She nodded and smiled. "He's so cute. You gotta see him. And he be driving his brother's car sometimes."

I couldn't believe how she was acting. But then again, yes, I could. She was always flirting with Taevon — *Buy me something from the store, Taevon. You should let me ride your bike, Taevon. Can I play with your dog?* But he ain't never pay her no attention.

"What's up with you and Monte?"

I smiled, but I ain't know. He was nice, but Monte ain't make my heart skip like

137

this other boy I seen in the neighborhood sometimes. "I don't know."

"You can't get past the pimples?"

I laughed at her. "No, it's not that. He's just okay."

"What then?"

"You know Clint's cousin?"

"Who?"

"The one that come around here all the time, with the dreads."

"Oh, the sexy dark-skin one?" she asked, nodding.

I smiled and closed my eyes at the same time.

"Damn, like that?" LaSheika asked, laughing.

I nodded. "I think his name Nine or something?"

"Girl, I'ma ask Clint for you. You gon' have to step your shit up, though. He fine like a mug."

"Oh my God. Don't put me out there?!"

"I got you, Tinka. I'ma hook you up. Trust."

I laid across the bed and watched TV on mute, while LaSheika called this Carlos dude. I half-listened to their nasty conversation. The music from downstairs was so loud the walls shook. I knew some of the songs, like "This Is How We Do It" and

"Get Ur Freak On." Then they started playing some Go Go. First it was "Wind Me Up Chuck" by Chuck Brown, then "Pieces of Me" by Rare Essence. People's voices got louder. A lot more people had come because I could hear different voices I ain't know, traveling up the stairs. They was laughing and shouting over the music. I heard somebody say "Sheeiit" real loud and laugh. I looked out the window and saw a couple cars pull up with more of Ma's old coworker friends.

When it was close to midnight, I got up so I could sneak me and LaSheika something to drink. Wasn't gonna be no toasting for the countdown without us. The air was so smoky and filled with the strong smell of weed, perfume, and sweat. *Oh my gawd.* Leon and Ms. Tracy was kissing on the steps. "Excuse me," I said when I squeezed passed them. Neither one of them stopped to look up. They just moved closer together. I smiled. Ooh, I couldn't wait to tell LaSheika when I got back upstairs.

There was so many people on the first floor that I could hardly move. What the heck was Mr. Duncan's fat butt doing over here? Too many arms, legs, hips, and sometimes coats in the way, for Ma to see me mixing two plastic cups of Patrón and fruit punch. I pressed my way past people I ain't know and inched my way back up the stairs, past Ms. Tracy and her new boo.

"Your mother having herself a ball," I said, handing her a cup.

"What you talking about?" She swallowed a big gulp like she drink alcohol all the time.

"Dag, girl. Slow down!"

She laughed. "What?"

"Save some for midnight!" I took her cup away. "Go look at your mother cutting up in the hallway."

She tiptoed to the edge of the stairs and then ran back in the room.

"Aww get it, Mommy," she said, dancing to the beat of Northeast Groovers' "Booty Call."

I hopped up and started dancing, too.

"Make a booty call, come on!" we sang together.

I twisted my hips and sipped my little drink just like I was in a video. They played "Da Butt" next and then they turned the music down. I could hear Teddy's voice starting the countdown: "Ten, nine, eight . . ."

". . . Seven, six, five . . . ," me and LaSheika screamed. "Four, three, two, one!"

"Happy New Year!" the whole house erupted.

LaSheika tapped her plastic cup against mine, and then we heard the bullets going off and car horns blowing outside.

"Niggas," she said, shaking her head.

"Exactly."

Somebody turned the music back on, blasting some old Rob Base and DJ E-Z Rock's "Joy and Pain," and the house finished partying. I danced until I felt a little dizzy. I laid down and ended up falling asleep. I woke up around three to use the bathroom. The music was real low and slow. I could hear Musiq Soulchild singing his butt off. A few people was still downstairs talking, but I could tell the party was basically over.

A loud slam, like someone fell down the stairs, woke me up the second time. LaSheika woke up, too. She looked at me, then we heard my mother yell, "No, Teddy! Stop! Please!"

I jumped up out the bed and ran across the hall, but the yelling was coming from downstairs. I skipped steps to see what was going on. LaSheika was right behind me. Ma was lying on the floor wearing nothing but a slip, holding her stomach. Tears rolled down her face.

"Oh my God. Ma, you all right?!" I asked, rushing down to help her.

141

"I know you fucking that nigga, Cola! How the hell you gonna disrespect me tonight in front of all these goddamn people?!" Teddy shouted, standing over top of her.

He ain't have his shirt on, and he was drenched in sweat. Teddy was twisted. I could smell the liquor on his breath when he yelled. His eyes was red and low. He looked down at her, but he ain't seem like he saw *me.*

"You ain't seen nothing yet, Cola. I know how to fix your ass!" he said lifting his leg, getting ready to kick her.

"No, Teddy!" I yelled and put my body in between the two of them. "Don't you kick my mother!"

"Fuck you, Tinka! You too goddamn grown as it is," he said, snatching me up by my arm. I felt like he pulled it out the socket, the pain hurt so bad.

"No, Teddy! Don't!" Ma shouted.

I was too stunned about him unbuckling his belt that I couldn't move.

"Your ass should've been my goddamn daughter any muthafuckin' way. Come here!"

He folded his belt in half. My feet was like cement attached to the floor, but my mouth fell open.

He swung his arm back, but wasn't nothing I could do in time to stop him from whipping me. I screamed at the top of my lungs when his belt ripped my arms and legs, like a razor blade slicing my skin.

"No!" I cried. I grabbed the belt with my hands, but it felt like fire. He wrapped one of my arms behind my back and hit me again. He hit and he hit until I was numb, like my body fell asleep. I heard Taevon's voice and LaSheika yelling when the whipping finally stopped, but then I blanked out and slipped into darkness.

When I opened my eyes again, I was in LaSheika's room. She told me how she ran to Ms. Shelia's to get Taevon and that an ambulance had to come get my mother, because she couldn't get up off the floor.

"I think she broke her ankle."

My body still hurt, like it was swollen all over.

"You probably don't remember, but my mother gave you some Motrin. You feel any better?"

"I feel like I'm on fire," I whispered.

LaSheika turned her lips up and shook her head. "Maybe you should soak in the bathtub. Come on."

She helped me get up and walked me to

the bathroom, then she turned on the hot water and poured a whole bunch of Epsom salt in it. I tried to undress, but my body hurt too bad.

"I'll help you, wait. I can't believe that man spazzed out like that! His ass need to go to jail, for real. I hope your mother press charges."

Me, too. How could she not, after what he did to us? "I'll never forgive her if she don't," I mumbled.

Who the hell Teddy think he was hitting me? I wished Marquan was here. He'd kill him, if he knew about this.

CHAPTER 14
NICOLA

That nigga almost had me fooled. I thought he would never ever hit me. He never did before. It was like he was a complete stranger. My whole body still felt bruised, and now my damn ankle got screws in it because of his ass. He *is* a fucking stranger to me now.

I ain't know how I was gonna ever get Tinka to trust me again. It was my fault she had to go through that. She won't even look me in my face no more. Almost like I'm the one who hit her. Maybe she forgot I'm the one who broke my damn ankle. I can't do nothing on my own no more. Either I gotta stay in my room all day or roll around downstairs in the kitchen or the living room until Taevon come to help me up the steps. I did the first thing I could think of to make Tinka feel better: put all of Teddy's shit out on the street. Well, Taevon had to do it.

I couldn't tell how Taevon really felt about

what his father did to us. He just stayed to himself about the whole situation. Even as pissed as I was, there wasn't no way in the world I could press charges against him. He was still my son's father, and Teddy had enough issues in his life. I ain't want him to lose his job behind this. Plus, not to make excuses for him, but Brian was in my face all night. I don't know why one of my old coworkers thought it was cool to bring him there. Brian Mickens worked in the mailroom, and he used to try and holler the whole time I worked at DPW. I kept trying to dodge him all night, but he kept finding a way to grab my hand or pull me by the waist. I knew Teddy saw him and I think he thought I liked Brian, because I was trying to still be nice about it, instead of making a big scene to get him to stop touching me.

Anyway, it is what it is and now I gotta stay off my foot until it's healed.

The fucked-up thing was that Eileen Wheeler couldn't wait for me to get better. Matter of fact, my company just laid me off. Talking about they tired of me not coming to work for this and that. But how the hell was I supposed to do any work when I couldn't even walk?

Renee and Matt offered to help us out for

a little while, and I accepted. I might be proud, but one thing I'm not is stupid. I let them cover some of our bills, but then I had to dead that, because I knew my sister. She'd never let me forget what she did for me.

One day Shelia wheeled me over to the welfare building on H Street to sign us up for more assistance. She was my girl, the only person who really helped me out. You find out real quick who in your corner when you can't do shit for yourself. Shelia cooked and helped me do the laundry, and she went grocery shopping for us. Whatever errands I couldn't get the kids to do, Shelia and Van did it for me. I was really thankful. Seemed like she always coming to my rescue.

After Teddy left, I stopped drinking and smoking as much as I used to, but I'm not gonna lie — them pain pills was like a godsend. My ankle still hurt like hell and if I ain't have them, I'd probably stay in the bed crying from the pain all day. I still slept a lot, but that was only because of the medicine. It made me sleepy.

Chapter 15
Tinka

"What's up with your mother? She all right and shit?" Monte asked before he sat next to me on the hood of Ms. Jackson's old green Saab.

I nodded, even though it was a lie. Ma been popping them pills from the morning to the night. Even after her ankle got better and she was finally strong enough to walk on it without crutches, she popped those pills. Her voice slurred, her eyes rolled to the back of her head until she nodded off. Sometimes me or Taevon had to help her up to bed, or we had to turn off a pot she left burning on the stove. It was hard watching her high like that.

Me and Monte was really cool now. He had a way about him that reminded me of Marquan. He was always checking on me or making me laugh. So even though I knew he was only asking because he cared about me, I couldn't bring myself to say the truth.

"Some people been talking. Not that you care, but I just thought you might wanna know."

I shook my head. I ain't wanna know. I already knew, for real. Ma was addicted to them stupid pills. Me and Taevon got into an argument about it.

"When you gonna quit taking them pills, Ma?" Taevon asked her one day when he helped her in the bathtub. "It got you acting like a crackhead."

"Don't say that, Tae," I said, because it wasn't crack. It was methodone.

"Man, whatever. I'm saying the truth. Look at her. Ain't nothing wrong with her ankle no more and she be feenin' for those motherfuckin' pills just like them *unks* be feenin'."

"Taevon, I still hurt. All over," Ma mumbled. "You don't know."

He looked disgusted. Taevon rolled his eyes and left me and her in the bathroom. I took her robe off and helped her sit down.

"He remind me of Marquan storming out like that," Ma said. "He don't understand, Tinka. But you do. Thank God you do."

But she was wrong. I didn't.

I watched as Monte looked at his cell phone for a while, then closed it shut. How could I tell him she couldn't get her same

149

job back taking care of old people once her ankle healed all the way back up? And that it wasn't just because she missed so many days from work. Ma said it was too much for her, but I think she just ain't feel like working no more. She got a little part-time job cleaning office buildings at night. She absolutely hated it and hardly went.

"What you gon' do later? I got that new *Saw* on bootleg. You think your mother gon' trip if I bring it over?"

Of course she wasn't. She was too damn high to care about what was going on. "Nah. Bring it."

"All right. Well, I gotta make a run real quick. I'll call you before I come, okay?"

"Okay."

CHAPTER 16
NICOLA

Teddy kept the pain away. Simple as that. He made me feel good. He apologized so many times that he made me dizzy. I believed him. Hell, I wanted to. I missed him. So much time had passed since New Year's. The springtime was always our season. We first met during the spring, back when it was just me and Marquan waiting at the bus stop on Fourth Street.

I had just picked him up from day care when Teddy pulled up and called me "Sexy in the Red." I ignored him then, but then he was there the next day, saying what's up again. He parked his car and got out to talk to me when I tried to ignore him. Teddy introduced himself and then pulled a tiny toy car out of his pocket to give to Marquan. I told Marquan he better not take it, and rolled my eyes. I don't know how I let Teddy talk me into letting Marquan have it, but he did. He ain't get my number that day, but he did the next week.

Teddy showed up at my new part-time job downtown where I had been cleaning office buildings overnight just to have some money in my pocket. His eyes actually watered up when he apologized about that crazy New Year's party. Teddy ain't never ever cry in his life for me. I knew he meant every single word. He promised to get some counseling. He *was* bent that night. We all were. Emotions was high. I ain't tell Brian he was wrong for touching me like I should have, and Teddy had a point. I made him look like a punk letting some other nigga rub his hands all over me in the place Teddy called his home. Plus, I fell down the steps — it wasn't his fault I broke my ankle.

We stopped by Van's job on the way home. It was a mechanic shop on Georgia Avenue with a small junkyard in the back. They was shooting craps and drinking beer in the garage when we pulled up. Somebody was grilling ribs and they smelled so damn good, like the kind where the meat was gonna melt off the bone. Music was blasting from the blue Tahoe parked next to us. Everybody was having a good time. I drank a beer and sat in his car while he watched them play and talked shit. It was just like how it used to be. I closed my eyes, inhaled the scent of

152

fresh herb, listened to Frankie Beverly and Maze sing about joy, then decided to forgive Teddy. I needed his help with the bills. It was tight around here with only a part-time job, plus Tinka need clothes and the fridge was empty as hell.

After an hour, Teddy asked me if I was ready to go. Instead of heading back to my house, he pulled up to a hotel on New York Avenue.

"Thought you might wanna get away from the kids for a second. You cool with it?" he asked, as we sat in the parking lot. "You can take a long hot bath. I'll rub your feet, massage your back . . . remind you why you miss me."

He smiled and I took a breath. It had been a long four and a half months with a cold, empty bed. I did miss him and it had been a long day.

"Come on, beautiful, let's go," he said.

Cleaning had a way of making me feel ugly all the time. It was basically my job to get dirty at work. Show up clean, leave dirty. I kept my hair covered and hardly wore makeup because I ended up sweating when I did it. Teddy made me feel like I was pretty, regardless, so I smiled and followed him into the hotel. I just wanted to be held.

I wanted him to apologize over and over again.

CHAPTER 17
TINKA

I came home from school to see Teddy stretched out on the couch with his feet up, talking about, "Hey, Tinka." I couldn't *F-ing* believe it! I ain't care if it was Taevon's father or not. He wasn't supposed to be here! Especially not after what he did to me. How could Ma really choose him over me — her own flesh and blood?

"I cannot wait until Marquan come back home!" I told LaSheika over the phone later.

"Girl, I should get Keion to shoot his bitch ass. He would never see it coming," she said. "I can't believe your mother letting that crazy nigga move back in. She think he ain't gonna try some wild shit again?!"

"She can't even look me in my face."

"Well, I know something that'll make you feel better. Guess who I saw today?"

"Who?"

"Nine!"

"Nine?!"

"Yes, girl! Him and Clint just went in Temple Courts."

Nine hardly ever came around the neighborhood. So every time he was around, it could easily be the last time I saw him.

"I'ma bring you something cute to wear so we can go outside and be seen."

"Okay, okay. Hurry up."

LaSheika was still there when I heard Ma come home. Her and Teddy was acting like nothing new was going on, like he ain't miss a beat or something. That's when I knew Ma must've been seeing him for a while now. Talking about she going here and there with a coworker, but all along she was with him, trying to see if he would move back. Every time I heard his voice and then Ma's laugh floating up the hall, it made me ill.

"Come on LaSheika. Let's go outside."

"All right," she said.

We both left the room, climbed down the stairs, and headed for the door.

"Tinka, you do your homework?" Ma said.

"Yeah," I said, letting the door slam. She was too high to even notice that I had on LaSheika's clothes. "She makes me sick," I said to LaSheika.

"I know she do, but try not to worry about it."

We walked up the block and headed to the basketball court across M Street. We watched Keion, Creature, Big Mike, Raynard, and Duane play basketball with some dudes we ain't know. Of course, Krystal was here, trying to get some attention from anybody with three legs. She was leaning against the fence with Angie and Mya talking to some boy on a bike. Taevon walked by with Hitler, Antonio, and Monte.

"I'm thinking about asking my aunt if I could stay with her for the summer. You think I should?"

"I don't know. I would be blown being here by myself. For the whole summer? Come on now. Hanging out with Laila every single day? Blah," she said, poking her finger in her throat like she wanted to gag.

I smiled. "I know, but I just can't be in that house with that man. I know he moving back in. I can't take the sound of his voice!" I shivered.

"I feel you."

We was quiet for a minute, watching the basketball game and the cars speeding down M Street and North Capitol.

"I gotta ask you something," LaSheika said, all serious. Her voice made it seem like it was something really important.

I looked at her sideways and said, "What's up?"

"So you can't tell nobody, okay?"

"I promise," I said, anxious to know what she was talking about.

"Me and Carlos did it."

My eyes got big.

"Okay . . . we did it three times."

"Three times?!?! How can you keep that secret from me?"

"I don't know. It just happened."

"When?"

"The first time was in January."

I shook my head. I couldn't believe this girl. "All this time . . . well, did it hurt?"

She nodded. Her eyes got as big as mine. "The first time it did . . . but after that it just seemed strange."

"But you let him do it again?"

She nodded.

I looked down at my feet. I wasn't ready for that yet.

"But that's not the only thing I wanna tell you."

I frowned. What could be more serious than that?

"Ummm . . . me and him not talking no more."

"Why?" I bet he used her, just like Aunt Renee warned me about dudes.

She took her sweet time before she said, "He gave me something."

My eyebrows jumped as high as they could go. I blinked and shook my head. "What?!"

She bit her lip.

"Your mother know?"

She nodded.

"What was it?"

"The doctor said it was trick-a-something."

"What's that?" I asked, but the whole time I was thinking, *Uggh, gross.*

"Well, when I told my mother how I was feeling, she said I probably had a urinary infection or yeast infection. Something like that. But when we went to the doctor, she asked me if I was sexually active. After I told her yeah, she did some more tests and then, that's what they said it was — trick-a-something."

"Dag."

We was quiet for a minute. I knew what I was thinking — did it itch or burn? Did it stink? Was she gonna have it forever like AIDS? — but I wondered what she was thinking. She looked sad.

It was killing me, though. I had to know if it went away. "You still got it?" I asked.

She shook her head. "It's gone now."

"Good." *Whew.* I can't be having no friends walking around with a fishy booty. That's just asking to get joned on. "I know you glad."

She nodded and looked at the guys playing ball. Then she said, "Don't tell nobody, Tinka. For real."

"I won't. I promise."

There was so much of my business LaSheika could tell somebody to hurt me if she wanted to, I could never put her business on blast like that. Anyway, it wasn't her fault that she was out there having sex already. Her mother let her do just about whatever she wanted, because she was too busy trying to act like she ain't have no kids herself. LaSheika got to spend the night out with her older cousins just about every other weekend, because her mother was headed to a club. It didn't take a genius to know why LaSheika wanted to be over there so much. They let her do the same things they was doing. Her sister, Laila, stayed with her grandmother around Kenilworth a lot, and Keion was on the block, doing his thing. And now with her mother dating Leon, Ms. Tracy seemed like she was paying even less attention to her kids. Ms. Tracy and Leon went out like twice a week, and she went by his place around Potomac Gardens whenever he wasn't in the neighborhood visiting his mother.

I just hope this trick thing makes LaSheika slow down. My mother ain't never got to worry about me asking her to take me to no dag-on clinic because of no issues with my coochie. I ain't having sex. Period. We never did see Nine or Clint. I guess I missed him again.

Two days later, Ms. Basque cornered me in the hallway at school. I tried not to look annoyed when she rolled all up on me like the police. She seemed like she loved looking me over from head to toe, like I was in military school or something. My own mother never even looked at me like that.

"Ms. Hampton," she said in her stern voice.

What now? "Yes," I said.

"I really like some of your writing."

Was I hearing her right?

"I want you to enter the District Youth Poetry Contest this month. I think you have a strong chance of winning . . . that's if you apply yourself," she said.

Is she serious? I never thought she paid much attention to my journal entries. Whenever I got my journal back from her, there was never any comments, just a check mark at the top of each entry. I couldn't believe what she was saying right now.

I opened my mouth to say okay, but I just ended up nodding.

"Did you hear me?" she asked.

"Yes," I was finally able to say.

"Okay. So, there's a five-hundred-dollar scholarship prize for first place, and the deadline is June fourth. Let me know if you need my help."

Five hundred dollars? There was so much I could do with that money. I could add on to the new wardrobe I been trying to build, for one thing. "Okay."

"And don't let this get in the way of your other class work, either," she said before walking the other direction.

I couldn't wait to get home to work on something new.

When school was over, I waited outside for LaSheika so we could walk home together. A couple minutes went by before she walked out the door with her other friend Melissa.

"Oh, Tinka. I'm going around Melissa's way today. My bad — I meant to tell you earlier."

I twisted my lips and nodded. "Oh, okay. See you." It wasn't the first time I walked home by myself, but the way Melissa was smiling seemed real suspect. I swear she looked like she knew something I didn't, but I tried hard not to seem jealous. Unlike her, I ain't mind sharing my friends.

"I'll call you later," LaSheika said.

Melissa smiled again and waved as they walked up Ninth Street toward Howard University.

I crossed Rhode Island Avenue and walked down Q Street. As soon as I got to the corner on Seventh, I saw a girl named Venesha standing in the doorway of the corner store. Besides the fact that she went to Shaw, I ain't know nothing about her, except at lunch today I found out Melissa had a beef with her. Five girls walked out the store one by one. Some was eating snacks and talking loud. Venesha said something to one of them and then she rolled her eyes at me. I tried to ignore them, but then her friends all looked me up and down. One with a blond boy haircut laughed and said, "Bitch, please."

I ain't have nothing to do with Venesha and Melissa's drama. I barely knew the girl outside of LaSheika.

"Where your girl at?" Venesha asked with an attitude. She stopped right in front of me and grinted again. Her clan surrounded her like they was backup. Some had their

163

hands on their hips.

"Who?" I asked, but I couldn't believe how much my voice cracked with just one word.

"Bitch, you know who!" Venesha shouted.

I ain't say nothing. All of those girls looked like they ain't care about nothing I had to say. Like they wanted to kick my butt just because. It didn't matter if I ain't know Melissa or not. All of a sudden I felt like crying. But I didn't do it, even though my eyes got watery.

"Tell that bitch I'ma split her shit the next time I catch her ass," Venesha said so close to my face that I could smell her Bubblicious chewing gum. I looked away.

She was a thick girl, and real short. She looked older than me, by at least two years.

"This corny bitch don't wanna fuck with *Diamond Mafia!*" a girl with a short red pixie haircut yelled at me.

Oh, no. Not the Diamond Mafia. Everybody knew about them. They was an all-girl gang like Most Wanted, X-Rated, and the Pussy Pound, who was good for slicing somebody up and robbing them. They was all ages, too. Most of them was in high school, but a lot of them had dropped out of school. I had even heard the Diamond Mafia lit some boy on fire with lighter fluid on Fifth and

Kennedy last spring. I ain't want nothing to do with them.

"I like them shoes," said the girl with red hair.

Oh snap. I looked at my cute black shoes with the tiny heel that I got from Gussini's with some money Taevon let me have for giving Hitler a bath once.

"Them joints hot as shit," said the big fat one with microbraids.

"Where you get them from?" said Blondie with the boy haircut as she stepped closer to me.

"Umm . . . they so old, I can't even remember."

"What size you wear?" Blondie asked.

"I wear a . . . a seven."

"Which one of y'all wear a seven?" Blondie asked, turning to her crew. Not only did she look like a boy, she acted like one, too. She seemed like she was the leader with her D.M. tattoo written in cursive on the side of her neck.

A couple of the girls shook their heads, while the others said, "Nah, not me."

"I wear a eight and a half," Venesha said.

"Damn. None of y'all can fit these joints?" Blondie asked, and then she crossed her arms and rubbed her chin, like she was thinking hard. "Well, I guess I want them anyway. Give 'em here."

My mouth fell open. "But what am I gonna wear home?"

"I don't give a fuck! Bitch, give me those muthafuckin' shoes! What the fuck I care about how you getting home?!" she said, jumping in my face and pointing her finger like it was a gun or something.

Venesha laughed hard and loud. I rolled my eyes and took a step back. It was six of them. What was I supposed to do? Ain't no way I could run from here all the way home or even to somewhere to hide. I couldn't believe LaSheika was not here. Of all times. All because of her fake new friend Melissa. Wasn't no way in the world I was gonna try to fight Blondie, either.

"What the fuck you waiting for?!" Venesha yelled.

But before I can make up my mind or even bend down to take my shoes off, I felt Blondie's fingernails scratching my face like a raggedy alley cat. Somebody kneed me in my stomach and I fell backward. A second later I felt somebody tugging at my shoes, while somebody else kicked my side. I felt the tears rolling down my face as I tried to roll into a ball. Ma's face lying at the bottom of the steps on New Year's flashed in my head. I held on to my bag as tight as I could and tried to cover my face, then I felt somebody yanking at the straps.

"Ay, ay, ay!" I hear a man yelling. "Leave that girl the hell alone!"

When I looked up, a dusty man with a construction hat and a neon orange vest was standing over me.

"Come on, sweetheart," he said, reaching down to help me get up. "You all right?"

I looked around, but those girls was nowhere to be found.

"Sweetheart, you okay?" he asked again.

I looked down at my bare feet. "They got my shoes."

"Don't worry about that. Are *you* all right?"

How could I tell this stranger that my stomach and my side hurt like hell? Or that some of those girls went to my school and I was gonna have to see them again, and maybe even have to fight every day until the end of the school year now? What was he gonna do about it? Nothing. So, I nodded like everything was okay and like I really would be all right.

"All right. Hurry up and get home safe," he said before he headed down Seventh Street.

I fixed my bag and mumbled "Thank you" before making my way barefooted down to the pay phone in front of the 7-Eleven on Rhode Island Avenue. Somebody had to come get me. ASAP. Wasn't no way I was walking all the way home like this.

Of course, Ma had to send Teddy when I called her at work. She couldn't ask Van or get Ms. Tracy to send Leon? It took an hour for him to show up. When he finally got there, he looked like he had just got off early because he still had on his work clothes. He ain't say nothing, thank God. I hated him, and deep down inside I knew he hated me, too. I rolled my eyes and climbed in the backseat of his Camry. I always felt like he blamed me just for being alive. Like I reminded him of the man who took my mother away from him. But it wasn't my fault. My father obviously ain't even want me anyway.

"You all right?" he asked.

I nodded.

"Good. Your mother would trip the hell out if something happened to you," he said so low from the front seat, I thought I was making it up.

CHAPTER 18
TINKA

LaSheika acted like she had no idea why I wasn't talking to her no more. She kept sending Laila by the house to ask me what was wrong, when she noticed I was avoiding her. I told Laila to tell her sister to ask her *new* best friend why we not talking. Then she came by the house talking about, "Oh my God. Why you ain't tell me what happened the other day?"

I ain't say nothing.

"So you gonna let me in or what?"

I rolled my eyes.

"Tinka, you know you can't blame me for that?"

I pressed my lips tight and blinked real hard. *Oh, yes I could.*

"For real, Tinka? We like that now?" she said.

She was right. I couldn't really blame her for getting jumped, but I *could* blame her for getting me into some nonsense because of her flaky new friend.

I sucked my teeth, and then opened the door all the way.

"Fuck that shit!" LaSheika said, smiling. Then she plopped down on the couch. "Tell the truth, you got at least one lick in, right?"

I smiled.

"Oh yeah, I'm not talking to Melissa no more."

"Why?"

"You know I heard she mess with Carlos?"

"Dag." *And you care after what he gave you?*

"Girl, forget that bitch," LaSheika said, rolling her eyes. "He a little boy anyway."

I wasn't so sure she even believed what she said.

Later after LaSheika left and I was alone in my bedroom, I wrote in my journal:

One person's nightmare can be another's
   dare
One person's refuge, another's prison
One gift, a curse

That little sixteen-word thing I called a poem and had the nerve to give Ms. Basque at the last minute ain't earn me no five-hundred-dollar poetry scholarship either. Later, Ms. Basque said, "You should've been embarrassed to hand that sloppy piece of crap to me in the first place, Miss Hampton, and I hope you learned your lesson when you saw the caliber of your competitors and the beautiful cleverness of the outstanding winner." *Blah, blah, blah.*

Ms. Basque even made me write the winning poem one hundred times in cursive. I wanted to kill her on the last day of school.

CHAPTER 19
NICOLA

The house was real quiet with Tinka gone for the summer. Taevon only came in the house to sleep and shower. He was spending so much time outside, running the streets. I stopped trying to keep up with that boy. He always had some slick shit to say nowadays, and he stayed on my nerves. Teddy and me did a lot of catching up. We went to Ocean City to the beach and we even went out West Virginia to hit the riverboat casinos. Teddy won fifteen hundred dollars that he let me spend at the Outlets. I brought everybody something. I got him and Taevon watches and tons of clothes for me and Tinka.

On the Fourth of July there was the annual block party Ms. Carmen threw every year. As usual she watched the action from her upstairs window. Everybody made sure to stop by and thank her for the food. She seemed like that was her favorite part of the day. She did hook the whole neighborhood up, though. There was everything. Fried chicken, hot dogs, hamburgers, chips, sodas. A couple times Ms. Carmen threw candy out the window to all the little kids. It was cute watching them running all over the place to catch it.

The U was closed and no cars could drive off of M Street to First Place. Cars could only leave out from First Terrace. Sammy and Duane's little Go Go band, DDB, played in the square beside our house, and they had the whole neighborhood rocking for a good minute. Then the fashion show started with a DJ playing, Keyshia Cole's "I Changed My Mind." Everybody was there. Even Ms. David and Ms. Jackson sat in canvas chairs near the back. Me and Shelia went over to watch it. Her daughter Krystal was one of the models. She had a bright blond bang. I couldn't believe Shelia actually let her have it. And I don't know who told her those tight neon green capris was cute on her thick behind.

Right after the fashion show, that monster-looking boy everybody call Creature and that sumo wrestler Big Mike jumped some poor homeless man because he had spit on one of Teresa's little girls since she was teasing him. They both was wrong, and yes, the homeless man was an adult who should've known better, but that little girl should've stayed in her place. Creature and Big Mike was real quick with it. They beat that man so bad, people made their kids go in the house, and when the ambulance and the police showed up, that was the end of all that.

Teddy came home from work earlier than usual. He grabbed a beer from the fridge and sat on the couch.

"What's wrong?" I asked. "Why you off so early?"

He shook his head and took his boots off.

"Everything all right?" I asked.

"Them niggas at work," he said, as he lit a cigarette. "Laying people off and shit."

Damn. I depended on his help around here. I only made seven dollars and fifty cent an hour cleaning them buildings. But I only worked thirty-two hours a week. That shit wasn't nothing. "You think you might be next?" I asked.

"Fuck, Cola, I don't know!" he snapped and got up to go upstairs. "Stop stressing me."

Now here we go again with this shit. I rolled my eyes and finished smoking my cigarette. I stayed downstairs for awhile to give him whatever space he needed to relax. Even on his worst day, Teddy was getting over living with me. Rent was next to nothing, even though he wasn't on the lease. If he wanted to move back with his mother, he wasn't paying nothing there either. Her house was paid for, his car was paid for. Teddy ain't have no real bills. He just liked spending money and going places. His ego probably hurt.

I went upstairs to see if I could make him feel better.

CHAPTER 20
TINKA

The weekend before the end of my summer break, Uncle Matt and Aunt Renee drove me back home from spending five weeks with them in Bowie. At first, Aunt Renee had said that I could spend the whole entire summer with her and that we was gonna have a ton of fun, but a day later she called back to tell me I couldn't stay the *whole* summer because Uncle Matt had already made plans for the two of them to leave the country. I was hurt for a little while, but then I got over it quick. I just wanted to go somewhere. Anywhere. Just the heck away from the Cordas and the noise and all the drama. And since visiting Aunt Renee's ain't cost us a dime, Ma ain't have a problem with it.

We ain't do much. I played in their pool as much as I wanted, even though it wasn't no fun playing by myself or with their dog Flower. Aunt Renee ain't get in the water one single time, talking about her hair getting wet and the chlorine messing up her skin. That's when I really missed Marquan and Taevon, because we would've had a ball together. I talked to LaSheika and Monte a lot, but it wasn't the same as being around the way.

I ain't realize how quiet it was out Bowie. No passing cars, no sirens, no radios, no people talking or walking by, no barking dogs or crying babies, no laughing or cursing. Just quiet. People came in the house and closed their doors, or people left out the house and climbed in their cars. Neighbors barely spoke to each other.

Uncle Matt was never home and when he was there, he was busy in his office with the door closed. Aunt Renee was no better — she stayed at the gym or watched QVC. On my birthday, she took me to a spa and then out to lunch at a fancy restaurant in a hotel in Baltimore, where we drank juice out of wineglasses and put napkins in our laps. There was even pretty designs in the butter. But other than that, me and Aunt Renee ain't do nothing together. She stayed on her side of the house, and I stayed on mine, reading the three books I brought with me. I read one each week: *I Know Why the Caged Bird Sings, A Tree Grows in Brooklyn,* and

The Diary of Anne Frank. If it wasn't for Marguerite, Francie, and Anne, I don't know what I would've done. Those books was the best part of my whole summer for real, and they all reminded me of me a little. Aunt Renee ain't seem to miss me when I was reading either. I guess she was getting tired of me asking her a hundred questions, like can I use Uncle Matt's computer and did she have any clothes she ain't want no more? I was starting to think maybe she really ain't want kids after all.

The Sunday night Uncle Matt and Aunt Renee drove down M Street to drop me off, I saw a lot of commotion going on in front of Ms. Carmen's house. Ambulances, fire trucks, and police lights lit up the corner on First Terrace and M Street.

"My God," Aunt Renee said, as she eyeballed Ms. Carmen's house.

"I swear I hate coming around here," Uncle Matt said and shook his head. "It's always something happening."

He was two seconds from saying, "It's always something happening *in the projects.*" I rolled my eyes at his comment, but I stared out the window, too. Uncle Matt made a right on First Place and then he stopped in the middle of the street behind a double-parked minivan blocking the way. I could see Ma, Ms. Shelia, Ms. David, and Ms. Jackson standing in front of our house, staring up the block at all the fuss.

Uncle Matt blew the horn at the person blocking the street, but no one came out to move their van. Whoever it was, was visiting Teresa.

"I can't believe somebody stupid enough to double-park on a one-way, single-lane street and then have the nerve to disappear!" he shouted.

People did it all the time around here. And ain't nobody complain. "That's okay, Uncle Matt. I can get out right here," I said, and unlocked the door.

"I don't want you walking around here by yourself," he mumbled angrily, and then he blew the horn again long and hard.

"Don't worry. I do it all the time. You can back your car back up the street. My mother's right there," I said, pointing, and then I opened the door.

"Tinka, you sure?" Aunt Renee asked, as she turned around in her seat to look at me.

I nodded. They was overdoing it. "Thank you for letting me spend the summer with y'all. I had a lot of fun."

"You're welcome. Let me at least give you a hug and watch you walk down the street," Aunt Renee said, getting out of the car.

Uncle Matt got out, too, and took the suitcase with wheels, which Aunt Renee gave me instead of the old book bag and trash bag I was using, out the trunk. I gave them both a hug and then walked down the U.

"Hey, Ma!" I yelled, as I got closer.

"Tinka?!" she asked. "Girl, what you doing walking down here by yourself? Where Renee and Matt?"

"Right there behind that van," I said, pointing.

She looked up the block and waved at them. "Oh, okay. You have fun?"

"It was all right. What's going on?"

"Ms. Carmen dead," Ma said.

"For real?!" I asked. Ma nodded her head up and down, then she told me the story she had heard. I stood the suitcase up and looked up the block where everybody else was looking.

Ms. Carmen's daughter Louisa found her mother sitting on the same old sinking couch she always sat on in the living room. She was sitting right in front of the TV dead as a doornail with a bullet in her head.

Who killed her?

Nobody had seen her for three days and all the neighborhood kids was wondering why she wasn't opening the door when they

180

knocked to buy candy. Some people said they smelled something funny coming from her house, but ain't nobody think to actually check on her.

"It might be her fat ass stanking in all this heat," Creature had joked to Taevon one day. And then today, Ms. David told Ms. Jackson, "I'm going to call the police if she don't open that door tomorrow." But tomorrow ain't have to come because Louisa showed up this morning and screamed at the top of her lungs as soon as she opened Ms. Carmen's door. She ran out in the street and screamed like a lunatic until Ms. Janice, who lived next to her, and Lynnda, who happened to be sitting on her porch across the street, ran up to see what was wrong. Ma said Louisa cried so loud the whole neighborhood stopped what they was doing for two seconds to look out their windows. And then, she said, a few minutes later the police showed up with a white van. But then two fire trucks rolled around, and all the firemen jumped off the truck, but nothing happened.

"All these people been here ever since, trying to figure out how they gonna get her big ass out of that house," Ma said, standing behind me.

"She ain't been out that house in years,

she done got so big," Ms. David said, shaking her head. "I ain't never seen one person eat until they are literally as big as a house. I can't believe it. How she let herself go like that and just grow and grow and grow?"

"But how somebody just walk up in her house and shoot her like that?" Ms. Shelia said.

"People stay running in and out of there. God knows who did it, that's for sure," Ms. Jackson said, shaking her head.

"She wasn't exactly being clever, *selling candy,*" Ms. David added, rolling her eyes.

"Let that woman rest in peace," Ma said.

Ms. David clucked her tongue and looked the other way.

I watched everybody shake their heads, then I took my suitcase in the house. When I walked upstairs, I heard huffing sounds coming from Ma's room. I looked over and saw Teddy watching a porno with his hand stuffed in his pants and the door wide open.

"Oh, you back home, huh?" he asked. "Welcome back."

His nasty self ain't even take his hands out of his pants. I went in my room and slammed the door. *I can't* believe *I'm back to this.*

On my bed was a birthday card and a gift wrapped in pretty paper and a letter from

Marquan. I didn't know which one I wanted to open first. Then I lied across my bed and flipped the gift box over. I ripped the paper off. *A camera!* Not one of those nice digital ones, but it was cool. I ain't never have one. I read the birthday card and the handwritten note at the bottom that said:

Tinka, I may not be able to give you the world like your Aunt tries to, and the way your father should be doing, but as long as you keep your head in them books you'll be able to see the world for yourself one day. Take plenty of pictures for me when you do. Happy Birthday!

Love,
Mommy & Teddy

Wow, Ma. I love it, but why you have to ruin it by adding Teddy's name? I put the card down, and then I opened the envelope from Marquan. His letter said:

Hey Tinka,
What's up homie? Haven't heard from you in a minute. I can't wait to come home. I'm sick as shit of this mug. What I been missing around the way? I know summertime be crazy, so I know I'm missing a lot. What Taevon been up to?

He told me his dog big as shit. I still can't believe Ma let him keep a pit in the house. How she doing anyway? Ced been back around there?

I read that new book you sent me. Took me longer than I thought it was going to, cuz they had me in isolation for a minute. I had to whip this bama nigga's ass from Baltimore for trying to test me and shit. He ain't know about me at first, but now he do. Forget all that. Anyway, I'm glad your teacher told you about *Dark* by that Kenji Jasper dude. It was better than that other one. Maybe cuz it was something like me. A boy from D.C. who just made a mistake that he wish he could take back. I know you said you ain't read it, but I think you'll like it if you do. Anyway, I'm counting down the days until I get out of here. The only people who write me is you and my father, but he ain't got nothing else to do, cuz he locked up, too, so he don't count. We writing about the same shit. (Smile) He finally supposed to be getting out next year. Ain't that crazy? We gonna be coming home like at the same time, if he make parole. I think that shit is crazy! I wonder if he's anything like I remember back when I was little.

Okay, well I gotta go. Send me a letter and another book soon.

Your big brother,
Marquan

P.S. Happy Birthday if this get there in time. You fourteen now, right? Your ass ain't grown, remember that!

I laughed and folded his letter back up, then slipped it back inside the envelope.

"Well, did you have fun?" Taevon asked, opening my door.

I looked passed him and saw that his freaky father had closed the door, then I stared at Taevon's tanned skin. "Boy, you got dark as I don't know what! You must've been outside all summer."

"You got dark, too!" he said, smiling.

"Yeah, right." I couldn't get but so much more darker.

"You have fun?"

"It was all right. Too quiet out there, though."

"I bet."

"You should've came."

"Nah, I would've been bored to death out there."

"Yeah, you would've been. I miss anything

around here?"

"You know something always going on. Antonio got locked up. They caught him with a couple dime bags and some bottles of water."

"Dag. He selling dippers?" I asked. It seemed like everybody was smoking embalming fluid–saturated cigarettes these days.

"What you think?"

"Selling, I guess."

Taevon nodded. "But he said he was smoking them so he could get probation, and maybe take some drug rehab classes."

"Oh."

"You hear what's going on outside?" he asked.

"Yeah, somebody killed Ms. Carmen," I said. "That's messed up."

"But how 'bout they knocking down her front wall right now."

"Stop playing!" I jumped up to look out the window. Sure enough, that's what was happening. A bright white light beamed on Ms. Carmen's house. A cloud of dust floated in the air and a big piece of wall was missing from where the window used to be. A couple of firemen had big sledgehammers by their sides, and some other men with construction helmets walked back and forth like they was trying to figure out how they was gonna patch the hole back up after everything was over. Mr. Duncan looked like he was losing his mind, talking to whoever would listen.

"I'm about to go back outside. I wanna see how they gon' bring her fat ass out," he said, standing beside me. "I bet you she extra heavy now, with all that dead weight. I see they done got a crane now."

I shook my head and watched him walk out my room and close the door. I ain't wanna see that. Ms. Carmen was stuck in the house like Anne and her family in that attic. I ain't wanna see her wheeled out like the Elephant Man, or that Hottentot Venus lady Ms. Basque told us about from South Africa, who everybody pointed and laughed at in London circuses just because she had a big butt. Ms. Carmen was always nice to me. Even if she was the one stocking Creature, Duane, and the rest of them up, she needed her privacy and her peace. She saw all kinds of things from her window, and she was probably taking all kinds of secrets to the grave with her.

CHAPTER 21
NICOLA

Tinka walked in the house looking like she been crying or something, but when I asked her what was wrong, she said "Nothing," like she always did. I wasn't no doctor, but it ain't take one to see that girl had issues. Probably the usual teenage girl stuff. Boys. Maybe her and that little pimple-faced boy got into a fight. I knew that was her little boyfriend — she ain't think I was paying attention, but I wasn't stupid. Little fast-ass.

I was sitting at the table playing Spades with Shelia, Van, and Teddy.

"Teenagers," Teddy said, laughing. "Damn, baby, are you renigging?"

"No. I got my books! Just make sure you got yours."

"No more talking across the table," Van said with a cigarette dangling from his lip.

"When you gon' marry my girl and stop playing with her?" I asked, looking at Shelia. I knew she really loved him. He was reliable and dependable, nothing like the father of any of her kids.

"Ask Shelia." He laughed. "How many times she gon' tell me no, is what you oughta be asking her."

Shelia rolled her eyes and looked down at her cards. I knew why she kept telling him no. The same reason I ain't never telling Teddy yes. Niggas full of shit. They say they want you, then they don't once they get you. I ain't stupid. Shelia ain't either.

"See how she ain't speaking up?" Van said. "She don't want me."

Teddy laughed and stood up. "Baby, ain't it time for your medicine?"

"Is it time already?"

He nodded, then he went to the counter and grabbed my pills.

"Wait. Let's finish this hand first," Shelia said. "I know how your ass get once you under that spell."

"Fuck you, Shelia. I need my medicine."

"Mm-hmm," she mumbled under her breath. "I bet you do."

"You got something to say?" She seemed like she had something she wanted to get off her chest and shit. "Just say it!"

Shelia sipped her drink and shook her head. "Girl, just play your hand. I ain't messing with you."

Later after Van and Shelia left, Teddy asked me if I was all right.

I nodded. He walked to the kitchen and opened the fridge.

"Hey, Cola!" he yelled. "I'ma need a couple dollars so I can get my brakes fixed. The alignment a little messed up, too."

This nigga. "Your ass need to get another job," I mumbled. He never even let me touch that damn car. Half the time, I'm catching the bus or the train to work.

"You hear me, Cola?" he yelled from the kitchen.

"I don't get paid 'til next week, Teddy."

"Then what am I supposed to do 'til then?"

"Ask your mother for it. I ain't got no money."

"Man, fuck!"

"Catch the bus! Where the hell you gotta go so bad?!"

Taevon burst in the house, looking pissed off, with Hitler running behind him breathing hard. Taevon sprinted up the stairs. Hitler's chain banged against the steps as he ran behind him. A few seconds later Taevon ran back down and straight out the back door.

"What the hell that boy doing now?" Teddy asked from the couch.

I ain't say nothing. A couple minutes later, a loud gunshot went off.

"Ahhhh!" I screamed, cuz the bullet sounded so close to our house. Then another two shots went off.

"What the fuck going on out there?!" Teddy shouted and crouched to the floor. I hit the floor, too. We stayed still for a few seconds, then Teddy popped up. "Where's Taevon?"

He went to the window like he ain't care if anybody saw him or not. "Aww, shit . . . Call the ambulance, Cola!" he yelled before running outside.

I grabbed the phone with my heart beating a hundred miles a minute. What in the world had just happened? I ran outside while I waited for 911 to answer. About ten guys stood in a circle in the alley behind my house, all looking at the ground. I pushed them away, then I saw Taevon bending over Shelia's son, Antonio.

Thank God it wasn't my son.

I told the woman on the phone to send an ambulance. Antonio was squirming on the ground, twisting and turning beside a bloody, dead pit bull.

"Ahhhh," Antonio cried out when Monte helped him sit up. His foot was bleeding.

"My bad, young," Taevon said. "I fucked up like shit."

"Damn, you okay, man?!" Teddy said.

"I'm calling your mother, Antonio!"

"Nah, don't do that, don't do that," he said through clenched teeth.

Like hell I wasn't. I dialed her up and stepped inside my yard. When I looked up, I saw Teddy take a gun from Taevon and then tuck it in his waistband. *What the hell?*

"Hello?"

"Hurry up and get over here. It's an emergency!"

I watched Monte and Sammy put the dead dog in a black trash bag, then carry it off to the big trash can. Ms. David stood in her back doorway, shaking her head the whole time.

"Somebody could've got killed!" she said as soon as Shelia showed up all hysterical with Krystal screaming behind her.

"What in the world?!" Shelia said, kneeling beside Antonio. "You okay?"

"Owww! Stop, Ma. That hurts!" Antonio hollered.

Duane and Raynard came over at the same time the ambulance pulled up. Of course, nobody admitted how Antonio got shot, when the paramedics asked. Taevon was fighting Hitler against another dog, and the other dog lost. He was trying to put him down, when he accidentally shot Antonio in the foot.

Them damn children trying to give me a heart attack. I lit up a cigarette and went back in the house. Every day it's something around here.

■ ■ ■ ■

PART III
THREE YEARS LATER

■ ■ ■ ■

CHAPTER 22
TINKA

A raggedy white pickup truck piled high with old furniture putt-putted down the block until the brakes screeched and stopped in front of Ms. Jackson's old house. A blue minivan pulled up right behind the pickup, and two women climbed out. One had sandy brown and blond dreads and two huge silver hoop earrings dangling by her shoulders. Three little kids ran out laughing and playing while the older, rounder lady went to say something to the men in the pickup. Everyone but the kids grabbed something before they carried it inside.

"Oh, we got new neighbors? Who's Miss Lady? She sexy as a mug." Taevon stood in the doorway behind me with Hitler. I could smell that dog from a mile away.

"When you gonna give him a damn bath?" I covered my nose with my hand and breathed with my mouth. "He stank, Taevon, for real!"

But before he could answer, we heard a bunch of screams coming from inside Ms. Jackson's house. Stephanie's scrawny naked body burst out the front door holding a bundle of clothes. Ms. Janice's crackhead niece been running in and out of Ms. Jackson's house ever since she moved out four months ago to live in South Carolina with her daughter. Stephanie flew down the street, high-stepping it. Hitler barked and yanked Taevon so hard he dropped the chain. Hitler's muscle-bound coffee-colored body went zooming down the block right on Stephanie's heels. She hollered again and ran faster. Hitler kept barking until Stephanie disappeared behind Ms. Shelia's house. Taevon ran behind them.

Wasn't no shame about being scared of Hitler — the whole neighborhood was scared. Even me sometimes. Taevon could barely control him. Hitler grew so strong, he looked like *he* was the one walking Taevon whenever it was time to be walked, and I ain't never seen a dog with a head as big as Hitler's either. It was like a small TV set, but his thick neck was strong enough to hold it up. Dudes came all the way from Baltimore to breed their dogs with him.

I cracked up laughing when I heard Stephanie's screechy voice scream from behind the house again and then I heard a loud *pop*. The sound came from Ms. Jackson's house. That's when I turned to see the gray-haired pickup driver limping out with a stream of blood staining his jeans. Creature stepped out the door, looked both ways, then he zipped up his pants. I shook my head. I couldn't believe he actually let Stephanie's nasty, used-up crackhead self touch him, and he was supposed to be a baller. *I think not. Uggh.*

"Tinka, get your tail in this house 'fore one of them bullets find you!" Ma yelled.

I stood up and went inside.

"Who them people 'cross the street?" she asked, peeking out the window.

"I don't know," I said, peeking beside her. "But I bet they 'bout to leave now."

Me and Ma stayed glued to the window, watching the police and the ambulance come and go. I guess our new neighbors ain't have nowhere else to stay since they kept on moving in like nothing strange had happened. Taevon came in the house with more details. He said the girl with the dreads was twenty-two, her name was Halima, and those were her three kids. The big lady was her mother Valerie, and the guy who Creature shot was Halima's uncle. They just moved from Barry Farms.

"Three kids? She look like a baby herself! Tinka, you better not even think about it!" Ma said, shaking her head from left to right.

"Two of 'em twins," Taevon said.

"What?!" Ma said. "Poor baby."

"How you know all this?" I asked.

"I got my ways," he said, smiling.

"Please, don't tell me you tried to holler at her?"

"I don't have to try," he said, flashing his cell phone.

"Uggh, boy." I blocked my nose with my upper lip, like something smelled foul. "You just as nasty as Hitler."

"Nah, I just wanted to welcome them to the neighborhood," he said, laughing. "Just showing them some Sursum Corda hospitality."

"Spell hospitality!" Ma said.

"What?" Taevon smiled. "H-O-S . . ." He paused and tried to start again. "H-O-S . . ."

"Mm-hmm. That's why you need to take your narrow ass back to school! Spell it for him, Tinka."

I hated when she did that.

"Go 'head, spell it!"

I leaned my head back and looked at the ceiling. Why she always have to make me seem like a Goody Two-shoes, like I knew

200

every single thing and like I ain't never do nothing wrong? "H-O-S-P-I-T-A-L-I-T-Y," I said.

"Good. Don't ever be ashamed of being smart. Hell, I wish I was. Don't ever be ashamed of making good choices in life either. I wish I would've done it," she said, and then she turned to Taevon. "I just want the best for all my kids. Always have. I want you to be better than me and better than what people expect y'all to be. And you can't be that if you don't finish school, Taevon. Even Marquan got his GED at Oak Hill, baby. Why you can't go get your GED? Ain't nothing wrong with that."

He shrugged his shoulders.

"What happened to you wanting to work at a pet store, huh?"

Taevon stared at the floor and then nervously scratched his head.

"You could go back to school and be more than a pet store worker. Maybe you can be a . . . a . . . a what they call it, Tinka? The doctor for the animals?"

"Veterinarian."

"Yeah, one of those. Come on, Taevon. The way you love animals? You could do that easy. What about that?"

He shook his head and said, "Nah. That's too much."

"What you mean, 'that's too much'?" Ma asked, confused.

"I just don't want to," he said, standing up and walking to the front door.

"That don't even sound like you, Taevon. Why not? You love animals. You can't stand out there on that corner all damn day for the rest of your life," Ma said.

"All right, Ma, damn!" he said, like she had worked his last nerve. "I'll see y'all later."

He disappeared outside. Ma shook her head. "That boy just like his brother. Can't nobody tell him nothing. I don't know what I'm gonna do about him."

"What *can* you do?" I said, then bit my lip. She was kinda right. It's funny how Taevon would go all out of his way to look up something about one of his pets on somebody's Internet, but didn't want to go to school. He even went to the library once to find out what he could feed some lizards he bought from a crackhead. Showed me the information he printed out and everything. The poor things died, though, because he never bought the special lamp they needed to stay warm.

Ma took a deep breath, looked at her watch, and then she stood up. "It's time for me to get ready for work. When Marquan come in, tell him I need twenty dollars."

Ever since Marquan been back home, one minute she telling him to stay in the house, the next she asking him when he gonna give her a couple dollars. I ain't see her nodding off as much, but she still mumbled every now and then, so I knew she was still popping them pills. Teddy was just helping her hide it better. Seem to me like he enjoyed her more when she was high or something, because he wasn't trying to get her to quit. Maybe it was because he was too twisted, too, most of the time.

It was weird around the house when Marquan first came home. He knew what had happened to me and Ma that New Year's when he was locked up, and he wanted to kill Teddy. He ain't express it to nobody but me. He told me he ain't know how to *not* be fucked up with Teddy. "I don't give a fuck about that nigga," he said. But he knew it would be a problem for Taevon and Ma. So he tried to keep his distance as much as he could. He stayed around Trinidad like he used to. Ced came to scoop Marquan up a few days after he got out of Oak Hill, and the next thing you know he was on the block with Creature, Big Mike, Raynard, Duane, Sammy, and Keion. Taevon was out there selling, too. Monte couldn't keep that secret from me. Him and Antonio sold it, too. But they ain't seem like they fit out there with the other dudes. They got distracted too easily, and I knew for a fact that Taevon was real sloppy about it. Every time I went in his room, little Baggies was all over the floor. I don't know how many times I heard Marquan tell him *not* to do something. I ain't think Taevon wanted to do it, for real. He just wanted to be like Marquan. He dropped out of school just like Marquan, and he even went to jail for stealing a car like him, too. Ma had plain given up on both of them.

Even though Marquan had most of his stuff in his room, he ain't really live with us. He stayed with his girlfriend, Jillian, around Trinidad a lot. Plus he was still cool with everybody around there. I think he felt more comfortable there than around here.

The phone rang while I sat watching TV in the living room. LaSheika's name popped up on the caller ID. As soon as I picked up the phone, she begged me to come outside.

"Nine out here with Clint. Come outside, Tinka, hurry up!" she screamed in my ear.

I been trying to get this boy to notice me for so long. We spoke whenever we saw each other, but I was too scared to do more than that. No matter how hard she tried,

LaSheika couldn't convince me to do anything more than make sure he saw me looking cute whenever he was around the neighborhood. On top of that, Marquan was giving me much grief about boys. "Don't be being pressed for no nigga, Tinka. They'll never respect you if they know you sweating them. You too good for these dudes," he said. But even still, I ain't know what I was gonna do if I missed Nine this time. His cousin Clint was Taevon's age, and he lived in Temple Courts on the K Street side near LaSheika's house.

"Wait 'til my mother leave," I whispered.

"You better not even think about having no boys up in here," Ma said, coming from nowhere, creeping up like a stalker. She scared the hell out of me.

"Ain't nobody thinking about no boys, Ma!" Like I really wanted to bring somebody up in here. I ain't even want LaSheika over here with Teddy around.

"You better not be. Let me borrow that handbag LaSheika gave you."

I rolled my eyes. I can't keep nothing. She always wanna borrow my stuff or try to squeeze her big hips into clothes she knew she couldn't fit. I went to my room and grabbed the camel-colored Louis with the broken zipper. LaSheika don't believe in

205

keeping broken or stained stuff; she just passed it on to me and I ain't have a problem with it, since I wasn't wasting my money on no materialistic crap. I mean, I'll wear it, but even if I *could* afford it, I wasn't buying it unless I absolutely had to have it. And that was rare. Ever since that time all our stuff got put out on the street like that, and we had to leave most of it behind, I tried not to get attached to nothing like that. Keion and whichever new guy she was dating was how LaSheika got her money anyway. If Marquan or Taevon had it, they would give it to me.

"Oh, I almost forgot. Tell Taevon to take this vacuum cleaner back over Shelia's tonight. Somebody done broke hers up," she said, fastening up her jacket.

Ms. Shelia and Van stayed having people running in and out, so her house was usually a mess. Now that she was a grandmother because Duane, Raynard, and Krystal had all popped up with kids, her place stayed a filthy hot mess, no matter how hard she tried to keep it clean.

"All right, I'm gone. Remember, Tinka, I said no boys in here. I'm not playing either!"

I rolled my eyes again. She just wanted to make me and Monte into something we wasn't. He was just my friend. I called

LaSheika as soon as the door closed. "I'm on my way."

I ran upstairs to change my jeans to the skinny-leg ones that made my booty look bigger, then I put on a cuter pair of earrings. The ones with the peacock feathers I got from a stand on H Street. I swiped my lips with some lip gloss I bought from the beauty supply shop — the gloss sometimes made my lips itch, but oh well — then I cut through my backyard to get to LaSheika's house. She was outside with her little sister Laila. They was leaned up against Keion's green Old School with rims.

"Hey, girl."

"Hey. See, they 'bout to leave. I was trying to keep Nine out here for you. Clint said they was about to run Uptop real quick and then back to the Southside."

"Dang." I was pissed.

"You need to let him know what's up 'fore I do," Laila said, blinking like a cat.

Why she gotta be so hot? I ain't a *roller,* by no means. Nine just had this cute, serious look that made me wanna hug him every single time I seen him. He made me wonder what he was thinking and why he ain't smile as much as everybody else.

Clint and Nine walked out and hopped into Clint's bucket. They both waved at me, before Clint pulled off.

"See," LaSheika said. "You don't know when the next time he coming back around here. You playing games."

She was right. "Next time I see him, I'll let him know what's up."

"Yeah right," Laila said. "I heard that before."

"Mind your business. LaSheika, get your clone please."

LaSheika laughed and nudged Laila away from us. "You want me to tell Clint you trying to holler or what?"

"Nah, that's okay."

"All right, girl. Don't be mad when you don't see him 'til next spring," she said, laughing.

Whatever.

"You heard what happened in Ms. Jackson's house today?" she asked. Her eyes popped open wide.

"Girl, I saw the whole thing!" I laughed, then told her the entire story. By the time I got to the part when Hitler chased Stephanie behind Ms. Shelia's house, I saw Clint's bucket pull up again.

"Look, look, look," I whispered. "They back."

LaSheika turned around. "Girl, this might be your last chance."

Clint's chubby self jumped out the car and ran back inside the tall sky-rise building. Nine got out, leaned on the car, and puffed on his Black & Mild.

"You got a girlfriend, Nine?" LaSheika yelled at him.

My face turned numb. No, this trick ain't just do that. I swear my heart just stopped beating.

He smiled and shook his head.

"You want one?" she asked.

I couldn't believe this heifer.

"Depends," he said.

"On what?" LaSheika asked.

I cannot believe this is happening right now. Right in front of me, though?

"A lot of stuff," Nine said, smiling. "Why you asking me all these questions? You know something I need to know?"

God, he is so fine.

LaSheika smiled. And then . . . *oh no, she didn't just nod her head toward me. I can kill her right now.* I felt my face getting hot. Nine walked over toward us. He looked so good. His dark skin was smooth and his slanted eyes so sexy. His dreads was freshly twisted, and his gear was fresh, too. He had on a gray hoodie, with a black North Face vest on top, some crisp Citizens with the faded fronts, and some old school Jordans I ain't

209

seen nobody with.

"How you doing, Tinka?" he asked, standing so close I could smell the Black & Mild on his breath.

I smiled, but I ain't say nothing. Not only was my heart beating now, it was beating so fast I thought I was gonna faint.

"Tinka, stop acting all innocent and shit," LaSheika said, as she tugged my arms from across my chest. They *were* locked kinda tight.

This chick got two heads coming out her neck. I can't believe how hot she acting right now. She blowing the heck outta me.

"Come walk with me real quick," Nine said.

"All right," I said, and followed him toward the end of the block.

"So what's up with you?" he asked.

"Nothing much. What's up with you?"

"Your girl got a lot to say."

"Yeah, she sure do," I said, staring at the ground.

"So what's up? You always this quiet?"

"Not really."

"So if I give you my number, you gonna call me?"

"Maybe." I knew girls had to always be coming at him. " 'Maybe'?" He looked surprised. "What you mean 'maybe'?"

I smiled. "I mean what I say. *Maybe.*"

"Oh, okay," Nine said, nodding. "Well, *maybe* I won't give it to you then."

"Well, don't," I said, confident all of a sudden. "I'll live."

Nine laughed and puffed on his cigarillo.

I surprised myself with that comment. "Maybe you shouldn't believe everything people tell you."

I walked back toward LaSheika. *What the heck was I doing?* I watched my feet so I wouldn't trip up because I knew Nine was still watching me. LaSheika's facial expression told it all. Shoot, I ain't care. Ma taught me one thing if nothing else. *Don't ever make nothing easy for no dude.* " 'Cause once they got you wrapped around their finger, they got you," she told me.

"What happened?" LaSheika asked, all pressed when I got back to her.

"Nothing."

"You get his number?"

"Not yet."

She crossed her eyes like a clown. "What you mean, not yet?"

"I'm playing hard to get."

"Girl, you crazy," LaSheika said, shaking her head. "Okay. Well, let me know how that works for you."

"Good night, ladies," Nine said, as he

walked back to Clint's car.

"Good night, Nine," LaSheika answered.

"See you," I said.

"Damn, you done fucked up," LaSheika said after Clint pulled off again. She shook her head.

"We'll see."

She shook her head.

"Ay, Tinka!" Marquan yelled from the corner.

I sucked my teeth, because I already knew what he was gonna say. "Let me go see what he want. He better not say nothing about me talking to Nine."

"You know he is."

I walked over near the market. Marquan walked away from Duane, Creature, and Big Mike.

"Who was that nigga?" Marquan asked.

As soon as he said it, I rolled my eyes. "Nobody. Just Clint's cousin."

"Where he from?"

"Southeast, I think." He always asked that whenever he saw a new face in the neighborhood. I knew he ain't trust nobody ever since he got locked up.

"What I tell you about being up in niggas' faces you don't know?"

I crossed my arms over my chest. Marquan

212

kills me sometimes. He so overprotective of me.

"You eat yet?"

I shook my head.

"Here," he said, handing me a twenty-dollar bill. "Go get us something from Yum's. See if LaSheika can go with you first."

I smiled and took the money. "She will. What you want?"

"Four wings and some fries. Get extra mambo sauce, too."

"Okay. I'll be back."

I walked back over to LaSheika, then we worked our way up to North Capitol and P Street. After I paid for our food, we headed back over to First Place.

"Look at my phatty, it's my phatty," LaSheika sang the new CCB song they kept playing over and over again on the radio. I kinda liked the hook, but that horn loop was a little annoying. But I guess it was real catchy.

I joined in.

We walked past Krystal and her little fake crew, who was walking up the street toward us. She rolled her eyes.

"That's why that bitch got a baby already," LaSheika said. "She need to be taking care of her daughter, instead of being out here

213

looking for some nigga."

"Exactly." I dug inside my bag to steal a fry. She still was beefing with me after all these years.

"Oh my God. Look, Tinka!" LaSheika whispered and nudged me at the same time.

I looked up just as two dudes with black ski masks stumbled out of the liquor store in front of us at the corner of Hanover Place.

"Move, move, move!" the thick one yelled. He had a gun by his side.

Me and LaSheika froze and waited for the two guys to run whichever way they was gonna run. As soon as they turned the corner on New York Avenue, I realized I had just seen those Jordans and the dude had dreads peeking out of his hat. My chest tightened. An Ethiopian man came out the store screaming something in his language before he went back inside pissed off.

"Was that who I think it was?" LaSheika asked nervously.

"You think so, too?"

She nodded. I shook my head. We kept walking home and neither one of us said nothing more about it. Maybe Marquan was right after all.

CHAPTER 23
NICOLA

"Y'all got one, too," Ms. David said, waving a yellow sheet of paper over her head like a fan as soon as she saw me walking down the block.

I saw the yellow paper wedged in the door. *What was this?*

"They talking about they gonna give us all this money to move out. Or so we can use it as a deposit for one of the new town houses they supposed to be building," she said with so much anger, her jaws got tight.

I snatched the paper off the door and read it over. What they mean "new town house community"? Then I thought about the burgundy Ford 150 pickup truck that stopped in front of Mr. Duncan's house like a month ago. Two white men wearing L.L. Bean khakis and Eddie Bauer jackets climbed out and pointed around the neighborhood. One of them took notes, and nodded, while the other one talked. It was the weirdest thing to see, but I never thought to mention it to nobody.

"I'll believe it when I see it!" Ms. David shouted. "Sursum Cordas been here for more than forty years. I done been here ever since they first built it back in the sixties. Back when them nuns lived around here. Before them white folks carried their behinds all the way uptown. I remember when them no-good hoodlums first started selling that crack mess that got them people stealing from their own relatives and before all this shooting and killing 'round here. I been here for a long time now. Done seen a lot of people come and go. Done seen a lot of killing, too. Police don't care. City don't care neither. Naw, they ain't gonna tear these projects down. They want us to kill each other."

I sat down. My head hurt just thinking about moving from around here. This was déjà vu. I looked down at the paper again. *Learn how you can get $80,000 toward your down payment for your GTI Community home purchase or for relocation expenses.*

But we can't move. Where we gonna move to?

"I heard it all before," Ms. David kept on talking.

She ain't have no family around here no

more. Her son lived in San Francisco and her daughter lived in Oklahoma or Ohio. Her husband died in Vietnam. She told anybody who would listen that he was white, but I heard on the low that he was really mixed but passed for white. I felt sorry for Ms. David sometimes, though. Because she spent way too much time looking out the window, sweeping her steps, or hanging clothes out on the line in her backyard, and ever since her best friend Ms. Jackson moved to South Carolina, she seemed even more lonely. She went to the church around the corner like five times a week, but Taevon told me he saw her buying lottery tickets on Florida Avenue once. I ain't believe him at first until one day, I overheard her telling Mr. Duncan she hit the number with Marion Barry's birth date. A straight-up hypocrite.

Ms. David knew everything about this place. She was the first to call the police if she smelled something fishy. They even knew her by name when they drove through. A couple of them, like the young fed who kept telling everybody he graduated from Dunbar, like anybody cared, stopped just to chat it up with Ms. David and everything. She gave them too much of her time and she ain't realize the police was just using her.

They stopped in front of her house, stared people down, and asked her lots of questions about what new things was happening around the way, and she told them everything they wanted to know just because she felt important and needed. Ms. David ain't keep it no secret that she was a snitch either, talking about she wanted them knuckleheads out the neighborhood and that she wasn't scared of them because God had her back. Teddy said, "She better mind her damn business before she be much nearer to Jesus than she wanted to be. All it's gonna take is for her to snitch on the wrong person," he said.

"I done heard it all," Ms. David went on. "First, it's we getting new management. Then them people say they gonna fix up our houses, then they come throw some cheap chalky paint up, fix a few broken stoves and boilers with used parts they done got for half the price somewhere because they bought in bulk, then two months pass and they done forgot about us. Got the nerve to ignore us when the mess is broken again!"

I shook my head and looked up the block.

"Now these GTI people talking about

they gonna tear it down and build town houses for us! Yeah, right. Ain't nobody 'round *here* gonna be able to afford no town house down the street from no Capitol Building. Them politicians gon' snatch them all up for their mistresses. I already see what they doing to D.C. now. All you see everywhere is them white folks moving back in the city from the suburbs in Maryland and Virginia. Now they walking they dogs and jogging in places where people used to hide dead bodies. Growing gardens where trash and homeless people used to be. The city ain't care nothing about fixin' it up for us!"

"Mm-hmm."

"It's that high yellow mayor. Rebuilding, renovating, and raising rent on what should've been rebuilt and renovated a long time ago!"

Ms. David had a point. I couldn't see them just tearing down this place. I knew people whose grandmothers grew up around here. Whole families, generation after generation, grew up right here. As much as I hated the projects when I first moved here, I saw it for what it was. A village within a village. It was way too much history here. There ain't no way they'd get rid of Sursum Cordas. *Why now? Where everybody gonna go?*

Ms. David was still running her mouth when I stood up to go in the house. "Okay, Ms. David. I'll talk to you later. I just got off from work and I'm tired," I said before closing the door.

I ain't mean to cut her off, but I had a lot to think about, and I couldn't do it with her yapping. I balled the paper up and threw it in the trash. *It's not true anyway. Some sort of scam.* I took my shoes off and sat down to smoke a cigarette. No sooner than I light it, when Taevon walked in with a big, long yellow snake wrapped around his shoulders. I dropped my cigarette in my lap and jumped up.

"Boy, get that shit the hell out of this house!" I shouted. "I know you done lost your mind!"

He laughed. "Man, it's just a snake."

"So what?!"

"You scared of a snake?"

"Get it away from me, Taevon! Now!" I screamed and ran out of the kitchen to the living room.

"Touch it, Ma," he said, following me.

"No! Get it away from me. I'm not playing. For real, Taevon!"

"It's just a snake, Ma. He not poisonous," he said again, inching closer. "He ain't gon' bite you."

"Stop playing little boy!" I screamed, running to the living room.

Teddy cracked up laughing.

"You think this is funny, but it ain't!"

"Okay, Ma."

"Stop messing with your mother, boy," Teddy laughed.

"You ain't got enough shit in here already?" I asked, feeling my skin crawling.

"I'ma put him in a tank, Ma. Monte said he got a hundred-gallon one I can have."

"Taevon, did you hear what I said? Bad enough you got that filthy dog running around here! And all them little critters in your room. Ain't gonna be no snake, too."

"Man . . . ," he said before he went back outside. But I knew what that meant. Just like with Hitler, and them gerbils and that big brown, hairy spider that was the size of a plum. As soon as he could convince his father, that nasty thing gonna be right up in here, too. Teddy was a sucker when it came to Taevon. Anything that little boy wanted, he got. I don't know why he couldn't have a simple fish tank. Nice and simple.

Tinka walked down the stairs and went to the kitchen. She ain't even part her lips.

"Well, hello to you, too," I said.

"Hey, Ma."

"You seen Marquan lately? I told that boy

I needed some money before they cut the cable off in here. Call him for me. I'm gonna get in the shower."

"Okay," she said.

I ain't like taking money from my kids, especially when neither one of them was working. But hell, they was gonna do what they was doing anyway. And if they taking from this house, then they needed to make a contribution. The cable and the electric ain't gonna pay for itself.

CHAPTER 24
TINKA

Teddy walked through the front door covered in filth. He threw his keys on the kitchen table all loud and hard, like he wanted somebody to notice him. I watched him do his regular routine of opening the refrigerator door and twisting off the cap of a Heineken, before he sat down in the living room beside me. His body straight-up reeked, plus he was making my skin itch. I stood up, so I could go to my bedroom.

"You ain't gotta leave the room just because I come in it," he said with an attitude.

I rolled my eyes and climbed the stairs. I guess it was one of those days again. Either I was gonna stay in my room for the rest of the night or I was going over LaSheika's. Wasn't no way in the world I was gonna stay over here with him drinking and having a nasty attitude.

"Cola!" I hear him yelling while I go in

my room.

"Yeah, Teddy?!" she screamed back.

"Them muthafuckers did it! They laid me off!" he yelled back up the stairs. "And they hired like three of them 'migos last week!"

I listened to Ma's footsteps going down the stairs, then I shook my head and got up to close my door. I ain't wanna hear her trying to boost his ego just so she could make him feel better. Let him suffer. Maybe if he stopped drinking so much, his boss wouldn't have even thought about going out and hiring no Mexicans.

The house phone rang. I picked up the cordless laying on my bed. It was Marquan.

"Tinka."

"Huh?"

"I had to make a run with Ced real quick, but go in my room and get a hundred fifty dollars for Ma for me. I might not be back until tomorrow. She keep talking about bills she need paid. What the fuck is Teddy doing and shit?"

"I don't know, but I just heard him tell Ma he got laid off."

"What?! That's that bullshit."

"Okay. Where is it?"

"Check in my second drawer."

I told him bye, then I popped up to go upstairs to his room. I hated going to the third floor. Taevon's animals had the whole upper level smelling rank and funky. He was trifling. He never wanted to change that stuff at the bottom of his gerbil cage. Dog food and blunt guts was sprinkled from the stairs all the way to his door. This was the one thing I ever heard him and Marquan arguing about and why Marquan told Ma he stayed over Jillian's house so much, even though he really just wanted to kill Teddy. Ma ain't argue with him about it.

"Marquan a grown man," she said.

I opened his door and was surprised to see how clean and neat it was. Marquan's bed was made up like he was in the military, and his walls was plain, besides one gigantic poster of Tupac's face that hung over the dresser. I opened the second drawer, where his socks was, and ran my fingers around to look for the money he was talking about. But I only found four twenty-dollar bills folded up. I opened the top drawer to double-check, but no money, just socks. I pushed the drawer in and headed to the door. "I'll just call him about the rest," I mumbled.

Maybe I should check the third drawer, just in case. I pulled the third drawer open and felt around his wifebeaters and folded T-shirts. I fingered some crumpled paper, so I pulled it from underneath an old school Madness T-shirt Jillian bought him for his last birthday on eBay. The paper was a yellowing, folded newspaper article. A picture of a boy in a school picture was underneath a headline that said: ANOTHER YOUTH SLAIN. Terry Jenkins was one of the boys from the Ivy City shooting and that stolen car Marquan went to jail for. I read the whole article, forward and backward. The dude was nineteen and had two kids, a two-year-old girl and a four-month-old little boy.

I wondered if Marquan blamed himself for what happened to Terry. Why else would he keep this paper all these years? The article said the last school he went to was McKinley Tech. His mother was in the article talking about how mad she was with the city for not doing enough about black-on-black crime and teens killing teens.

"I been trying to keep my son out of trouble since he was thirteen," the paper said. "All he been trying to do is put a little bit of money in his pocket and take care of his kids. What was he supposed to do? He can't get hired nowhere. Ain't no jobs for black boys in this city."

I shook my head and closed the drawer. On the way downstairs, Terry's face stayed in my head. He looked like a tiny, slim guy,

like the rapper Pharrell with a short haircut.
I opened my journal and laid across my bed,
then wrote the first thing I felt about Terry:

Alone you rest
In the smallest of places
Crouched on your knees you prayed
Bullets tearing through flesh
Your life once precious, now gone
Your heart still sings
Loud for all to hear

I got stuck after that last line. *Loud for all
to hear* what?

A voice once strong
Now a whisper

No, I ain't get it.

~~In the smallest of places~~
~~Crouched on your knees you prayed~~
~~Bullets tearing through flesh~~
~~Your life once precious, now gone~~
~~Your heart still sings~~
~~Loud for all to hear~~
~~A voice once strong~~
~~Now only a whisper~~

I scratched every line out and closed my

227

journal. The only thing that kept popping up in my head was poor Marquan instead of poor Terry. Clearly if he had that paper stuffed in his drawer, he was still trying to deal with it. Everybody made bad choices. It sucks that somebody lost their life because of one. I thought Marquan was dealing with it okay. But I see he wasn't. I knew he was blown when his father never made parole. He was pissed for a while after he first found out. Him and his father had gotten close again through all that writing when Marquan was in juvie. But I think he really needed his father around, the same way I wished mine could be.

CHAPTER 25
NICOLA

"They shooting outside again?" Shelia asked Tinka when she walked in the door.

Tinka nodded and walked upstairs like it wasn't no big deal. Me and Shelia was sitting at the kitchen table talking about that yellow piece of paper and the $80,000 promise with Van and Teddy.

"How they think somebody gonna be able to afford some fancy town house, when they know everybody around here low income or no income?!" Shelia said, twisting her lips.

"But you know Temple Courts got a different offer from another company, right?" Van said about the other apartments on the block. "So maybe we shouldn't be complaining."

"I say we just take the money and move to Charlotte or Atlanta," Teddy said, sipping his beer. "I can probably get a job quick down there, and you, too, Cola."

What?! Charlotte or Atlanta? Teddy must've

bumped his damn head. I'm not trying to move all the way down there. I rolled my eyes and took a long sip of Rémy. I remembered when we first moved around here because we ain't have nowhere else to go. It was supposed to be temporary. That was seven years ago when we left Trinidad. *If we do have to move, then so be it, but not all the way the fuck down South. Teddy's crazy.*

After Shelia and Van left, the phone rang. When I answered it, the person hung up. I looked at the caller ID. The name with that number said Monica Cannon. I had no idea who that was, so maybe it was the wrong number. I started washing dishes. About an hour later, an Unknown popped up on the phone. Now it wasn't the first time, nor was it the fiftieth time, an Unknown popped up on my phone. I don't make it my business to answer them, but since it happened a second time in the same hour, I did.

"Hello?"

Nothing but silence, followed by a dial tone.

Ten minutes later, the phone rang again.

"Hello?" I asked.

Nothing.

"Who that?" Teddy yelled from the living room.

"They keep hanging up."

230

The next time the phone rang, Teddy answered it.

"Hello?" he said, snatching the call mid-ring.

"Yeah. Okay," he said before his voice got lower.

"Who is that?" I asked from the kitchen.

"Um . . . nothing. I gotta make a run real quick."

Now I'm not a genius, but I know a repeat when I see it.

"You goin' to meet a bitch?" I asked, walking to the living room.

"What?!" he said, looking at me like I was dumb. "Whatever, Cola."

"Where you going then?"

"It's a poker game up at the shop they say I need to get in on. Where my keys?"

"Teddy, that sounds like a bunch of bullshit. Who's the bitch? What's her name? Monica?"

"Stop, Cola. Just stop!" he said, pushing passed me.

"No, you stop!" I said in his face. "If you leave, don't come back, Teddy. I'm not playing."

"Cola, calm down. I'll be back in an hour. Can't I leave and go kick it with my friends without you making a big goddamn fuss about everything?"

I rolled my eyes. We had been down this road before. Too many times. Just because he lost his job, he needed to feel like he was somebody. Monica must've been doing a better job than me. "Bye, Teddy."

He kissed me and walked out.

CHAPTER 26
TINKA

The phone rang, but I ain't recognize the number.

"Hello?" I said.

"Hello, can I speak to Tinka?" the strange voice said.

"This is she," I said, confused.

"Hey, Tinka. How you doing?"

"Who's this?"

"It's me, Nine."

My heart froze.

"Hello?" he said again.

"Hey." Of course, I was confused.

"Oh . . . you trying to figure out how I got your number, ain't you?" he asked, laughing.

"Yeah."

"LaSheika gave it to me the other day."

I could kill LaSheika. "She did?"

"You don't sound all that happy to hear how hard I'm trying to see what's up with you."

I was too shocked to be happy. This ain't seem like the kinda thing he would do. "Why you trying so hard?" I asked, lying across my bed.

"What you mean?"

"Why you going all out your way to find me?"

"Whatever, Tinka, you know you a cute girl."

My stomach flipped over.

"Plus, I heard you real picky. I like that shit."

"You do?" *Now I get it. He must think I'm a virgin.* Even though I was, I ain't want him to think something was wrong with me for not doing it already.

"Yeah, I do . . . so what's been up with you?"

"Nothing much. I just been chillin'."

"Chillin', huh? Why you always so quiet when I talk to you?"

"No reason," I said, but I was really wondering how far I was gonna let this conversation go. I mean, Nine made my voice quiver. He was so secretive and sexy, and it was something about the tone of his voice, and the dark look in his eyes whenever I saw him. Plus, I wasn't *absolutely* sure that was him and Clint at that liquor store that day. I took a deep breath and said, "I heard you from Barry Farms, is that true?"

He laughed. "Something like that, but why you gotta say it like that?"

"Like what?"

"Like it's something bad about that."

"Nah, I don't mean it that way. I'm just saying, I heard it's terrible out there."

"And it's not terrible where you live?"

"True. I guess some people could say that," I said, laughing.

He laughed a little, too. "So . . . you don't have a boyfriend?" Nine asked.

My stomach flipped again. "I got friends," I lied a little.

"What kind of friends?"

"The kind I like."

He laughed and then said, "I see you slick with your words. I heard about you."

Glad he noticed. "What you hear about me?" I asked, sitting up on my elbows. I wanted to pinch myself. I still couldn't believe we was actually talking right now. I couldn't handle no face-to-face conversation anyway. My confidence was up like I ain't-know-what over the phone.

"I heard things. Don't worry about it," he said, laughing.

"No, tell me," I said, smiling.

"I'm just messing with you . . . When you gonna let me take you out somewhere?"

"Ummm . . . I don't know." *Oh my God.* I hoped it ain't sound like I was smiling from ear to ear, because I was.

"What you doing later? Want to get something to eat somewhere."

He had a car? "Ummm . . . I guess so."

"Cool. You gonna be ready in like an hour?"

An hour? Oh my God. "Yeah, I will."

"All right. Take my number down. I know y'all got caller ID," he said, laughing.

"Whatever." I laughed.

"Bye."

I hung up and rolled over on my back. I had to think about what just happened. Then I jumped up to find something to wear. After I got dressed, I headed over to K Street. It was bright and sunny outside, but still cold. March was funny like that. Nine was leaning against a beautiful black Impala. He was wearing a black hoodie with a silver graffiti-style skull-and-crossbones print etched on the front and a black Nationals fitted cap. He smiled and opened the door for me like a gentleman. As soon as I climbed inside, a rich whiff of marijuana filled my nose. I watched him walk in front of the car, not sure what to think about the blunt burning in the ashtray. As soon as he was inside, he offered me a pull. Both of my brothers smoked weed, all of Ms. Shelia's sons smoked it, too, but I never tried it. Never felt the need to. Nobody ever offered it to me before either, though. LaSheika told me she smoked it a couple times and it made her feel relaxed.

"Come on, hit it," Nine said, passing the brown rollup to me.

"No, thank you. I'm good."

"Oh, so it *is* true?"

"What you mean?" I asked, confused.

"I heard you're a Goody Two-shoes for real," he said, smiling.

I rolled my eyes. Here we go again.

"You need a little danger in your life," he said, staring at me. "You act like it's crack."

I *was* feeling a little nervous and it *did* grow from the ground. I took it and puffed a little. I didn't think I was doing it right, because I ain't feel any less nervous than I did before I smoked it.

"How you feel?" he asked. His eyebrows danced at the top of his forehead like he knew I was high.

"All right, I guess." But I ain't know what the big deal was. Nothing different had happened to me.

"Good," Nine said, and then he turned TCB up on his speakers. He nodded his head to the heavy percussion beat before pulling off to make a right on North Capitol. He made another right on H Street and then we drove under the Third Street Tunnel.

"I ain't know you had a car," I said, as I looked out the window.

"It's a lot you don't know about me," he said as he merged onto 395.

"Where we going?"

"Cheesecake Factory. You like that?"

"Never been there."

"You'll like it."

We crossed into Virginia and took the exit after the Pentagon building.

"How old are you?" I asked.

"Twenty. How old are you?"

"Seventeen."

"Oh . . . so are you worth me taking a charge?" he asked, smiling.

"What you talking about?"

"You a minor."

"Whatever," I said, smiling.

We rode without saying anything for a while. Nine tapped his thumbs on the top of his steering wheel to TCB's thumping beat. When we got to the restaurant, he got a burger platter and I got some chicken pasta. He didn't say much, and I was too nervous to really eat, let alone to start a conversation. I hoped he ain't think I was boring. There was so much food left over when we got up to leave I took a to-go bag home with a slice of cheesccake.

In the car he said, "You really is quiet."

"You, too."

He smiled. "I guess so. Well . . . let's see. Tell me what you like to do for fun."

"You gon' think I'm a nerd," I said, shaking my head and looking out the window.

"Unless you tell me building computers, no, I'm not."

I giggled. "I like to read a lot and sometimes I try to write poetry."

"Okay . . . seems a little boring, but I can dig it."

Boring? "What about you? What you do for fun? Snatch purses?" I asked with an attitude.

He looked at me sideways, like I had disrespected him or something. I felt stupid for saying something so messed up. This wasn't going the way I hoped it would. We was both quiet for a long time.

"I like playing video games and riding my motorcycle," he said when we went under the tunnel.

"Do you work?" I asked, turning my body toward him.

He looked at me sideways, then looked back at the highway. "Yeah, I work."

"What you do?"

"Detail cars with my cousin."

Right.

"What school you go to?" he asked.

"Dun."

"Oh, okay. Dunbar. You got any brothers or sisters?"

"I got two brothers. You?"

"Nah. It's just me."

"And your cousin."

"And my cousin Clint," he said, smiling. "You wanna go to Hains Point?"

At this point, I wanted to go home. There was something definitely up with this dude. My heart told me that *was* him and Clint at the liquor store. "Nah, I'm ready to go back. I gotta finish my social studies paper," I lied. "It's due tomorrow."

"Oh, all right," he said, sounding disappointed.

We rode in silence back to the neighborhood.

"You want me to drop you off at the corner, or in front of your house?"

"K Street is cool."

He nodded and turned down K Street from New Jersey Avenue. When he stopped the car, he put his hand on my thigh and said, "I hope I ain't piss you off when I teased you about reading and stuff. I think it's cool for real. I got a bunch of dummies for friends." He smiled. "It'll be nice to have a smart one for a change."

I half-smiled and opened his car door. "Thanks for lunch. I'll talk to you later."

"You mean that?" he asked.

I nodded, but I wasn't so sure.

When I walked in the door, Marquan was sitting there alone, shaking his head. The TV was off and nobody else was around. The only thing I could hear in the whole house was the refrigerator humming. Him sitting there like that was haunting.

"Boy, what's wrong with you?"

"I fucked up," he whispered, staring at his hands.

"What you mean?" I sat down beside him and dropped my handbag and my cheese-cake on the coffee table.

"I don't wanna talk about it."

"You sure?" I asked, confused. I ain't never seen him like this before. His hands was shaking a little bit. "You looking real crazy right now, sitting here all by yourself."

He was still quiet.

"Marquan?! Boy, snap out of it. What's wrong with you?!"

He shook his head even though he looked like he wanted to tell me whatever it was, then he said, "Nothing. I'ma be all right."

But he ain't seem like it. "Well, where everybody at? It's quiet as I-don't-know-what in here."

He shrugged. "Taevon outside. And I think Ma and Teddy over Ms. Shelia's."

"I ain't see Teddy's car."

"Well, I don't know," he said, all cranky.

"Where Jillian?"

"I think she at the crib."

"Well, I'm about to go upstairs. You acting like I'm getting on your nerves or something. If you wanna talk, you know where I'll be."

He nodded.

"All right." I stood up. It wasn't like him to act that way to me. Even if he was feeling some kind of way, I ain't think he would come here instead of going over Jillian's first. Maybe they had an argument. She probably caught him with another girl. He'd be all right. I stopped at the stairs and turned around to look at him. "Did you cheat on Jillian or something, Marquan?"

He shook his head.

"Then what?"

"I just fucked up, that's all," he said, standing up. "But I'm about to be out. I might be gone for a minute."

"Where you going?

He shook his head. "I'm over Jill's if

anybody asks."

"Okay, but where you gonna be at for real?"

He looked at me long and hard. "With Ced."

I bit my lip. Something was really screwed up. "All right."

I watched him grab a big duffle bag I ain't notice at first from the other side of the couch, and then he stood up. The look on his face made me feel like it wasn't nothing I could say or do to stop him from leaving.

"Bye," I mumbled.

He tilted his head and walked out.

Marquan was tripping me out. I looked out the window, watched him get in Ced's car, then they disappeared. I shook my head.

CHAPTER 27
NICOLA

Somebody killed that little boy while he was sleeping in his own damn bed. Some random shooting in the middle of the night that left two people dead, one a nine-year-old boy. The shit ain't make no kinda sense. You can't even sleep in your own damn house no more. That poor child never even knew what hit him. The news kept showing his mother crying over and over again, on every single channel. He was a straight-A student, a little basketball star at his rec center, and all his friends loved him. Like a dozen candles was still flickering in front of all the flowers and teddy bears outside his apartment building around Carter Terrace. The mayor and the chief of police looked exhausted on Channel 7, talking about how they was gonna catch whoever did it. I hoped the hell they did.

I hadn't seen Monica Cannon's number on the caller ID, and there hadn't been no late-night disappearances from Teddy, but I still ain't trust him one hundred percent. I thought about calling Monica and finding out the whole story. But I knew that could go more than one way. Some women tell the truth, some lie. She might not think it necessary to tell me a damn thing. Wasn't like me and Teddy was married. Who knows what he told her about us. I just needed to know that the man who was sleeping next to me at night wasn't out there purposefully trying to hurt me. I had enough nonsense in my life. All I wanted was for Teddy to respect what we had.

I stared at the stripes on the wallpaper in the kitchen. They went up and down. Some stripes was fat with tiny dots, some skinny and dark yellow. Flowers appeared here and there. Sometimes they all blurred together, like a kaleidoscope of colors. I swallowed the last sip in my glass and got up to get some more.

CHAPTER 28
TINKA

Ma looked at me and shook her head. I could tell she wanted to get something off her chest. She'd been drinking and cursing under her breath for a good two hours before she finally said, "Tinka, I already see you the only one gonna be somebody in this family. Please don't screw it up."

How come she never talked to Taevon and Marquan like this? And why I gotta be the one who better not screw it up? What about them? Why they get to keep doing whatever illegal stuff they doing and she don't say nothing about it? She could play dumb if she wanted. Taevon had a gun, and nobody acted like it was a problem. Ma knew neither one of her sons had a job, so what else they doing to make money? Marquan stay fresh, and Taevon don't do too bad either. Let me miss one day of school and it's like I slapped a teacher.

And Teddy ain't no better. He act like Taevon a saint around here. Since Teddy lost his job, he even got the nerve to ask Taevon to give him a couple dollars here and there. Neither one of my brothers wasn't making no plans to do nothing special with their lives. Yet I was the one who better not screw it up. It wasn't fair.

One day, I was on my way home from school when I saw smoke billowing from the top-floor window of Teresa's house. I could smell the charred, burning odor in the air all the way from Dunbar. Fire truck and ambulance sirens echoed through the streets. Gray, thick smoke darkened the sky above my neighborhood. I practically ran down N Street to see what was happening. The streets was blocked off by trucks and police. Teresa was screaming at the top of her lungs, "Not my baby! No, not my baby!"

I covered my mouth and inched closer. Two firemen aimed water hoses at her house while others tried to keep half the neighborhood back. They was all watching. Some crying, some in a daze. All just a few feet away. Ramont was standing with two of their kids, wiping his face. Then Lynnda snatched the kids' hands away from him and headed down the street. Ms. Hooper and Ms. Janice held Teresa's arms as they tried to calm her down. I almost ain't wanna ask Keion what happened, but he was the first person I saw.

"Everybody got out the house but De-Shawn," he said.

"Oh no."

"She been screaming like that ever since she ran out the house. You should've seen them flames coming out the windows earlier. That shit was crazy," he said, all sad. "Ramont said he thought he smelled gas, and Ms. Hooper said their water heater worked when it wanted to. So who knows . . ."

All I could do was shake my head. I closed my eyes for a second and said a tiny prayer for the little boy who looked so happy playing in the community room two days ago.

A news crew showed up and started taping. I couldn't bear listening to Teresa's cracking voice. She screamed and twisted out of her mother's and Ms. Janice's grips, then she ran back toward the burning house. A fireman snatched her up and carried her over near an ambulance, where a paramedic shot her up with something. Her cries stopped, then she sat quietly rocking back and forth on the gurney.

The first community meeting about GTI

and the little yellow fliers was postponed, of course. Ma took off work just so she could go, but now she was sitting at the table sipping from a glass and smoking a cigarette. Teddy was in his favorite spot on the couch watching TV. I sat down across from her with some math homework. She was in deep thought. Probably thinking about losing us like Teresa lost DeShawn, but she ain't say that. She just stayed quiet, plucking ashes in the tray.

"Your aunt called me this morning," she said after a few minutes.

"She did?"

Ma nodded and puffed again. "She said Matt put in a transfer and it got approved."

My mouth fell open.

"They moving to Italy next month."

"Italy?!"

Ma nodded.

"Why Italy?"

She shook her head. "She said he ain't join the military to be stateside forever."

Wow. What was I gonna do now that Aunt Renee wasn't gonna be here to save the day? I bit my lip and looked at Ma. Maybe she was thinking about how Teresa and Lynnda was. Even with all the drama they had over Ramont, in the end they was there for each other. Teresa was probably gonna move in with her sister now, or split the kids up to stay with their grandmother Ms. Hooper.

I tried to work on the next math problem, but I couldn't. Aunt Renee's was my own private hiding place whenever I wanted to get away from all the drama around here. Now where was I gonna go?

A few days later, Nine showed up at Dunbar. He was leaning up against Clint's car looking sexy as ever when me and LaSheika walked out the front door. Thank God, I looked cute today. I had on some little black stretch jeans, a hot pink hoodie underneath my fitted leather jacket, and the pair of Nike boots Marquan bought for me.

"You see your boy?" she asked, smiling.

"Yeah, I see him. Why you think they up here? Can't be for me."

"I don't know."

We walked near them, but LaSheika saw her new boo waiting across the street in his gold Caprice.

"Oops, gotta go, Tink. There go Larry. Call me later," she said, smiling and sashaying across the street.

"All right. Call me."

She stayed juggling dudes around and skipping school these days. Sometimes, I felt like we was growing apart, because chasing dudes and money seemed to be the only thing she ever wanted to do.

"Tinka," Nine called out.

I turned toward him and walked over, wondering what he wanted.

"Oh, you was just gonna walk by like you ain't see me and not say nothing?"

"No. I was about to —"

"Why you ain't call me yet?"

I bit my bottom lip. "Where Clint at?"

"So you gonna change the subject?"

I nodded and then leaned on the car, too.

"Oh, okay," he said, nodding. "I ain't know we was like that now."

I smiled and then I saw Clint talking it up with this girl in my science class. "Where y'all about to go?"

"I'm 'bout to get my car out the shop."

"What's wrong with it?"

"Nothing. I just got some rims put on it."

"Oh, okay."

"What you 'bout to do?"

"Nothing. Go home."

"It's Friday. You can't just sit in the house. You wanna do something?"

"Like what?"

"Something . . . It'll be fun. Trust me," he said, flashing a smile.

"Hmmm . . . I don't know, Nine."

"You can do your homework and read all

251

day tomorrow," he teased. "Come on, girl . . ."

"You got jokes?" I rolled my eyes, but smiled. "All right."

"It shouldn't take long. You wanna ride with us now, or you want me to pick you up after I get my car?"

I kinda liked the attention I was getting. I could feel people's eyes on me. Nobody at school ever really knew who I talked to, and Nine was cute and tall with pretty chocolate-smooth skin, so I knew they was really trying to get in my business. It was always LaSheika getting us rides here and there. I was eating it up, so I said, "I'll ride with you now."

He smiled and opened the door. "Ladies in the front," he said.

I smiled and climbed in, while Nine sat in the backseat. Clint got in the car a few minutes later, then we rode up to Rhode Island Avenue to get Nine's car. The rims looked tight. Big and bright like jewelry. I see he got some darker tint put on the windows, too. It looked good.

"You hungry?" he asked, as soon as he started the car.

"A little bit."

"You like Checkers? I gotta taste for their shakes."

"Yeah. I like them," I said, but I hoped that wasn't the *fun* thing he was talking about.

We grabbed some food on New York Avenue, then Nine hopped on 295 headed toward Southeast. For a second, I thought maybe I should've told Ma where I was going or something, but she would be on her way to work soon anyway. When we got off the highway and crossed the train tracks on Firth Sterling, Nine turned onto Sumner Road. He lived right across the street from the rec center. I could feel myself tensing up. I ain't think going to his house was gonna be the "fun" thing either.

"Wait right here. I'll be right back," he said, disappearing inside the house.

Good. At least he had better plans than humping on his couch. I relaxed and laid my head back on the headrest. I looked around his neighborhood. Barry Farms ain't seem too different from mine. There was houses and tiny yards. There was more grass over here, though. Some little kids played with skateboards in the middle of the street. A cluster of guys stood at the corner, cracking up at something. I ain't never been around here before, but everybody knew this was where Junk Yard Band came from and that this was where you could get the best dro, dippers, and O cups — filled to the brim with your favorite mixture of cough syrup, Cîroc, and whatever else. People said Southside dudes was more ruthless than everywhere else in D.C., because they was used to getting the shortest end of the stick. I'm not gonna lie, Southeast was the countriest part of D.C. Stuff that wasn't in style no more, people was still wearing. Some girls went to the grocery store in bedroom shoes, headscarves, and last night's club clothes and ain't think twice about it. Dudes was still rocking cornrows, when everywhere else every single body was rocking dreads. Most dudes over here looked grimier, like they ain't care about nothing. Just straight-up goons desperate for a better situation. Southeast was way different than where I lived and supposedly the poorest part of the city. I mean, Barry Farms was literally right on the other side of the train tracks. My social studies teacher taught me what that usually meant.

Nine came out the house, carrying two motorcycle helmets. One black one and one silver one.

"Oh, uh-uh," I said.

He was grinning from ear to ear. I looked at him like he was crazy.

"Come on, Tinka," he said, opening the

car door.

"You must've lost your mind. I ain't getting on no bike, boy."

He laughed. "Why I gotta go through this? Come on. You gon' have some fun today," he said, more like a threat than a fact.

I always did the right things to please everybody else. Not because it's something I necessarily wanna do. For some crazy reason, I always wanted to be one of those girls riding on the back of a bike, with my hair blowing in the wind. But I'd never admit that to nobody. I'm usually the first person to say when something's dangerous or not safe or illegal.

"Tinka, I'll go real slow. I promise," he said, taking my hand. "We're just gonna go for a ride, hang out, and then come back."

I looked at him sideways. "No poppin' wheelies, racing, or nothing crazy like that, right?"

He nodded.

"You promise?"

"I promise."

He looked so sexy lying. I took the helmet, then slid it on. Thank God, I wore jeans today.

"You look tight like shit in that."

My heart skipped a beat.

We walked over to the bike that was

255

covered up with a beige cloth and chained to a tree. It was silver with black sparkling accents. I took a deep breath and closed my eyes when I climbed on the back. He wrapped my arms around his waist and then he revved the engine. I leaned on his back and squeezed as close as I could. He pulled off smoothly, crossing Martin Luther King Avenue so we could get on Suitland Parkway. As soon as he merged on, I squeezed tighter. So many people tried to race on this two-lane parkway. I don't know if it's because of all the trees and the little bit of traffic lights or what, but I held on tight, just in case he wanted to show me his Evel Knievel side.

Nine surprised me, though. He was smooth and steady, even when he changed lanes and dipped past potholes. The sun was going down, and it was a little cooler than it was when we first pulled off, especially with the wind forcing its way through my jacket. We rode all the way to the end of Suitland Parkway in Maryland, passing Andrews Air Force Base on the right, and then he made a left on Pennsylvania Avenue, heading back to the city.

When we stopped at the traffic light, Nine yelled out, "Are you okay?!"

"Yeah!" I shouted back.

"Am I going too fast?!"

"No, just right!"

"You want me to speed up a little?!" he said, revving the engine.

"No, you good, you good!" I punched him in his stomach a couple times so he could get the point.

The light changed green. As soon as he could move ahead of the cars in front of him, Nine turned on the speed. We took off like a Jet Ski zipping across water. I squeezed him hard until my hands got numb. I heard the loud wind in my ears, and cool air crawled down my chest, but I felt like I was flying or free-falling through the air. And it was unbelievable. I never felt like that in my life. Nine ain't slow down until we had to stop at the light on Alabama Avenue. I thought I would've been mad at his little stunt, but I wasn't. Actually, I was thankful for it.

"Too fast?!" he yelled.

"Nope!" I shouted back.

"Good!"

But there was too many lights for him to speed without being ridiculous and cutting people off or just straight running lights, so he cruised the rest of the way down Pennsylvania Avenue. He stopped at a gas station near Anacostia Park. Nine looked so sexy taking his helmet off. His dreads spilled out and fell across his dark chocolate face.

"You ready to go home yet?" he asked.

"No." I smiled. "I'm having fun like you said I would."

He smiled, too.

I watched him buy two rollups at the window and then we hopped back on the bike. We rode up to the Capitol Building and then down M Street, up to Hains Point. It wasn't too many people in the park like I thought it would be. A couple of boats was out on the Potomac River, and a few people rode their bikes around for some evening exercise. I could tell Nine ain't wanna stop until I said so.

"Let's stop!" I shouted.

I was glad he heard me, because my throat was starting to hurt from all the yelling. He pulled up on the side of the park across from Reagan National Airport. Airplanes took off and landed while the sun took its time setting. I don't know if he planned it or not, but stopping here, especially at this exact time of day, was definitely romantic. We walked over to a picnic table and sat on top of it.

I smiled. "I'm not gonna lie . . . you was right."

"Told you," he said, grinning. "I told you,

258

you was gonna have fun."

"I ain't expect it to be like that. I'm usually not into risking my life . . . but that just felt like . . ."

"You was flying?"

"Yeah, just like I was floating almost."

"That's why I love it. I get this crazy rush whenever I pass by people."

We both got quiet and stared at the planes for a while, and then at some of the early buds popping out on the cherry blossom trees.

"So why you don't have a boyfriend?"

"I don't know."

"How you not gonna know?"

"I'm picky, I guess. Why don't you have a girlfriend?"

"I'm picky, too."

I smiled and shook my head from left to right. "Okay, I'll give you a real answer, if you promise you goin' do the same."

"Bet."

"I got two brothers who ain't goin' let me settle for just an average dude. And to tell the truth, I don't want one either."

Nine raised his eyebrows and tucked his lips down. "I understand."

"Your turn."

"Okay . . . um . . . I'm not the easiest person to get along with, number one. Plus,

I want a girl who keeps me guessing about what she's thinking," he said, looking at me with the most delicious-looking lips. I ain't expect that answer from him. "So far, I'm intrigued, Tinka."

I could've just screamed. Ab-so-lute-ly F-ing screamed. But I had to play it cool. I nodded and looked at the next plane taking off. Who would've thought when I woke up this morning, I'd be sitting here with Nine watching the sun go down and planes taking off? I closed my eyes and opened them to see if I was dreaming.

CHAPTER 29
TINKA

The first thing out of LaSheika's mouth was "Freak bought me this!" I couldn't believe she was actually dealing with a dude who called himself Freak. That nickname was just as bad as Creature's, except he ain't choose that nickname. I bet Freak did. I'm not gonna fake, her Dooney & Bourke saddlebag was cute as I-don't-know-what, but she was dealing with a dude who I knew she *had* to know wasn't gonna be faithful to her with a name like that. He had been buying her all kinds of stuff, getting her hair done every week, and a couple times he even let her hold his little S-Class Benz. LaSheika ain't even have her license yet. Only her learner's. They had only been dating for three weeks — almost as long as me and Nine been talking — but you would've thought it was three years the way they was acting. All bunned up with each other every time I turned around. She wasn't really going to school much no more either. Too busy chasing dudes and dollars.

"You like it?" she asked, waving her bag back and forth.

"Of course."

"I got it from Nordstrom's!" she said, like I asked.

"He sure is doing a lot for you."

LaSheika smiled so big, I could see every tooth in her mouth. But LaSheika had become one of *those* girls. The kind that had to have whatever the magazines said she had to have. She got her nails and hair done every week, but ain't been to the dentist since she was twelve. She was buying her self-esteem at the makeup counter. I knew she had already let Freak smash. Wasn't no way in the world he wasn't tapping that.

"Don't be jealous, Tinka. Nine need to step up his game. That's all."

"First of all, he ain't my man and Nine doing just fine."

"That's the problem. You need to go 'head and let him hit, so *you* can get that monkey off your back and so he can get you one of these!" she teased.

"Whatever, LaSheika!" She was my girl, but come on. I'm not a whore.

"Well, I'm about to get ready for our little

date. He's taking me to Jasper's."

"Oh, okay," I said, not hating in the least. "Have fun."

"We will!" she chirped.

I shook my head and walked back in the house. Teddy was sitting on the couch watching TV with his funky feet up. He been in his usual spot ever since he got laid off, wearing out the sofa cushions and leaving wet beer stains on the coffee table. I ain't see this dude try to look for a job once. I never seen him look in the newspaper or hear him make no phone calls for one either. He was just trifling. I heard him tell Taevon he was waiting for a job to find him this time. What man tells their son that? He was so pathetic. How could Ma allow him to just lie around the house doing nothing? All day at that? He had the nerve to be playing PlayStation sometimes when I got home from school. Talking about he in a tournament, and "nobody bet' not fuck with his team." Pa-thet-ic. He ain't even take the trash out. He waited for Taevon to come in the house to do it, and since Taevon was hardly ever in the house, Ma basically took it out whenever she was on her way out to work. I couldn't believe her. But I bet if Marquan had been around, she would've asked him to do it and he would've done it, thinking he was just helping Ma out.

I hadn't seen Marquan since that day he sat looking crazy in the living room. He called twice from an unknown number to say he was all right, and that he was hanging out of town with some friends, but that was it. He ain't say where he was at or who he was with or when he was coming home. He talked to Taevon for a little bit and told Ma he was sending her some money through Western Union. I was worried about him.

"Somebody called for you," Teddy said.

"Who?"

"Some dude," he said, scratching his chest through his raggedy gray wifebeater.

Okay, so I guess he ain't take a message.

"He sounded too damn old for you, I know that much."

I rolled my eyes and picked up the house phone. "What number they call from, Teddy?"

"Tinka, hell, I don't know. He called like twenty minutes ago."

Thanks a lot. I went upstairs and called the 804 area code number back on caller ID three times, thinking it could only be Marquan, but got no answer.

"Who was that? Your punk-ass daddy?"

Teddy was standing in my doorway, grinning and holding a beer bottle. If he wasn't in the way, I'd slam the door dead in his face. What was he talking about?

"What that nigga want?"

All up in my business.

"He wanna come see you? He wanna play daddy now?"

"What?!" I rolled my eyes. If Teddy had any sense, he'd know to shut his damn mouth. He knew I ain't have a relationship with my father.

"You heard me!" he said, his breath smelling like tart beer.

I just shook my head, and tried to close my bedroom door.

"Oh, you gon' act like I'm not talking to you?!" he said leaning forward, daring me to close the door. "I'm the closest thing to a father you ever had!"

I wasn't scared of Teddy. I hated him so bad it made my head hurt. *Try to touch me again, nigga. I'm not my mother. I'll have his ass killed or locked the hell up.* I hoped my eyes spoke the words I ain't dare say. I stared at him so hard he knew I wasn't afraid.

"Man, fuck your little ass." He laughed, then turned around to go across the hall. I knew he was drunk, but it wasn't no excuse. Between him and Ma always having something in their system, her popping them pills and drinking Rémy, or him smoking weed and whatever else, they was both making me crazy around here.

Nine called an hour later, like he knew something was wrong with me. He threw out a plan like he knew I needed it.

"Let's ride up to Atlantic City for the hell of it."

"Okay. Let's do it," I said, so fast he thought I was playing.

"Stop faking, Tinka," he said. "I'm serious."

"Me, too. I need to get away from here, for real."

"What your mother gon' say?"

"I don't even care. I just wanna do what I wanna do for a change and right now, Atlantic City sounds cool." Like I dipped in and out of town like this all the time.

"That's a bet," he said. I knew he was smiling, and I could tell he still ain't believe I was gonna go, especially when he said, "I'm on my way to get you, so be ready, okay?"

"I'll be ready."

As soon as I hung up, I threw some jeans, a top, and some cute underclothes inside my pink-and-white Puma bowling bag. I grabbed my toothbrush, deodorant, soap, and lotion. Then I sat on the bed and waited for him. I ain't even call LaSheika and tell her like I usually did. Ma was at work. She wouldn't be looking for me until tomorrow after school anyway. I'll make up a lie by then.

When I saw Nine pulling up forty minutes later, I ran down the stairs and straight out the door, before Teddy could try and act like he was somebody's father. I knew he was confused and probably goin' to exaggerate and tell Ma that I left in the middle of the night. Whatever. She'd just have to be all right.

"I thought you was bullshitting," he said, as soon as I got inside.

"I told you I'm not as Goody-Two-shoes as you think I am." But I really just ain't care. Even if Ma gets pissed, this ain't nothing like the stunts Marquan and Taevon pulled.

"Well . . . shit, let's be out then." He turned the radio up and let TCB pump through the speakers while he pulled onto New York Avenue. We was on BW Parkway when he lit up a blunt. This time when he passed it to me, I smoked like a pro.

"I can't believe you going hard like this. On a school day, too? I'm impressed, Miss Good Girl Gone Bad." He merged onto 95

North. He nodded his head to the beat, poked his bottom lip out, and tapped the steering wheel with his thumbs. I could tell this was his song the way he was rocking to the beat. "This must be a brand-new you."

"I just get tired of doing what people expect of me all the time. It's too much pressure. Why I gotta be the only one in the family who goin' finish school? With decent grades at that? And why I gotta be the only one who listen to my mother? I do whatever she say and it still don't seem like it's enough. I always do what I'm supposed to . . . and I don't ask for nothing from nobody. I never get in trouble. I'm tired of that!"

"Damn, shawty. Get it off your chest," Nine said, smiling. "You definitely need to hit this joint again."

I was really mad at Teddy, pointing out the fact that my father wasn't in the picture, and sweating me about my life like he was really somebody. Nine passed the blunt over and I inhaled long and deep.

"I'm just frustrated about everything . . ."

"Damn," Nine said, shaking his head.

Tears came from nowhere. "I just got so much pressure on me . . . all the time." I wiped my face, before they got out of control, and then stared out the window.

"Tinka, it'll be all right."

I chewed the inside of my cheek and shook my head. Why was I telling him everything about me?

Nine paid a two-dollar toll when we came out of a tunnel in Baltimore. I knew the lady who took his money could smell weed, but I wasn't even worried about it.

"I ain't know you was going through so much . . . ," Nine said. "I thought you had it made. You never complain about nothing whenever I talk to you. Plus, you always be smiling and shit like everything copacetic."

I laughed. "Copa-what?"

"Copacetic," he said, laughing too.

"What do you know about that?"

"Whatever. I read, too! It mean *all good.*"

He blew my mind with that one. I had to hit the J again.

"See, that's what I like about you," he said, looking at me. "We can laugh at silly shit. Plus, you cool as shit, man."

I smiled and took another pull from the tightly coiled blunt. I felt good. I watched the trees blending together in the darkness. "You know, whenever I'm on the road like this, and the trees disappear behind me . . . I just be thinking about all kinds of stuff."

"Like what?" he asked.

"I mean like look at these little cities we

269

passing by . . . What the heck is a Joppa-towne?"

He laughed at the big green sign we was passing.

"You never really think about the people living in these towns. We just trying to get where we trying to go . . . but all around us drama be unfolding. And we just passing through. Somebody probably just woke up because they can't sleep."

"True."

"Right now somebody probably getting stabbed to death over a twenty-dollar debt or something. It'll be in their little local newspaper in the morning and we just driv-ing by like ain't nothing happening."

"True," he said, nodding, and then he blew a cloud into the air.

"Somebody probably getting pregnant as we speak! A little life being created."

Nine laughed so hard he snorted like a pig. "You high like shit right now, young."

"Nuh-uh. I'm good. I'm being deep, Nine," I said, feeling a little dizzy at the same time. "You feel me?"

"Okay, okay, let me be deep with you . . ." He thought for a minute, then he said, "Okay, okay. A dude probably making a choice right at this very minute that's gonna change the rest of his life."

270

I nodded and puffed. Nine seemed like he was thinking about something serious, so I ain't say nothing else. We listened to the music and stayed quiet for a while, then somewhere in Delaware, Nine pulled off at a rest stop to get some gas, use the bathroom, and grab some Black & Milds. He bought me a hot sausage and some salt-and-vinegar potato chips like I asked for, then we got back on the road.

"Tell me something you ain't never told nobody," I said, hoping to break the long silence between us.

"Hmmm . . ." He looked over at me, like he ain't trust me or something. "That's hard."

"Come on . . . it gotta be something."

I watched him light his tiny cigar and smoke it for a while before he stared at the white car with New Jersey tags in front of us.

"There gotta be something, Nine," I said again. "Stop holding out."

"All right . . . Ummm . . . Well, I can't sleep."

My face went blank. "What you mean you can't sleep?" I asked, confused.

"I mean" — he blew a cloud of smoke in the air — "I try, but I can't. It's been like that for a long time."

271

He kept staring at the long stretch of highway in front of us. A couple cars floated in and out of lanes like the drivers was having problems staying awake.

"Why not?" I asked, turning my body toward him. I ain't never know nobody who couldn't sleep.

"I can't do it. I mean . . . I sleep, but I always wake up, sweating. Nightmares and shit."

I wasn't expecting to hear that. He said it so seriously that I almost ain't wanna ask nothing else. But I was curious. "How long it been like that?"

Nine let go of a deep breath and ran his hand across his forehead and up over his dreads. "Since I was thirteen. Off and on."

"Do you remember what you be dreaming about when you wake up?"

He nodded, but he ain't tell me what it was, and for some reason I knew this time it wouldn't be cool to ask, so I left it alone and looked back at the road. I don't know why I wasn't nervous about the fact that we was gonna sleep in the same bed together. Well, I guess *I* would be sleeping. I ain't feel weird about it at all. Nine didn't seem like the type to be pressed about getting some. He never tried to touch me like that before, anyway . . . almost like he ain't wanna cross the line for some reason, and I ain't have a problem with that at all. Shoot, as cute as he was, I know he ain't have no problem hooking up with some slutty broad who was down to do whatever for a little bit of attention. However, I'm not The One.

A few long quiet minutes passed by, so I said, "Well, what you do while you're up?" *Because I might just have to sleep with one eye open now. Forget all that.*

He shook his head and said, "Whatever there is to do. Sometimes I play PlayStation or watch TV. Sometimes I just stay out with my friends until they ready to call it a night. I don't know."

"So you really can't sleep at *all?*"

"I mean . . . eventually I fall asleep, but not for long. Maybe two or three hours at the most."

Three hours? No. I looked at him sideways.

He nodded when he felt my eyes burning a hole in his face. "It's your turn . . . Tell me something."

I sighed. Wasn't nothing as strange as what he said. "I don't keep too many secrets."

"There ain't nothing?"

"Nah, not really. I already told you enough of my drama."

"It's all good," he said.

273

CHAPTER 30
TINKA

We crossed a huge bridge that went up and down like a mountain with four lanes going in both directions. I panicked a little when we hit Jersey. Ma was gonna flip out on me when I got home. And did Nine think we was gonna do it or something? I ain't have a single dollar on me. What the hell was I thinking coming up here?

But Nine proved to me he was a gentleman. I mean he snuck a little kiss after we ate breakfast in an all-night diner on the strip, but it ain't really count because it was on the cheek. I was starting to feel like he looked at me like his little sister or something. Not cool at all. I mean, I ain't want him to slam his tongue in my mouth, but a kiss on the cheek? Come on now. By the time I get home, Ma probably won't let me out the house for the rest of the year. Teddy and Taevon probably gonna have something to say, too. And by the time Marquan hear about my little disappearing act, it'll be a wrap. So I'm not taking nothing less than a kiss on the lips before we head back home. Forget that. LaSheika would really laugh me out, if I didn't.

Me and Nine was about to put some quarters in the slot machines in Caesers just when a corny, skinny white security guard came walking toward us with an attitude, so we dipped out. I was blown that we couldn't really go to none of the casinos with our premature IDs, but Nine did his best to make it fun. We walked around for a little while, looking at the colorful dancing lights on the buildings and checking out the boardwalk. It was kinda dead out because it was in the middle of the week, but there was a few couples nuzzled together. When Nine stopped a guy who was selling flowers to all the other couples and bought me some, I knew I wasn't in the "little sister" category no more. I loved the way he looked a little nervous when he handed them to me.

"Thank you," I said before I smelled the three white roses.

He nodded and lit up another Black & Mild.

I was getting sleepy. We had been on the road for three and a half hours and now we was going here and there, like it was one in the afternoon instead of one in the morning.

"You tired, ain't you?" Nine said after he saw me yawning a lot.

I nodded, glad that he noticed, even though he ain't look like he was tired at all. He grabbed my hand and we walked back to his car. He paid for a room at a motel right off of Atlantic Avenue. We got settled in the room quick. I put on my tank top and shorts and climbed in the bed. He had on a wifebeater and some basketball shorts. The entire time I laid beside Nine, all I kept thinking about was what he must've been thinking. I knew he wasn't asleep.

"You wanna turn the TV on?" I asked him.

"You gon' be all right?" he asked, sounding relieved.

"Yeah, I can sleep through almost anything."

I heard the TV cut on real loud, then he turned the volume down a bit. I heard the channels flipping. He watched ESPN for a little while, then he started flipping channels again. I was shocked when he stopped at CNN. I fell asleep listening to the news.

I woke up when I heard the toilet flushing. I almost forgot where I was when I opened my eyes. I sat up and looked around.

Motel. Atlantic City. Four o'clock. A pistol. Wait — a pistol? What the —

"Damn, my bad. I ain't mean to wake you up," Nine said, coming out the bathroom.

"What the heck is that?" I asked, nodding at the nightstand.

He took a deep breath. "I'll put it back up."

"Why the heck do you have that?!"

He shook his head. "Long story."

I wiped my eyes, turned around to fluff my pillows up against the headboard, then I sat all the way up. Now I really felt like that was him and Clint robbing that liquor store. "And I got plenty of time." Clearly, I wasn't comfortable with no gun just laying right there.

"I don't go nowhere without it — especially not out of town."

"Why you got it for?"

He shook his head again. "All kinds of reasons. I never know when I might need it."

I shook my head and planted my arms on top of each other right in front of me.

"What?" he asked.

I couldn't stop shaking my head, no matter how hard I tried.

"Tinka, you acting all innocent and shit. You got two brothers who I know for a fact

277

on their grind. They do what they gotta do, don't they?"

How he gonna try and twist this up on me?

"Clint told me all about Hit *and* Taevon."

"Hit?" I asked, confused.

"Yeah," he said, putting the pistol inside the nightstand.

"Who is that?"

He looked at me like I was crazy.

"Who is *Hit?*" I asked again.

"Your brother." He said it like I was stupid.

"Marquan?"

"That's his real name? Clint told me his name Hit."

"No?"

"Don't he be around Trinidad all the time?"

I nodded.

"Ain't his father the one who used to work for Rayful Edmond back in the day?"

"Yeah," I said, confused.

"Okay, then so you know what's up."

"No, I don't," I said, shaking my head. "I don't have a clue what you talking about. I wish you hurry up and fill in the blanks, because I'm lost."

"Man, Tinka . . . why you acting like I'm making this up?"

"Because I really don't know what you talking about!"

"If you don't know, then I don't wanna be the one to tell you."

He climbed in the bed and pulled the blanket up to his shoulders. Nine closed his eyes and was out like a light. Snoring and everything. For somebody who never sleeps, when he finally do, ain't no stopping him. But now I couldn't sleep. I stared at the TV until *I* couldn't keep my eyes open no more.

In the morning, Nine woke me up running the shower. I stood up and went to iron my clothes for the day. I ain't even have nothing to say. At this point, I just wanted to go home. ASAP.

"What you wanna do today?" he asked when he came out the shower smelling fresh like that kush oil them Africans on the corner be selling. His body was still wet, and his chest made me think he used to play basketball or something. His towel was slipping off his waist and I could see those sexy indents like D'Angelo had in that video.

"Umm . . . whatever you wanna do," I heard my voice say.

"I wanna hit the shops. That's cool?"

I shrugged. "Cool with me." But I couldn't stop looking at his body dripping water everywhere.

"You gon' get dressed?" he asked.

"Of course," I said, embarrassed. I grabbed my bag and the ironed clothes and headed to the bathroom. I couldn't believe he still ain't try nothing with me. Let LaSheika tell it, dudes jump on her as soon as they get her by herself.

After I was dressed, we went to brunch at another diner and then we spent the next four hours going in and out of stores. Ralph Lauren, Movado, Gucci, and Louis V. He bought a watch and two pair of Gucci jeans for hisself and he bought me a Louis bag, and he even picked out two slamming dresses from White House Black Market. All he had was cash for this and cash for that. I felt like Julia Roberts in that old movie walking down the strip.

"You wanna stay another night?" Nine asked me later.

I thought long and hard. It wouldn't be nothing to stay another night. I had clothes. Evidently, he had the money. Plus, me and him could get real close this time. For some reason, I wanted him to hold me when I slept. But Ma would flip the heck out if I was gone for two days.

"Nah, I think I'm already in deep trouble," I said, sounding more disappointed than I wanted him to know.

"You sure?" he asked.

I nodded.

"Cool."

We ended up hitting the road at three o'clock, the same time I would've been leaving school. Ma was probably getting ready for work. By the time we get back it's gonna be after six. We might as well have stayed another night, but I ain't wanna end up doing something I ain't have no business doing. My name ain't LaSheika.

PART IV

CHAPTER 31
NICOLA

"So you grown now, Miss Thang? Where the hell you been for two days?"

"Huh?" Tinka said, trying to act dumb.

"You heard me?! Where the hell you been at?!"

"Nowhere."

"She a damn lie!" Teddy said, coming in the hallway. He was right. Here her grown ass was, wearing makeup and clothes I ain't never seen, and she was carrying shopping bags.

"Tinka, your ass better tell me something!" I shouted.

"I was with my friend, dag." She rolled her eyes.

"A grown-ass man, I bet!" Teddy yelled.

I wish he would shut up and let me handle this. "Who the hell called you from Richmond yesterday?" I asked.

"I don't know. I never talked to the —"

"Was that where you was at all this time?"

285

I asked, cutting her off.

"What? No," she said, and ran up the stairs.

"Oh, so you old enough to be disrespecting me now?" *That little wench.* I ran up the steps behind her. I shoved her door all the way open and stood in the doorway. "Teyona, listen . . . I'm only gonna say this once. If your little grown ass get pregnant, you getting the hell out my house! I'm not gonna be raising nobody's baby. You hear me?!"

She sucked her teeth and kept acting like I wasn't even there. Hanging her new clothes up in her closet.

"Do you hear me?!"

"Yes, Ma, yes!"

"You better check your attitude!"

She rolled her eyes again and turned her back to me. But maybe she ain't know I could still whip her ass if I wanted too. She in *my* goddamn house! "So whoever you was with, little girl, they better be able to take care of your behind if you turn up pregnant. And whoever the hell it is don't seem like they care much about you, if he don't even care if you going to school or not!

"I tell you what — you can throw your life away if you want to . . . but not while you

286

living here! I thought you would've learned something from my mistakes by now."

And if she haven't, then she'll probably just have to find out the hard way just like I did. Life ain't everything niggas whisper to you when they fucking. I hope Tinka was smart enough to know that. I went back downstairs.

"You need to put her ass out now, Cola! She don't have no respect!" Teddy snapped. "How the hell she gon' be gone like that and not even tell nobody nothing?! Out there ho'ing around. Put her ass out and let her see what it's like not to have a place to stay."

Tinka's bedroom door slammed shut upstairs. Sometimes Teddy really knew how to work my nerves. He just ain't know what to say sometimes or when to say it. Sometimes, he said everything I needed to hear. Like how moving to Charlotte might be just what we both needed. How houses were cheaper there, plus it was less crime and not as much drama day in and out. Teddy made me feel like leaving probably wasn't such a bad idea. D.C. was changing so much anyway. The whole city was changing.

Ever since that little boy got shot while he was sleeping around Carter Terrace, it seemed like the police was everywhere. The police chief kept talking about All Hands on Deck. She wanted every police officer on staff from recruit to lieutenant spending the whole weekend stopping everybody who looked suspicious or who had out-of-state tags, or who just fit whatever description they wanted to harass. At first I thought it was a good thing, until I realized the only people being harassed was young black boys.

So many new people moving to D.C. who don't look like me or nobody I knew, and they ain't seem like they was having a hard time finding jobs. All my old coworkers from DPW done moved out P.G. County, Maryland, now. Hell, we 'bout to be next, if we don't make that move down south. Can't none of us afford to live in D.C. And the worst part about it is the sky-rises going up everywhere, with luxury mortgages and ridiculous rents, are being named after Duke Ellington, Langston Hughes, and Frederick Douglass. Wonder what they gonna call Sursum Cordas next.

CHAPTER 32
TINKA
___

I called LaSheika to tell her about my drama, but she ain't answer her phone. Seemed like I could never get in touch with her these days. I laid across my bed and relaxed for a little while, then I heard Taevon's voice outside. I got up to look out the window. Him and Antonio was laughing with Krystal and Mya in front of our house. What was so damn funny? I was two seconds from calling his cell phone to interrupt. Plus, I wanted to tell him about my Atlantic City trip and to see if he knew why Nine called Marquan Hit.

I reached over and grabbed my journal, then I opened it to the last thing I wrote about: LaSheika and Freak. I flipped a page and wrote:

Well, I did it. Something bad on purpose and it felt good for a little while, but now I feel strange. Ma pissed at me. She even threatened to kick me out. I feel like she don't trust me no more. It's my fault. No more sweet and smart Tinka, I guess. But for real, it's not fair. Compared to everything Marquan and Taevon do, I ain't do a hint of what they be doing. Why she treat them so different from me? Like she expects them to fail, and she expect me not to ever mess up. She always on my back. When Marquan and Taevon quit going to school, she ain't threaten to put them out on the street! Taevon got a gun in this house and he's still up in here! Marquan went to jail and she still wash his clothes when he here. Teddy beats her and even he still living here! It's so not fair.

Ma looked at me sideways for the next couple of days, like she was waiting for me to do something else extreme. I came straight home from school every day and went to my room. I did my homework, wrote in my journal, and read one of the books I checked out of the library. I only talked to Nine a couple times. He wanted to hook up, but I needed to get back in good with Ma. I couldn't stand the way she been looking at me, like she thought I was pregnant now or something.

I ain't know what was up with Nine's mother Roxanne. The first time I met her was crazy. I was sitting on the couch waiting for Nine to grab something from his room, when she walked in the door.

"Uggh. Why it smell like that in here?!" she hollered.

I watched her cover her nose and look at me crazy. We had only been in his house for a couple minutes, and I ain't smell nothing.

"How you doing?" I said when she looked me up and down.

"Hey." She rolled her eyes, then looked at Nine, who came down the stairs with a jacket in his hand.

"Why it smell so funky in here?! You been having sex in my house, boy?!" she shouted.

My eyes almost fell out my head.

"What?!" he yelled. "This your dirty-ass house smelling like that. Come on, Tinka, let's go!"

What was she trying to say about me? She ain't even know me. Nine apologized as soon as we got out the door, but I wasn't never gonna forget her saying that. It ain't take long for me to see she smoked crack the next few times I was over his house. I always felt like I had to watch where I left my stuff whenever I was over there. Roxanne asked way too many questions, too.

Not like she cared about the answer — it just seemed suspect, like she was trying to distract me so she could rob me blind. She gave me the creeps with her spaced-out eyes and her nervous hands. She asked him for money every time we walked in the house. Even though he gave it to her, he ignored her mostly, and he never left me in the house with her by myself.

I was lying across his bed watching TV, when he said, "You know how embarrassing it is to have a mother like her?"

I stayed quiet. How was I supposed to answer that? My mother had her addictions, too.

"I used to get picked on and shit, when I was little. Everybody know my mother smoke that shit."

I stayed quiet.

"That's why I first got my pistol. Fuck that. As soon as I could get one, I did and dared a dumb muthafucka to fuck with me again."

He told me about all the different voices he heard coming from her bedroom all hours of the night and how it messed with his head when he was little. Nine rubbed his forehead like it ached for a long time, and then he drink some of the bottled water sitting on the nightstand beside his bed.

"That shit still be fucking with me," he whispered.

I wondered if that's what he dreamed about when he was asleep. Maybe it was something much worse. When he put his arm around me and pulled me close, I let him. I ended up cuddled close to him through the night, and when he tried to peel my clothes off, I ain't stop him. Nine kissed every inch of my skin. I wanted him to feel better about whatever was messing with his head. I wanted him to be relaxed and to forget about other people. If all I had to do was let him feel the inside of me so he could be back the way he was before, then it was okay. I ain't stop him when he pulled my panties down. I let him slide inside of me on his sheetless mattress, stroking and arching my body until we was both tired and our voices was hoarse. Nine laughed and rolled over on his sweaty back when he was finally done.

"What's so funny?" I asked.

"You." He took a deep breath and laid his head on his pillow.

"What?" I asked.

"I thought you was a Goody Two-shoes, but I thought wrong."

I smiled. Nine was back to hisself again. But for some reason, I ain't feel like me. I

293

don't know why Marquan popped in my head when I stared at the ceiling, but he did.

About an hour later Nine took me to get something to eat, and then we stopped at a hole-in-the-wall spot off of Good Hope Road called the Roc Soul Café. Some new all-girl Go Go band named Sticky Sweet was rocking. Clint's girl played the keyboards in it, and he was up there, too. The band was kinda tight, playing Jay-Z beats with their lead rapper flowing. She had a crazy song with a hook that went, "I got my pussy into something my heart can't get out of/this can't be love," that made me think about me and Nine. I hoped I had made the right choice by sleeping with him and that things would still be all good with us.

Marquan's girlfriend Jillian showed up on our doorstep the day me, Ma, Taevon, and Teddy was about to ride out to Bowie. Aunt Renee and Uncle Matt was leaving the next day for Italy, so they was having a huge dinner at their house. Clearly, Jillian was the one who was pregnant.

"Damn, Marquan keeping secrets like a mug," Taevon whispered in my direction.

"How y'all doing?" Jillian said, as she rubbed her stomach.

Ma looked like she wanted to cry.

"Oh boy." Teddy laughed and lit a cigarette.

"Have you seen Marquan? I haven't heard from him . . . in a minute," she said, looking away. "I'm really starting to get worried now."

"Honey, how many months are you?" Ma asked, shaking her head like her day had been ruined.

"Eight."

Ma shook her head and walked to Teddy's car.

"Have you heard from him?" Jillian asked, sounding desperate.

"He called a couple days ago. But I haven't seen him for a while. But he's grown, child. I don't pay him no attention when he come and go."

Jillian looked down at her stomach, and then up the block where Creature, Big Mike, Keion, and the rest of the dudes Marquan be with sometimes was hanging out. Of course he wasn't there.

"I talked to him yesterday," Taevon said. "Don't worry about him, Jill. He's all right."

"You sure?" she asked. "Does he realize his baby can come any day?"

Taevon nodded. "Trust me, he knows. Go home, Jillian."

She shook her head, her highlighted long twists swaying back and forth. She was still worried. "All right."

Ma and Teddy was already sitting in the car, when Jillian walked back to her old BMW.

"What's up with Marquan?" I asked Taevon once we was seated in Teddy's backseat.

"That nigga on the run," he whispered.

My forehead tightened. "For what?"

He shook his head, and said, "Don't worry about it."

I knew not to ask nothing else. I watched the highway, while Teddy sped up Route 50 like a demon. Something was definitely strange about Marquan being MIA, and I wanted to know what the deal was.

"So you 'bout to be a grandma?!" Teddy teased Ma.

She sucked her teeth. "Don't start with me, Teddy."

I leaned over to ask Taevon, "Do people call him Hit?"

He looked stunned for a second, then he said, "Who told you that?"

"Clint's cousin, Nine."

"Clint know that?"

"Yeah, why? What it mean?"

"That's what Ced and Bear be calling

him, but I wonder how Clint know," Taevon said. His forehead was tight like mine now.

If anybody knew anything about Marquan's whereabouts it was Ced, and more than likely Bear, too, since he been staying up under Ced for as long as I can remember. Bear never really said much. Just a big dude who used to play football up Spingarn, and who ain't go nowhere with his talent but straight to the block. I was still confused though. "Why they call him that?"

Taevon raised his shoulders up and looked out the window. He knew why. He just wasn't gonna tell me. I ain't say nothing else. I sat back in my seat and looked out my window, too. I was willing to give him some time. Just not that much.

Aunt Renee's house was packed with Uncle Matt's family and friends. We was the only ones there for her. I was surprised how big a deal they had made it. Two servers with little black bow ties filled and refilled champagne glasses. A caterer had made the baked chicken and roast beef that sat in big metal pans heated by little flames. Shrimp and oysters chilled on chunks of ice with lemon slices. Garlic mashed potatoes and sliced green beans sat in glass bowls.

Aunt Renee actually looked happy she was

leaving. She gave all of us something to remember her by, even Teddy. I got an Ann Taylor charm bracelet. Real white gold, too.

"I can't believe Marquan didn't come, Cola. How could he not come say good-bye to his favorite aunt?" she said after a lot of people had left.

"I don't know what's up with that boy," Ma said, shaking her head. "His little girlfriend showed up at the house a little while ago, talking about she eight months pregnant."

"What? Wow," she said, surprised. "So I'm about to be a great-aunt?"

Ma cut her eyes and then she sipped her champagne. I was counting, and this was her fifth glass. "I'm about to be the youngest grandmother you know!" she snapped.

Aunt Renee laughed. "You'll be all right. He's a man, Cola. You don't have to have nothing to do with him taking care of his child. Just be the grandmother. Don't even think about raising his kids."

Ma nodded, then she said, "And this one right here." She shot a hard glance at me. "Your favorite. Been spending the night out in the middle of the week, not telling nobody where she been and missing school . . . like she grown!"

I looked away.

"What?! Tinka? Come on, sweetie. What you doing with yourself? You are so close to graduating, why you messing up at the end?" She sounded so disappointed.

I ain't say nothing.

"I know you know better. I hope that's the last time I have to hear about you doing something crazy like that."

I nodded.

"Hmmm." Ma sighed. "She better not. I already told her she bet not bring her ass to my house with no damn baby. She gon' have to go. I'm not kidding either."

"Why you ain't tell Marquan that?!" I said.

Ma looked at me like a snake crawled out of my mouth. "Excuse me?"

Aunt Renee's eyebrows went up, then she said, "Tinka, you wanna talk before I go?"

About what? They already had my life planned out. I shook my head.

"You positive, sweetie?"

I nodded.

"Well, just because I'll be overseas don't mean I'm not going to be checking up on you. And I hope you know, I'm coming to your graduation next year."

"You are?"

"Yes, I am. Me and Uncle Matt want to be able to help you go to college, if that's what you want to do."

"For real?"

"So you better get your head back in them books, and off of them boys!" Ma snapped.

I gave Aunt Renee a huge hug. I was gonna miss her so much.

When we turned off M Street, I saw two police cars in front of Ms. David's house with their lights flashing. We only been gone three hours and the police here and Ms. David was giving the feds a mouthful as she pointed to her front door.

"Look at this shit," Teddy said, shaking his head.

"Wow," I said. "Look at all them bullet holes."

"I know she pissed," Ma said.

"That's what her old ass get!" Taevon snapped. "She too busy running her fucking mouth off to everybody. Look at her now! Running her mouth."

"Watch your mouth!" Ma shouted.

Taevon climbed out the car and walked to the front door. I heard footsteps *click-clack*ing behind me. I turned around and saw Krystal walking up the walkway behind us.

"Hey, Ms. Cola. Hey, Tinka."

What the hell she doing over here? Don't be

fake. I mugged her and she looked away, smiling.

"Hey, Krystal. How your mother doing? She was supposed to call me yesterday."

"She doing good. She in the house."

"I'ma call her right now." Ma went to look for the cordless, while Krystal went upstairs with Taevon.

I couldn't believe this. Taevon and Krystal. Right in front of Ma and Teddy. And nobody was gonna say nothing? I shook my head and went to my room. Here he was about to screw that tramp, probably smoke some weed, and ain't nobody saying nothing. Let that had been me. *And here I am trying to be on my best behavior, so I can make her happy. Oh no.*

CHAPTER 33
TINKA

I called LaSheika, but she ain't answer the phone again. She never answered her phone when she was up under some boy. I called Monte, but he said he had to call me back. I was feeling bored in the house. Since me and Nine got tight, Monte ain't really like hanging with me like he used to. When he did he just wanted to smoke weed. I was getting tired of that. I was tired of hearing Teddy and Ma fussing and making up. Tired of hearing Krystal and Taevon's bed rocking and floor squeaking over top of my room.

Plus, it was just too nice outside to be in the house. I called Nine to see what he was doing.

"Me and Clint 'bout to go to Budds Creek in a little bit. You wanna go?"

"What the heck is a buzz creek?"

He cracked up laughing. "Budds Creek. It's a racetrack out Maryland. I'm thinking 'bout racing my bike."

My eyes popped open. "Race?"

"Yeah, race!" he said, all eager. "You down? You can be my own cheerleader. You want me to come get you?"

"Yeah. I wanna see you smoke somebody."

"See, that's why I need you out there rooting for me." I could hear the smile in his voice.

I bit my lip. "Okay."

When Nine showed up late in the afternoon, I was all ready to go. I had my sunglasses, a small umbrella like I saw people on TV carry when they was at a racetrack, and I had two frozen bottles of water packed away in my bag.

"Ma, I'm going out with Nine. I'll be back later."

"Why he can't come in here and say hi?" She was sitting at the kitchen table sipping from her cup already.

I rolled my eyes. "He's just my friend, not my man, Ma."

"I don't care."

"We in a rush."

"He should've planned better. Tell him I said bring his ass in here. As much as he call my house for you? I wanna see who you been spending all your free time with."

I breathed hard and put my handbag on

303

the back of a kitchen chair. I ain't want him to see her for real. She ain't have it all together, and who knew what she was goin' say. Nine looked like he was ready to pull off, when I walked to the car.

"My mother wanna meet you," I said.

He looked at the time on his radio, then he said, "Okay. What Mom wants, Mom gets."

I smiled and waited for him to lock his car up, then I led him inside the house.

"Ma, this is Na'eem," I said as he said hello.

"Nice to meet you," Ma said, taking another sip. She made me nervous by the way she looked him from head to toe, so I knew he was, too.

"And that's my brother Taevon," I said, pointing in the living room.

"What's up?" he said, barely looking away from his game.

"You ain't gon' introduce me, Tinka?" Teddy said.

"That's Taevon's father," I said, rolling my eyes.

"How you doing?" Nine said.

"So you gon' move her ass up out the house or what?" Teddy joked.

Nine looked confused, like he ain't know if he should comment or not. I rolled my eyes, then grabbed his hand and headed for the door. *Teddy can kiss my ass.*

"What's up with Slim?" he asked, as soon as we got to the car.

"He makes me so damn sick. I can't stand him," I snapped.

Nine shook his head and smiled. "Well, get him out your head, cuz we 'bout to have a good time."

I leaned back in the seat, closed my eyes, and listened to the music seeping from the speakers.

When we pulled up in front of Nine's house, Clint and another dude, who looked way too big to be riding a bike, loaded up a white trailer with a sloppy black paint job.

"Wait right here," Nine said, then he hopped out the car and walked over to see if they needed help. I heard him say, "Y'all straight?"

I had no idea he was really into racing like that. I was shocked since most dudes I knew ain't have real hobbies. Playing PlayStation ain't count at all. Maybe I *could* count Tae-von collecting animals, but even that wasn't doing nothing unusual.

I looked around Nine's car while I waited. His ashtray was filled high with ashes from Black & Milds. Bootleg CDs covered in Magic Marker lettering was scattered across

305

the backseat. Some old receipts was peeking out of the armrest. He was too junky to be so cute. I turned around to see what they was doing, but Nine was headed back to the car.

"All right. Let's be out," he said, climbing in. "You need to use the bathroom, cuz it's a long ride."

"How long?"

"About a hour."

"Nope. I'm good."

"Bet," he said, starting the engine.

Nine followed close behind the black trailer. He lit up a blunt as soon as we turned on 295. I could tell we was heading to no-man's-land out Route 5. Him and Clint traded places a few times, and now the trailer was following us. There wasn't that much traffic. We passed by a lot of trees and houses that were spaced apart by long stretches of fields or trees. Some had cars in the yard for sale close to the road for people to see. Plastic animals posed beside bushes. We dodged a dead deer smashed on the road that big black birds kept trying to pick at. When we turned down Budds Creek Road, we had to slow down, because of a man riding in a buggy with a brown horse trotting in front of us. The man had a long beard, and he was dressed in dark clothes with a big straw hat blocking the beaming sun.

"What the heck?" I said.

"He Amish," Nine said when he saw my confused face.

"Oh . . . I ain't know they lived this close to D.C."

"Yeah, they do."

"They're so weird."

He turned and looked at me like I said something strange, then he said, "Sometimes, I wish I could be more like them."

I frowned. "Uggh. Why?"

"Look how peaceful it is out here. They don't have to worry about nothing. They make everything they need with their own bare hands." He took a pull from his blunt and blew the smoke out. "They can build just about anything. They grow their own food, make their own clothes, and they don't get no help from the government for nothing."

I ain't know all that. Nine offered me the blunt and I took a quick pull.

"Plus, whenever one of them need something . . . they get it from their neighbor. And they trust each other. They don't have crime like we do either. Everybody know each other. It's like a little village. I like that shit."

He crazy. Not me. "But they don't even have no phones or no Internet. They don't even have electricity. Do they use the bathroom in the woods?"

He cracked up laughing. "I don't know about that part, but I know plenty niggas who ain't got none of that other shit and can't none of them get up and build a house from scratch!"

"True, true." I giggled.

"See, they self-sufficient. Why my people can't be like that?"

I rose my eyebrows, cuz he had a point. "I bet they know how to grow their own weed, though."

He laughed, then the car got quiet.

"Are you self-sufficient?" I asked.

"Hell yeah. If I ever need anything, I go out and get it. Fuck that," he said, staring at the man slowly trotting down the road. "Can't get no more self-sufficient than that."

I watched the Amish dude turn down a long path that disappeared into thick green woods. Nine kept going straight. When we got closer to the racetrack, I heard loud engines making harsh ripping sounds. A charred rubber smell filled the air. I saw a long line of trailers and bright-colored cars waiting to get inside. Families sat under umbrellas in the stands eating hot dogs and drinking Cokes.

Clint and the other dude, whose name I found out was Reggie, helped Nine unload two bikes from the back of the trailer. Backyard Band pumped from their loudspeakers. Nine and Clint put on some padded gear and gloves, and then Nine put some iPod earbuds in his ears.

"What you listening to?" I asked.

"T.I.," he said, smiling. "Got to."

I nodded.

"Here, babe" — he passed me a twenty-dollar bill — "go get something to eat while I go smoke these niggas real quick."

I smiled. He kissed me and then put his black-and-yellow helmet on. "Make sure you cheer real loud for me, too."

I rolled my eyes playfully. "All right. I'll be the one spelling your name out with my body."

"Aww shit . . . I wanna see that. You gon' make me lose the race doing that shit."

I spun around and headed toward the concession stand with a big smile on my face. *He's silly.* It was so bright, hot, and sunny that I pulled my umbrella out and put my shades on. I bought some chicken tenders and fries, then I climbed the high metal bleachers. There was a lot of people here, black, white, Spanish. Young and old. I had no clue about this place. There was a long line of bikes and cars waiting to get their chance at the starting line. I saw Nine's new black-and-yellow bike inching up, too. By the time him and another dude reached the starting line, I was so anxious I stood up. Their engines made loud cracking sounds like thunder when they revved it. How fast was Nine's heart beating right now? When the light went from red to yellow to green, Nine whizzed past the dude on the neon bike.

"Yay, Nine!" I yelled.

That's what I really liked about him. He knew how to make me have fun, and he lived life like he ain't have a care in the world. I was so jealous of that. I wished I could forget about everything and go just like he did.

CHAPTER 34
NICOLA

When I unlocked the door, I thought I heard Marquan's voice. I walked in the house and looked in the living room, and saw him talking to Taevon and Teddy.

"Oh my God. Marquan, where the hell you been at, boy?"

"Hey, Ma," he said, smiling and reaching out to hug me. I couldn't remember the last time Marquan gave me a hug. I squeezed him back. He was so slender and frail now, like he'd lost at least fifteen pounds.

"Boy, what you been eating? Look at you!"

Marquan looked away. Something else was different about him. He looked sad, almost depressed or something. I wanted to cheer him up somehow. See him smile again, so I said, "And who said you could go and make me a grandmother already?!"

"I know, Ma. My bad." He half-laughed. "I was gonna tell you a long time ago, I just got caught up."

"Yeah, right."

"Well, why you ain't call Jillian? She worried about you."

"I know. I'll call her in a minute."

He lit a little cigar, and watched Taevon and Teddy playing PlayStation. I sat on the couch and watched them play for a while, waiting for a chance to ask Marquan where he been, but it ain't seem like he wanted to talk about it. All of a sudden, my head started throbbing. I went upstairs and took two pain pills. Those pills always made me sleepy.

When I woke up the news was on and Teddy was lying beside me, rubbing my arm. The reporter was talking about a dead body they found wrapped up in some carpet in an alley in Southeast. They thought it was a teenage girl who was around the same age as Tinka. I sat up and listened.

"You all right?" Teddy asked.

"Where Tinka?"

"I think she gone somewhere with that nigga."

I climbed out the bed and went across the hall. Tinka's door was closed, but I opened it. Her bed was messy. Clothes thrown everywhere, like she was in a rush when she left out. She was getting so grown. Never stayed her tail in the house no more. All up under that little boy.

I called Tracy's house to see if LaSheika knew where she was. Tracy said LaSheika never home either no more, but she gave me LaSheika's cell phone number. I tried to call her, but she didn't pick up. I looked through the caller ID for that boy's number and then called him. I hoped my baby was okay.

"Hello?"

"How you doing? This Tinka's mother. She with you?"

"Ahhh . . ."

"Don't ahhh me. Is she with you right now or not?!"

"Hold on . . . Tinka, it's your mother."

"Hey, Ma. What's up?"

My heart felt relief the minute I heard her voice. "You okay?"

"Yeah."

"Oh . . . well, tell that boy he need to buy you a phone or something if you gonna be staying out with him all the time. You scared me."

"Huh?"

"I got enough problems than to be worried about you all the damn time. The least he can do is make sure I can get in touch with you. You hear me?"

"Ummm . . . okay," Tinka said, like I had

313

said something outrageous.

"That don't mean it's okay for you to turn up pregnant either."

She ain't say nothing when I said that.

"Did you hear what I said, little girl?"

"Yes, Ma."

"Good."

I went back to Tinka's room and cut the light on. I couldn't remember the last time I came in her room when she wasn't in it. The picture of me and her father sat in a frame on the nightstand beside her bed. I remembered that night like it was yesterday. We was at the Legend having a good time. Next to the picture was a book by Terry McMillan. I kinda remembered reading it back when I used to work for DPW. Shelia gave it to me. A story about a single mother with a whole bunch of kids. Surprised Tinka reading it, though. She's really growing up.

I picked up a handful of tops and jeans from her bed and folded them into neat piles. I hung up all of her dresses, then put her jewelry into tiny plastic box containers on the dresser. She had three books underneath her blankets. I put them on the bookshelf and made up her bed. I felt her journal under her pillow. I pulled it out and read the words on the front: "Confessions and reflections."

I sat down on the bed and flipped the pages so I could read a little bit. It was mostly poems. Some crossed out and some half done. A few lines I couldn't understand because her handwriting was so terrible. She wrote about hating Teddy, about Taevon's nasty habits, missing Marquan. There was one she wrote called "Forgetting." I knew it had to be about me. I read it twice and then closed the journal shut. That was always Tinka's problem. She knew more than her little grown ass should have, yet she ain't know a damn thing at all. I left her room and went back to bed.

CHAPTER 35
TINKA

She had her nerve. I should be telling *her* what to do. She only acted like she cared about me when she wanted to. Surprised she noticed I wasn't home. She so far up Teddy's butt, and so high out her mind, she never notice when I'm gone. This was my fourth time sneaking out the house late to be with Nine, and she ain't even get that pissed. Which didn't surprise me at all. I don't know who she thought that phone call was fooling.

"Let's go," Nine said, reaching for his jacket.

"Where?"

"A quick ride somewhere."

"Okay."

Quick rides always meant bike rides. He must've known that I needed to clear my head. He passed me my helmet and I put on my jacket. Nine hopped on his bike, and I climbed on behind him. He headed toward

316

495. When we crossed the Woodrow Wilson Bridge into Alexandria, Virginia, I felt a chill crawl down my back. When we got to the Van Dorn Street exit, Nine pulled over at an Exxon to get some gas.

"You wanna drive?" he asked with a big smile on his face.

I flipped my visor back. "Me?"

"Yeah, you." He smiled.

I shook my head.

"Come on, Tinka. Man up."

"Who said I wanna be a man?"

Nine smiled. "Look, all you gotta do is squeeze this right here for gas and this for brakes."

"And then what?"

"That's it."

"Boy, you crazy. I ain't driving this thing. I be done flipped us over somewhere. I don't know how to drive."

Nine laughed. "Okay, okay. But I need you to do something."

"What?"

"I need you to be ready when I'm ready to go, okay?"

"What you mean?"

"Just be ready."

I shook my head, straight confused.

"I'll be back. Just be ready."

I sat sideways on the bike and watched

317

him go in the store to pay for the gas.

Before I knew it, Nine was running back with his gun in his hand. He stuffed it in his jacket, then yelled, "Watch out, watch out!" He jumped on the bike. "Come on!"

My heart thumped so hard I thought it was gonna stop.

"Come on, Tinka!" he barked again and then he revved the engine.

Oh my God. Oh my God. I made my feet move somehow, then I jumped on the back, wrapped my arms around his waist, and shut my eyes tight. Nine balled out and hopped back on the highway toward D.C. He had robbed that gas station, just like I knew for sure now he robbed that liquor store last year.

As soon as he turned the bike off in front of his house, I pushed his back with all my might and jumped off. I snatched my helmet off. "Are you crazy?! Why you do that, Nine?!"

He ain't say nothing.

"I can't believe you got me in the middle of that!"

"Go 'head. Get it off your chest," he said, taking his gloves off.

"How could you do that to me?" I screamed.

"Calm down, Tinka. Ain't shit gonna happen."

My eyes stretched wide. Why was he acting so nonchalant, like he ain't just rob a damn gas station? With me on his bike at that? I ain't never been in trouble before, and now he got me in the middle of this mess. I took a deep breath and counted to three in my head. "But Nine, what if the police find out?! Then what?"

"Then nothing."

"They can trace the tag, Nine."

"No, they can't. The bike's stolen — they can't trace it to me. Just relax."

What? My eyebrows froze at the top of my forehead, before I took a long blink.

"This ain't nothing new for me. I told you if it's something I need, Tinka, I make sure I get it."

I shook my head.

"You was with me when I did it before."

I could feel my forehead folding into creases. "When was this?"

"Remember Atlantic City? When you was sleeping, I got us some money so I could take you shopping."

"You did what?!" I asked, shocked.

"Look, you gon' stop questioning me," he said, walking up the walkway to the front door.

I ain't want him to be mad at me, for some reason. Even though I knew what he was doing wasn't right, I guess nobody got hurt.

"You coming in?" he asked in the doorway.

I dragged my feet as I walked up the sidewalk.

CHAPTER 36
TINKA

Now there was two people I couldn't stand, always up in my house. I see Taevon done lost his mind letting Krystal and her loud crybaby stay the night. Bad enough his damn father got on my nerves. At least Krystal kept out my way for the most part, unlike Teddy, who stayed answering my phone calls and not delivering the messages. Marquan was sleeping here more than usual this summer, ever since the police started having All Hands on Deck weekends. They kept pulling people over and locking them up for stupid stuff like cracked window-shields and unpaid parking tickets. The first weekend they did it, the police made 786 arrests. A lot of people got hemmed up on outstanding warrants. Now the police been driving around thinking they The Shit.

Whenever I try to talk to Marquan about where he was at for over a month, he tells me not to worry about it.

"Just be happy I'm back," he said, all nonchalantly.

So I left it alone. I ain't even ask him about that Hit stuff. I couldn't talk to him about nothing no more. He was too busy getting excited about his little man being born. Him and Jillian been filling up Marquan's room with all kinds of baby stuff. Evidently, she was gonna be living with us soon, too.

One day when I got home from school, I noticed how much our house had become noisy and busy like Ms. Shelia's. Teddy and Van was drinking in the kitchen. Taevon, Monte, and Antonio was playing PlayStation in the living room. Hitler was laying on the floor beside them. Krystal was on the couch putting barrettes in her daughter's hair. Ma was in the kitchen washing dishes.

"I just got off the phone with Aunt Renee," she said.

"Dag. For real?" I always miss her whenever she calls the house. "What she say?"

"Nothing. Just that her and Uncle Matt are doing fine. She said she was gonna send us some pictures as soon as she get settled."

"I still can't believe she gone," I said, leaning on the counter.

"How you think I feel? She was my only family."

322

"You still got us, Mommy," I said, kissing her cheek.

She smiled.

I went upstairs and started reading my new Walter Mosley book. I had only read the first four chapters, when I heard Ma screaming her lungs out. I popped up the minute I heard her voice.

"Marquan got shot!" Krystal said, running up the steps.

"Oh my God!" I jumped out the bed and ran downstairs.

"Jillian said he's at Washington Hospital Center," Taevon said while he helped Ma out the door. She looked weak in his arms.

She was crying and saying "No, no, no" over and over again. Teddy started the engine.

"I'm coming, too," I said, running out the door without thinking or even grabbing my bag. I had to know if Marquan was okay.

The ride to the hospital seemed like it was taking forever. I prayed the whole time. Ma couldn't stop looking at her watch no matter how hard she tried. She kept twisting her hands back and forth and combing her fingers through her hair. Taevon shook his leg nonstop and stared out the window. Teddy turned the radio on to break the silence, but it wasn't helping. He hummed the whole song about some dock on a bay 'til we got there.

As soon as Ma found out he was in surgery, the police said, "Your son's under arrest for capital murder." Her knees buckled, and Teddy caught her and led her to a chair. My knees got weak, too, and I needed to sit down. Taevon shook his head and helped Jillian to a seat. Teddy got all of us some water from the cooler in the corner, and then he said he was going outside to smoke a jack. That was the first time he did something nice for me, but I was too drained to tell him thank you.

We sat in the overheated tiny room waiting for Marquan to get out of surgery. Ain't nobody been back out to tell us nothing since they first told us Marquan got shot in his back. The bullet was real close to his spine. Two police officers and one detective in a suit waited in the hall. We all stared at the clock while the hours crawled by. Jillian kept rubbing circles on her belly and walking back and forth. I watched Ma rubbing the lines out of her forehead, then she walked back and forth like Jillian. Back and forth, back and forth, they kept going. They was making me dizzy. My chest was hurting, and I ain't even notice I was squeezing my shirt until a nurse asked me if I was okay. I went outside to use my cell phone. Nine would know what to do.

"Damn. Try not to worry, young," he said.

That's it? I tried not to, but that was impossible.

"You want me to come up there?"

"Not now. Maybe later."

"He's gonna be okay," he said. I closed my eyes and tried to believe him.

When I came back in the waiting room, Ma was looking crazy.

"Capital murder," she mumbled, and scratched her neck when I sat back in my seat beside her. "I need a cigarette right now."

She dug in her purse, but then she looked at Teddy.

"That was my last one," he said.

"Well, I'ma get a Pepsi from the vending machine," Ma said, counting out change.

"I'll run to the store for some smokes then," Teddy said.

Ma rolled her eyes in his direction, then she stood up. I looked over at one of the ladies on the other side of the room. Her blond hair was barely in a ponytail. She kept rocking back and forth with one hand covering her mouth. I felt like how she looked. Terrible.

"Turn to Channel 5. It's on the news,"

Ma said, rushing back in the room.

Taevon stood up and pushed the button on the TV mounted to the wall above us until he got to the right channel.

The reporter said: "The seventeen-year-old was airlifted to Children's Hospital in critical condition. Two other victims are at Washington Hospital Center in serious but stable condition. One man was found dead. His identity is being withheld by police awaiting family notification. This is the third tragic shooting in the last five weeks, but the ninth fatal shooting this year for the Trinidad neighborhood. Local residents are begging the police department to step up their new initiatives to put an end to the violence."

"My children can't even come outside no more. They need to do something about this. What am I paying taxes for?!" said a brown-skinned lady who looked like somebody I knew from a long time ago.

"That's why we moved from around there," Ma said. "This is ridiculous. I don't know why Marquan keep hanging around there!"

"Everybody can't just up and move!" snapped the lady with the blond hair.

"Was I talking to you? You all over here," Ma said, rolling her neck.

"Ma, calm down. Calm down," Taevon said, reaching across my lap to squeeze her leg.

"People all up in my damn business," Ma said, turning back to us.

"You just worried, Ma . . . Marquan's gonna be all right," I mumbled, more to cheer up myself than her. Capital murder wasn't nothing to play with, and this time we wasn't gonna have Uncle Matt and Aunt Renee's lawyer.

"It's your son's fault mine up in here!" the woman screamed. "He's a muthafuckin' terror!"

"Excuse me?"

The woman rolled her eyes and shifted in her seat when one of the officers stepped in the room. She looked like she wanted to say more, but she didn't. Biting her tongue must've hurt like hell, because she groaned and looked the other way. Everybody else ignored her, but I couldn't. I heard what she said. Loud and clear. I stared at her every time she looked up at the TV.

A couple minutes later, the same doctor who spoke to us before stepped into the room. Jillian wobbled over just as the doctor said, "The surgery went well."

"Thank God," Ma said, and then she let out a deep breath.

Marquan was still unconscious and they wouldn't know whether or not he could move until he woke up.

"Mom? You can come with me to the recovery room," the doctor said.

A police officer followed them. When Ma left, I leaned my head on Taevon's shoulder. I felt worn out all of sudden, like I had been holding my breath and jogging in place. God kept taking my brother away from me. If he had died . . . I wouldn't have been able to take it. But now capital murder? My brother? What was we gonna do?

CHAPTER 37
NICOLA

There was other people back in intensive care, too, laying in beds plugged up to machines that beeped. The beds were separated by colorful curtains. A cluster of doctors stood around monitors in the middle of the floor. I could smell sickness and disinfectant all around me. Marquan's hand was handcuffed to his bed, and a police officer with a twisted facial expression stared at me. I looked away and then inched closer to Marquan. A clear mask was over his mouth, and the machine beside his bed seemed like it was helping him breathe by the rhythm of the suction and clicking sounds it kept making. I could tell my son was in pain. For the first time, the freckles across his face looked dull to me.

"Hey," I whispered near his ear.

He opened his eyes and blinked three times. I smiled and rubbed his arm. "I'm glad you okay."

He looked like breathing hurt like hell. He had wires connected to stickers on his chest and a bag of something clear flowing from a bag above his head. Even his finger was taped up and connected to monitors. Wasn't nothing I could do to help him. I took a deep breath, because I couldn't think of nothing else to say. What could I say — *Everything gonna be all right?* How did I know that was true? My son was headed to jail and wasn't nothing I could do about it.

He blinked again.

"I need you at home, Marquan."

He kept his eyes opened for a couple seconds, and then he closed them tight. When they opened again, I felt like I knew what he wanted to say — that he ain't kill nobody, that he was getting set up, that he was coming home. I touched his face and bent down to kiss his cheek. I looked at the police listening to my every word. His forehead crinkled up before I walked out the room.

In the waiting room I thought about how much all of our lives was about to change. Did my son really kill somebody like his father did? I felt sick to my stomach and like I was about to faint. Tinka, Teddy, and Taevon all hugged me when the sobs poured from my throat and wouldn't stop.

CHAPTER 38
TINKA

"Ma, you left the rice burning again!" I yelled, snatching the searing pot off the stove before I ran cold water over it. Smoke filled the sink. It smelled so bad, I threw up on the floor. Ma ain't even look up. Her head was nodding backward as she sat on the couch. She looked like she was about to go to sleep, but she wasn't. She was in that weird spaced-out place those damn pills took her, and she was breaking my heart. I grabbed some paper towels and the mop to clean up my mess.

We couldn't afford a good lawyer for Marquan. To make everything worse, the lawyer the court gave him ain't seem like he knew nothing about the law. He hardly ever opened his mouth — like he was ashamed of his Indian accent — and when he did open it, he mumbled. I had never even thought lawyers could be shy until I met this dude. When Ma called herself asking him if Marquan was gonna get out of this mess, the lawyer said, "I don't know. Probably not."

We all kinda lost it after that. Ma started nodding and leaning in midsentence, and that's when I knew she was back popping pills tough. I slept mostly. Ma was too busy dealing with her issues to even ask me why I wasn't going to school. Taevon was different, too. He stayed out on the block more, and when he wasn't outside, he barricaded hisself in the room with Krystal. It was like nobody wanted to deal with what we all knew was gonna happen. Marquan was gonna go to jail just like his father did, for killing one dude and for attempted murder on another.

The same day Ma called herself going back to work, I watched Krystal's ghetto self mixing water and strawberry soda in Kayla's baby bottle in the kitchen.

"You don't think that's too sweet for her?"

"She love it. Watch," Krystal said, smiling. "Here Kay Kay."

Sure enough I watched that little girl suck down the bottle as fast as Krystal used to throw back those NyQuil caps back in the day.

"You gaining weight?" she asked.

I looked at her like she was crazy.

"Them jeans ain't used to fit you like that."

I looked down at the jeans Nine bought me awhile ago. Maybe they *was* tighter. I ain't even have them buttoned. But why she sweating me?

"How long you gon' be over here freeloading and fucking my son?" Teddy said, walking into the kitchen and scratching his nuts.

I knew he was drunk, but he ain't have to talk like that in front of that little girl. I watched Krystal snatch Kayla up with the quickness and then she stormed upstairs. Two minutes later Taevon came running down the steps, furious. "Why you disrespecting my girl and shit?!" he yelled.

Teddy looked at Taevon sideways, then he cracked up laughing. "Go sit your young ass down somewhere," Teddy slurred. "What the fuck you gon' do?"

"The fuck you mean, what the fuck I'm gon' do? I'm getting sick of you 'round here."

"Who the fuck you talking to?! You *my* child!" Teddy burped, then he laughed again. "Little nigga think he gon' do something to me."

"Yeah, all right," Taevon snapped. He nodded his head at Teddy like he knew something Teddy didn't, then he went back up-stairs.

I guess everybody was feeling some kind of way about Marquan, because I ain't never hear Taevon talk like that. Or maybe he really liked Krystal's no teeth-having-self. He was already making Hitler sleep in the doghouse whenever Kayla was there. Plus, he got rid of that snake Ma ain't know he actually kept. I can't wait for the day when Teddy crossed Taevon's line. It'll be a wrap. Krystal got Taevon acting brand-new. I wonder how she got his nose open like that. Teddy better beware.

I saw Ced and Bear talking to Taevon near the basketball court on M Street. I don't know why I wasn't surprised because I should've been. I hadn't seen Ced in a while, and he looked like life was still treating him real good. He was fresh from head to toe. As soon as I got close enough, he said, "What's up, Li'l Sis?"

"Hey, Ced."

"You been all right?"

I nodded.

"Good. Just hollering at Tae about your brother and shit. Trying to see what's up and if it's anything I can do. You need anything?"

I shook my head. "I just wish he was out, that's all."

"Me, too."

Bear stayed quiet, like he was Ced's bodyguard. He kept looking around at every dude that came anywhere near us. Taevon ain't even look at me.

"All right then. See you later," I said. I kept walking down the street. Ms. Shelia waved me over. She was sitting in a chair outside her house watching her grandkids play in the yard.

"How your brother doing?"

I bit my lip and looked across the street at Creature, Raynard, Duane, Big Mike, Keion, and Monte shooting craps in front of Ms. David's house. She was looking from her upstairs window on the phone. Me and Monte hardly talked anymore since me and Nine got so tight. I don't know if it was my fault or his, I missed him a little bit.

"He all right, I guess. He getting physical therapy now, but he still in D.C. Jail."

"Oh, he is?"

I nodded.

Ms. Shelia shook her head. "Your mother doing okay? She ain't called me back in a couple days."

"Ma is Ma."

Ms. Shelia shook her head and frowned.

"I know she in there blaming herself like she always do about everything. But she can't do that. I stay trying to tell her that. How you holding up?"

I took a deep breath. How do I tell her that I feel like somebody got their hand over my nose and my mouth smothering me? My mother in there going out of her mind, and my brother ain't gonna never see this neighborhood again. Marquan was more like my father than my brother. I couldn't. So I just said, "I don't know."

She half-smiled, then said, "You ain't pregnant, are you?"

I looked at her confused.

"Your breasts ain't never been that big, girl. You ain't fooling me."

When was my last period? My mind raced back over the past few weeks, and I couldn't remember having one this month. I leaned on her fence and watched Jevin, Naomi, and Niobia playing in Ms. Shelia's yard, then at the cars passing up the street. All of a sudden, Creature stole Monte in his jaw and snatched up a fistful of money. Raynard, Big Mike, Keion, and Duane backed away and watched Creature going down the street.

"Oh my God, you see that?!" I asked.

"Girl, I try my best not to see half the

mess that happens around here," she said, shaking her head.

Monte held his jaw and ran across the street, pissed. I watched him run in his house.

"Let's get in the house, y'all," Ms. Shelia said, rounding up her grandbabies. "Who knows what craziness gon' happen now."

I hoped Monte wasn't thinking about doing nothing stupid.

An hour later, Nine called and said he was on his way. Good, I needed to get out to take my mind off everything. Plus, I was feeling physically sick staying in the house. There was so much bad energy. Everything around me felt so depressed and negative, but now Ms. Shelia had me wondering. Was something else making me feel sick? I walked to the market and bought me a pregnancy test.

CHAPTER 39
TINKA

Ma floured and seasoned some chicken she was about to fry up. She kept flipping the same chicken wing over and over in the flour like she ain't realize it was the same piece. I wanted to talk to her, but she looked high.

"You need my help?" I ain't trust her cooking no more. Something was always ending up burned or undercooked.

"No, I'm okay," she said, studying the food she was working with like a book. She was high.

"You all right, Ma?"

"Yeah, I just got a lot of stuff on my mind."

I knew she wasn't gonna tell me no more than that, so I left her alone. If the chicken turned out burned, then I'd just eat cereal. I was so bored that I went out the back door and cut through our yard to go to the market for some munchies. LaSheika was getting out of a burgundy Tahoe.

"Where the heck you been?!" I asked. "You don't answer your phone or return your phone calls no more?!"

"Girl, I lost my phone," she said, smiling and waving bye to whoever was in the Tahoe.

"Where the heck you been?!"

"You wouldn't believe it if I told you. Give me a hug."

The Tahoe pulled off when I hugged her. "You look like you had a ball. Where was you?"

"Miami."

"What the —"

"LaSheika Curtis, get your ass in here!" Ms. Tracy yelled from the window.

"Uh-oh. I'll call you later. Promise."

"You better. I gotta tell you something, too!"

I went inside the store and grabbed me a hot sausage, a honey bun, and a Sprite. I paid the Korean lady and left the store thinking about how I was gonna tell Nine I was pregnant. What was he gonna say? Would he be happy or freaked out? I still hadn't really thought about it. Monte was leaning on the gate when I crossed the parking lot, drinking a bottled water.

"What's up?" he said.

"Hey. You okay?"

"What you talking about?"

"I saw you and Creature the other day in front of Ms. David's house."

"Man, fuck that nigga."

I nodded, feeling his pain. Nobody liked Creature for real, people just kissed his butt for the most part so they could stay on his good side.

"You been straight, though?"

I smiled. "Guess what?"

"What?"

"I'm pregnant."

"For real?" he said, surprised. I thought he looked sad, and not happy like I was. "You ready to be a mommy?"

"No, not really. But God must be ready or something."

He smirked and then looked up the street. "I always thought you was different than all these other chicks."

"What you mean?" I said, offended.

He shook his head and said, "Nothing."

But I wouldn't let it go. "No, Monte, what you mean?"

"What was wrong with me?" he asked, in a way that made me feel sorry for him. "You and me was . . . you was supposed to be my girl . . ."

He stopped hisself from finishing his sentence. I ain't know how to answer his question anyway. I never thought Monte still looked at me that way. Every time he flirted with me, I shot him down. Monte was no Nine. He was my friend and that was that.

"Anyway, I gotta go. I'll holla at you later," he said before I could say anything. He walked away.

I thought about what Monte said on my way back home. Creature and Keion was in the alley arguing about something serious. I said "What's up" to both of them, but they was too busy yelling back and forth to pay me attention. Creature was always mad about something. I thought I saw a gun in his hand, but I wasn't sure. I turned around to double-check, but I couldn't tell.

That fried chicken smelled so good when I walked through the door, I couldn't wait to eat. Teddy was already chomping on a piece like he couldn't wait until Ma finished cooking the rest of dinner.

"Ma, it's almost done?"

"Yeah. Like ten more minutes."

"What else you cooking? Smells good," I said, looking in the pots on the stove where there was yellow rice and cabbage. I could smell biscuits in the oven.

"Why you can't wait 'til it's done? All in your mama's way and shit."

I frowned. What the heck he thought *he* was doing? "Whatever, Teddy."

"Don't *whatever* me, girl. You better get her, Cola, before I teach her ass how to respect me."

"I got laid off," Ma blurted out. "Yesterday was my last day."

"Aww shit," Teddy said, shaking his head. "I knew it. You so busy worrying about that spoiled motherfucker who gon' spend the rest of his life locked up that you done forgot about us!"

"And when the hell you getting a job?!" Ma shouted, the first time in I don't know how long.

Three loud gunshots went off. We all froze. It sounded like it was coming from the alley behind the house, but ain't nobody go check.

"Let Ms. David call the police like she always do. I got my own damn problems," Ma said before she put another piece of chicken in the sizzling grease.

"I tell you what, I'm moving if shit don't change around here," Teddy said, sucking the hell out of his chicken bone.

Are you serious?

"Leave then, Teddy! Do everybody in here

a goddamn favor and get the hell out! I'm tired of your lazy ass anyway. Save me a headache," Ma said.

"Bitch, you done lost your mind?!" he said, jumping up with his eyes bulging.

Teddy knew nobody was in the house but me and Ma, so he was showing off. Taevon wasn't here, and Krystal had went to get Kayla from Ms. Shelia's before I left out earlier. If he thought he was gonna do something, I swear to God I'da grabbed the frying pan. Hot grease and all. I walked over and stood in between both of them. I looked Teddy over and he smiled.

"Oh, what you gon' do, bitch?"

I ain't say nothing. I just stood in front of Ma and stared him down. I was *not* afraid of Teddy, and I knew by the way he looked away from me that he knew it, too. He dropped his bones in the trash can and walked into the living room. Me and Ma both let out a huge breath of air. I guess we was both waiting to exhale.

"Everything gonna be all right, Mommy. Let him go, if he wanna go."

"I know, Tinka. That's exactly what I'm trying to do," she said, holding on to the sink for balance.

This wasn't the first time she told me she ain't want Teddy around no more. But on the other hand, it *was* the first time she ever said it to him, and I believed her.

I ain't want to disappoint her even more by telling her my news. So I just kept it to myself.

CHAPTER 40
TINKA

Keion was dead. He bled to death in the alley behind our house and I felt so guilty. Two seconds was all it would've took me to call 911 when I heard them gunshots going off in the middle of our standoff with Teddy. Somebody killed Keion after I had just said hi to him not even ten minutes before. I thought about how Keion looked out for me whenever my brothers wasn't around and how he was just plain cool. He knew everybody and everybody liked him, even Creature, I thought. I kept replaying my walk through the alley and if I really did see Creature holding something black in his hand. But they was friends and they been friends for as long as I could remember. *Creature wouldn't do that, would he?*

I called LaSheika, but nobody answered the phone. After the police made their rounds knocking on doors and asking hundreds of questions, I found the nerve to go over her house. LaSheika opened the door and started crying as soon as she saw my face. I threw my arms around her, and my best friend sobbed until her body felt weak next to mine.

"I'm so sorry," I whispered.

LaSheika nodded and stepped back to make room for me to come inside. I could hear Ms. Tracy moaning upstairs.

"Y'all need something? Anything I can do?" I asked, feeling like a stranger.

Laila looked up and half smiled, before her mouth disappeared into a straight line.

"Umm . . . ," LaSheika said, wiping her face. "I don't know, Tinka. We just been so . . . fucked up about this. What we gon' do without Keion?"

She cried again until her whole face was wet, and wiping tears with the back of her hands wasn't enough. Even though I just went through something like this with Marquan, I ain't know what to say to make her feel better. Laila started crying, too. I was helpless watching them take turns pouring their hearts out, wiping away tears and blowing snotty noses. I did the only thing I could think of, I got up and grabbed some paper towels from the kitchen and gave both of them some. I knew how they felt a little bit. When I found out Marquan got shot, my whole world felt like it was slipping away. He did more for me than my father did, and I know that's how they saw Keion, too. He was the man of their house and now he was gone.

I wanted to tell them what I knew so bad — that Keion and Creature looked like they was near blows and that I thought I saw Creature with a gun when I saw them arguing in the alley, but I couldn't. Creature *knew* I saw them arguing and I was probably the last person to see them. Wasn't no way in the world I could put myself out there . . . even if it was my best friend's brother.

"He told me they was fucking with him ever since he got out of jail. Talking 'bout he was an informant and shit cuz he got out so fast," LaSheika said with an attitude. "If these ignorant niggas knew anything, they would've knew he got out cuz the police ain't have shit on him, but a dub bag."

"For real?"

My stomach flipped. Maybe I ain't never have to say nothing. LaSheika was upset and I felt real guilty about what I knew, but I wasn't gonna risk my life by running my mouth. Sorry.

Ms. Tracy's slippers shuffled down the stairs. She looked horrible. Her face was swollen up, her eyes was bright red, and her hair was all over the place. She closed her robe and tried to smile.

"How you doing, Ms. Tracy?" I asked, trying not to make her cry again.

She just shook her head like there was no words in the English language to say how she was doing. So I said, "My mother said she wanna make y'all some dinner, if it's okay with you."

She took a deep breath, like her soul was hurting, then she said, "I don't have an appetite, but the girls might want it. Tell your mother I said that would be nice, and thank her for me."

"Okay," I said, standing up to leave. "I'll be back later on."

"All right." LaSheika walked me to the door. "Please come back, Tinka, for real."

I nodded and then turned to leave. I felt so sorry for her, but wasn't nothing I could say that was gonna bring Keion back.

I opened my journal and wrote:

Listen to the sounds of a dying
   neighborhood
Police lights brighten the night
Fatherless children play surrounded by
   yellow

ribbons blowing in the breeze
Defeated mothers scream whispers and
   endless
prayers into the crowded streets
Men curse the night and smash beer
   bottles
Houses broken from years of stress lean,
porches sag, front steps crumble
Memories of better days fade away
Trash scatter like confetti at a party for
   neighbors
long forgotten
Listen to the last breath of a place
   beloved
Now silenced

None of the guys Keion used to hang with showed up at his funeral. Not one single one of them was there, not even my own brother Taevon. I ain't know if LaSheika was pissed about that or not. She just looked hurt. Period.

"I never really fucked with him like that," Taevon said when me and Ma came back home. Now that I thought about it, I ain't never see them hanging out.

"You still could've came. That's my best friend's brother, Taevon. She would've came for you."

"Whatever." He took his bowl of cereal to

the living room where Teddy was playing PlayStation. All I could do was shake my head.

CHAPTER 41
NICOLA

Every channel I flipped to was playing the same news story: military-style checkpoints around Trinidad. This was the feds' big, bright idea for stopping the violence over there. If somebody tried to drive through the neighborhood who ain't live there, work there, or worship there, then the cops wasn't letting them in the neighborhood. Period. People was pissed about this all across the city. Some was even trying to sue.

I couldn't believe it, either. I mean, the police was tripping when they first started leaving their lights flashing even when it wasn't an emergency. "Criminals should know we in the area," the police had said. Whatever. Now how in the world did they think they was gonna catch somebody breaking the law if they announced they coming first? "Preventative measures," the police kept saying. It's bad enough they keep having these All Hands on Deck weekends, but the checkpoint mess was even more outrageous. Lock down a whole neighborhood. Really? Make everybody show ID for proof they belong there. Are they serious? It's like the gestapo in Germany. Soon the police gonna make people wear that Star of David on their arms like they made the Jews do.

If the police really wanted to, they could've probably easily locked down Sursum Cordas. All they had to do was block off First Place. Trinidad was different. It was made like a regular neighborhood. A ton of streets, apartments, and houses of all sizes and shapes smashed in a one-and-a-half-mile area between Bladensburg Road and West Virginia Avenue on the east and west, and Mt. Olivet Road and Florida Avenue from the north and south. Some houses was brick, some wood panel, some stone. Tons of trees and yards. Traffic flowed up and down streets. Some one-way, some with stop signs at the end of each block. Schools, churches, and corner stores. On first glance, Trinidad seemed quiet and peaceful, like a *Leave It to Beaver* type of neighborhood, but it was far from it. Some of the houses was for crackheads and dope dealers. Trap houses. Because of all the crime and drama, it was easy to forget there was a lot of hard-working people who lived there.

"She ain't here right now," I told Taevon's little friend Monte. "You want me to tell her to call you or that you stopped by?"

"Nah, that's okay," he said, walking away.

That was strange.

I told Tinka she could visit, but she couldn't live with me no more. Since she was pregnant, that nigga she fucking needed to be taking care of her ass, not me. Ooh, she was pissed when I said that. But I tried to tell her a long time ago how it was going down. She ain't think I knew her ass was pregnant, but I was still the person buying our tampons and pads. Her stock was at the same level it was two months ago.

She gonna have to find out just how different women are from men. She just gonna have to find out the hard way when that nigga she think she love so much get ready to leave her ass and she stuck raising a baby by herself. She should've had them damn books open, instead of her legs. She ain't wanna do nothing with her writing no more either. When she left, she ain't take none of her journals. They was scattered around the room.

One day she came by, I told her something came in the mail for her from that District

Youth Poetry place. She rolled her eyes and put it on the counter. Everything got on her nerves, but I just knew this would be something she wanted to do.

She said, "Ain't no big deal. Ever since I was in that contest back at Shaw, I get an invitation to enter every year."

"You gon' send them something this time?" I asked.

She shook her head, like she was so over it all. "Nah, I don't think so," she said.

"Why not? You don't think your stuff good enough?"

She sucked her teeth and rolled her eyes again. "No, that's not why."

"Then why not? All that writing you do in them composition books and you not gonna do it? I don't get you sometimes, Teyona." I shook my head. "You think I liked cleaning office buildings? I'd rather be cleaning my own house than cleaning up after strangers. You like doing all that writing. You do it for no other reason in the world than the fact that you love doing it. You keep on and your ass gon' end up just like me. Doing a job you can't stand, just to get by."

Tinka rolled her eyes again and went upstairs. I put the letter under a magnet on the fridge, so she could remember what she was giving up.

I try to teach her ass, but she don't want to listen. She think she knows it all, and I guess now that she pregnant she really think she don't have to listen to me. That's why I put her behind out. Now that she gotta take care of herself, Tinka gonna get good practice for what's about to happen. I hope she know it ain't easy raising a baby when you ain't got nothing to promise it, but prayers and dreams and love. If she was as smart as I thought she was, she'd just get rid of it and call it a day.

I grabbed my bottle and took two pills, before I laid back across Teddy's lap. He was knocked out, and that's exactly how I wanted to be. I had so much on my mind. Those GTI people was hanging around the neighborhood taking measurements like we ain't even live here no goddamn more. Letters kept coming in the mail, telling us how long we had to decide if we was going to take the money and go or if we had questions, what number to call. I ain't feel like dealing with it. I had more than enough shit happening in my life.

CHAPTER 42
TINKA

It's funny how fast my life changed just from two little pink stripes. Nine told me he wanted me to be more close to him so he can make sure me and the baby be okay. Seeing as Ma put me out, that wasn't a hard choice to make. Ma acted like I was purposely trying to hurt her, by getting pregnant. "Ain't no such thing as getting pregnant on a accident, Tinka!" she yelled at me. "You fuck with no protection, you get pregnant. Simple!"

I took most of my stuff over his house, and moved in his little room. Anything I needed, he went out and got me. He was putting together a dresser for me, so I could get rid of all the plastic bags crowding his room. We watched *The Boondocks* while he worked. After he was done, I stuffed all my clothes in the drawers.

"A crib can still fit right there," Nine said, pointing to the space between the dresser and the window.

I nodded and smiled. Nine was proud. I never seen him smile as much as he had since I told him I was pregnant. He went with me to the Family Health and Birth Center on Seventeenth and Benning Road so I could find out how far along I was. He even went to orientation with me. Only him and one other dude came with their baby mothers. He asked questions and everything.

"You wanna go for a ride?" he asked, playing with my feet.

"You think it's okay for me to do that?"

"I'll be careful. The baby gonna have to get used to it anyway. That's all his pops like to do."

It was hard for me to get used to the fact I couldn't do everything the same like I could before I got pregnant. Maybe once I start to show, it'll seem more real. "All right, let me use the bathroom first."

We hopped on his black Yamaha. It seemed like every time I turned around Nine had a different bike. He said him and his cousin Clint knew somebody at a dealership and they could switch whenever they wanted because they detailed all the used cars there for free. Nine drove past the Anacostia train station and straight onto the highway. The breeze felt so good snaking down my back. I squeezed Nine tighter and he revved the engine, making my butt vibrate. We flew down 295, dipping passed slow cars that had no business being in the fast lane. I was so glad I had him to take my mind off everything. He was treating me exactly how I needed to be treated. Smothering me with attention and love. Whatever I needed, he got it for me.

I spent more time in the house alone with Nine's mother than I wanted to, whenever Nine was out with Clint doing God knows what. It was weird being in the house with her and nobody else. Sometimes her funny-looking crackhead friends came to the door, and Roxanne ran out behind them, itching to get high. That was one of Nine's rules. She couldn't have nobody in the house, especially when I was there. Roxanne ain't like me and I ain't like her. I think she ain't like me because Nine gave me money she used to get high with.

There wasn't much to do at his house but watch TV. I got bored easily. There wasn't a book in the house besides the Bible. I couldn't even find a pen, let alone something to write on. I started cleaning the house to pass time. It made me feel like I had some goals. First, I cleaned the kitchen from top to bottom — the refrigerator, the stove, and inside all the cabinets. The next day, I scrubbed the bathroom with bleach (even though I wasn't supposed to be around strong chemicals). Even the walls — I wiped them down and washed the shower curtain and towels. I scrubbed all the windows, washed and ironed the curtains. When I was done there, I worked on Nine's room. He had stuff everywhere. The bottom of his closet was nothing but dirty clothes and tons of tennis shoes. He had crap underneath his bed, spilling out of his drawers and dangling off the top shelf of his closet. I straightened out papers and pictures in his drawers. I washed and folded clothes. There was four bags of trash in the kitchen when I was done cleaning. I was spreading his clean comforter across the bed when Roxanne popped up in the doorway.

"It look good in here." She rubbed the back of her neck and her eyes darted around from left to right. "Thank you for cleaning up, Tinka. I know I let this place go."

"No problem," I said while I put pillows in the cases.

"I'm serious. I don't know how I let it get like this," she said, looking all around the room.

"That's okay. I needed to take my mind

off some stuff, so . . ."

I tried to ignore her staring at me but I couldn't, so I said, "Excuse me" and walked out the room.

"You know Na'eem had a brother?" she said to my back.

I stopped and turned around. "No. He did?"

She nodded, then I saw her eyes fill with water. "His name was Anwar."

"What happened to him?"

Roxanne wiped her face and shook her head. "Something I wished could've happened to me instead."

I looked at Roxanne for the first time. She was hurting, just like my mother. I didn't wanna make her hurt no more, so I left the subject alone. I ain't know what was worse — Nine's mother doing crack or Ma popping pills to cushion her pain all those years. Something in me suddenly made me want to hug Roxanne, so I did.

CHAPTER 43
TINKA

A few weeks later, the neighborhood was buzzing when I dropped by after school. The feds had snatched Creature up to press him out about Keion. I was so glad I ain't have nothing to do with them fingering him, but since they ain't have enough to charge him with, Creature was back out two days later, and *pissed* wasn't the word. He was so mad, he had half the neighborhood scared to even look his way when he walked down the street.

Monte saw me in the market and told me if I knew anything about what happened I better keep my mouth shut. I felt uncomfortable. Why would he think I might know something? Did he see me that day when Creature and Keion was arguing? Could he tell I was keeping my distance from him?

I told Taevon what he said, and he got real pissed. Almost like Monte threatened me or something. But I ain't take it like that. I took it like he was just warning me. Monte used to have a crush on me. I mean I looked at him like a cousin or something, because he was so close to Taevon and Antonio. But Taevon seemed like he was ready to break Monte's jaw or something. I told Taevon to calm down. That it wasn't nothing. A couple days after that, Creature and Big Mike fought in front of Teresa's old burned-up house. Ain't nobody try to stop them or jump in it, and Big Mike ended up stabbing Creature in his side. He had to be rushed to the hospital. I never found out what they was arguing about and I never understood why Taevon was so pissed off.

"Good," LaSheika said, when I told her what had happened. "I know that nigga had something to do with my brother." I ain't say nothing. I ain't know for sure. She wasn't the same since Keion died. She hardly talked, and I never seen her smiling no more. She wasn't even fixing herself up like she used to do. It was like she ain't care. LaSheika was always in the house now, too, and I ain't never hear her mention no dude's name she was seeing either. I guess she wasn't feeling nobody. I couldn't blame her. Who could she trust, really?

The first time I saw Creature after he got stabbed, he was wearing a black hoodie over his head like he was trying to hide from somebody, but it wasn't working. We all knew it was him. He seemed so paranoid. I couldn't tell if he thought somebody was trying to kill him or if he thought somebody was setting him up. I just stayed the heck out of his way.

CHAPTER 44
NICOLA
___

Shelia banged on my front door like somebody was chasing her. Hard, fast, and loud. "Oh my God," she said, looking scared and out of breath when I opened the door. Krystal stood behind her, shaking.

"Come outside. Hurry up," she said.

"What?" I asked, confused. "What's wrong?"

"Just come."

I followed her outside and around the corner. My hands was shaking. I should've grabbed my cigarettes. Lord knows I can't take no more bad news. I can't. The police was everywhere, pouring down the street, swarming the neighborhood, taping off the block. Most of the commotion was in front of Tracy's house. A small crowd was gathering across the street and staring at the house.

"What's going on?" I asked.

"They all dead," Shelia said.

"They who?" I mumbled.

She nodded at the house. My mouth fell open. No. Not true. I shook my head, and closed my eyes. This was a dream. I was gonna open my eyes and everything was gonna be normal. But when I opened them, two people was carrying out a black body bag, then another one was being carried out the house. They was all dead. Tracy, LaSheika, and Laila.

"Oh no . . . What am I gonna tell Tinka?" I mumbled.

The minute the third bag came out, a gust of wind blew strong enough to flap some of the police tape loose. Leaves pushed back and forth against the curb. Trash swam down the sewer. The cool air took my breath away and forced a chill down my neck. Ms. David's skirt curled up around her ankles. I couldn't believe her mean, nosy ass was actually wiping away tears. Teresa pulled three of her kids closer, but she ain't stop them from looking away either. Mr. Duncan said what was on everybody's minds. "This shit don't make no goddamn sense!"

As soon as he say it, I looked over at Tinka, who had come from nowhere. Her eyes scared me so much, I wrapped my arms tight around her as she bawled in my arms. A noisy helicopter shined a huge bright light, tracing all of our bunched-together houses. I told Shelia to take Tinka back in the house, because I ain't want nothing to happen to the baby. As much as she needed to learn a lesson, her baby was still gonna be my grandbaby.

I stayed outside to find out what happened. We watched the police come in and out of Tracy's house with brown paper bags, then some worked their way around our street knocking on doors and asking everybody questions. I looked at the guy they called Creature, shaking his head and smoking like he was innocent or like he ain't know what happened. Everybody 'round here knew he was a pure monster and that he had something to do with it.

CHAPTER 45
TINKA

The neighborhood was gloomy the next couple days. When I looked out the window, I ain't see nobody on the block. Even Tae-von stayed in the house. I hung around the house, trying to remember the last thing I said to LaSheika before she was killed. I couldn't remember our last conversation, and it was making me sick to my stomach. I spent most of the day curled in bed, looking at old pictures of us or talking to Ma. She actually made me feel better, and she ain't seem like she wanted me to leave. Maybe she was really worried about me.

I just didn't know who would do that to them. Why? I thought about all the guys LaSheika messed with over the past few months and wondered if any of them had something to do with it. Or maybe even one of the guys that Ms. Tracy was seeing. Who knew? Could Creature have had something to do with it? Did LaSheika say something to the police about Creature and Keion beefing over something? Did she? I couldn't figure it out. Thinking about it made my head hurt. I knew I had to stop trying to piece everything together.

The funeral was held in Bible Way on the corner of New Jersey and New York Avenues. Seemed like the whole city came. The mayor, the police chief, Dorothy Height, and Marion Barry, and just about the whole Sursum Cordas neighborhood was there. I saw people I knew from Sibley Plaza, Tyler House, and even people who used to live in Temple Courts. I felt so sad. Seemed like bad things kept happening to everybody around me. There was three caskets in the front of the church, covered in yellow, purple, and white flowers. While people talked, I scribbled on the back of my program. Drawing flowers and birds. It was hard to be here and listen to all the speeches from people who didn't really know my friends. To hear all the promises about them trying to catch who did it, and the promises to end crime.

I wrote:

Promises, promises
Unkept and uninsured
Nobody cares when the cameras are off

Jillian called the day after the funeral. She said she was bringing Jordan over to see us. We hadn't seen her since she had the baby at Washington Hospital Center three days after Marquan's pretrial, so we couldn't wait to see him again.

"This baby look just *like* Marquan!" Ma sang, reaching out for him when Jillian showed up. "He's so handsome."

Jillian and Jordan made me take my mind off of everything. It was good to see Ma not buzzed up off them pills for a change. I was sitting in the living room across from Krystal and Kayla. Taevon stood next to Ma, smiling.

"How old is he now?" I asked.

"Seven weeks," Jillian said, beaming.

"He been keeping you up at night, ain't he?" Ma asked, adjusting Jordan's receiving blanket.

"Ba-by?" Kayla asked, pointing. Krystal nodded.

"Little man do look like Quan, though," Taevon said. "Look at his eyes."

Even Taevon seemed happy, but lately, he was looking burned out to me. His lips was already dark brown from smoking a lot of weed, and his eyes was turning yellow.

They used to always be red whenever he was high, but now he looked like he wasn't getting no rest either. He was even letting his beard grow in, something I ain't never seen him do. It wasn't shaped up, so his face looked scruffy. I don't know when the last time he let Ms. Shelia twist his dreads, either. He was really looking crazy. I don't know how Krystal put up with him like that.

"I wonder if he gon' have his freckles when he get older," Taevon said.

"You ready?" Jillian asked me.

I rose my eyebrows and smiled.

"She better get ready, cuz that baby coming," Ma said.

"How far are you?" Jillian asked.

"Eleven weeks," I said.

"Here, get your practice in," Ma said, passing the tiny powder puff to me. He smelled so good. I held him softly and thought about what me and Nine's baby was gonna look like. Would it have my eyes? The kind Aunt Renee told me was filled with stories. Would it be like me or Nine?

"You doing so good, girl," Ma said, looking up at Jillian. She rubbed Jordan's cheeks with her thumb. "I know you miss Marquan, but you doing real good. He all nice and chubby."

Jillian blinked back tears and smiled. Ain't no way I could be in her shoes. Jordan probably was never gonna see his daddy not behind bars, because Marquan's case wasn't going too good. His next court date was months away, and from what Ma told me, the lawyer ain't sound confident about it at all.

"When the next time you gonna visit Marquan?" I asked.

"I was thinking about next Wednesday. He ain't seen the baby in a while."

"I wanna come with you, if it's okay."

"Yeah, okay," she said.

"I remember when Marquan's father first got locked up," Ma said, shaking her head and staring in Jordan's eyes like she was trying to see if Mark was in them. "I ain't know what I was gonna do. We was living with him on Florida Avenue, and I depended on him for everything . . . food, clothes, bills. I ain't know how the hell I was gonna pay the rent. I ain't have a job, my mother already told me not to call her for nothing when I got pregnant, and my sister was too busy chasing Matt, so I ain't have nobody."

Funny how Grandma told Ma the same thing she told me, and look where it got her.

"What you do then?" Jillian asked.

Ma let a deep breath come from her throat and then she shook her head. "I met Tae-von's father and he let me lean on him for a little while. We stayed in his mother's basement and he took care of us until I got a job."

I rolled my eyes.

"So you'll be all right. I mean I ain't got much, but I ain't gonna let you and my grandbaby have no worries, you hear me?"

Jillian nodded.

"Oh y'all ain't gotta worry. Trust me," Taevon said. "My nephew gon' be straight."

He sounded way too convinced for somebody who ain't have a job. I ain't wanna think about Marquan or the son he left behind without a father, so I kissed Jordan on his forehead, told everybody bye, and headed upstairs to lie down.

"Stop! Get off of me Taevon! I'm not playing, for real."

Krystal's loud voice woke me up, but the *boom, boom, boom* sound made me jump out the bed. Ma's door was closed across the hall, but I knew her and Teddy could hear the noise from downstairs just like I could. As soon as I got down the steps, I saw Krystal's bare feet flailing around in the air and Taevon sandwiched against her with his hands around her throat.

"Oh my God, Taevon! Stop it! Let her go!" I screamed and ran over to get him off of her. Krystal's muffled breathing scared me so much, I pushed Taevon away as hard as I could. He ain't move that much. "Taevon, stop it! Let her go!"

I tried to pry his hands from off her neck, but I didn't want him to brush against my stomach, so I stepped back.

"Boy, get the hell off that girl!" Teddy yelled, and jerked him by his waist.

Taevon let go, but the look in his eyes was something I had never seen before. Krystal rubbed her throat and tried to catch her breath. Taevon smelled like he had been drinking all night long. Two empty Patrón bottles on the coffee table told it all.

"What the fuck's wrong with you, boy?" Teddy shouted.

"What the fuck wrong with you, putting your muthafucking hands on me?!" Taevon yelled.

"Who the hell you think you talking to?!" Teddy bucked in his face.

"Taevon, calm down," Ma begged from the hallway. She had her nightclothes on and tried to cover herself with one hand.

"Nah, fuck this nigga!" Taevon barked back.

"Oh, that's how you gon' talk to me?" Teddy asked, taking a step closer. "Like I'm a stranger? I ain't one of your little friends."

Krystal crawled toward the couch and pulled herself up.

"Baby, don't talk to your father like that," Ma said.

Taevon's eyes jumped and got real wide. "You let this muthafucka do the same shit to you!"

"What, nigga?! I'm telling you, you gon' stop disrespecting me in here." Teddy took two more steps closer to Taevon. "You think you big shit 'round here, but you got the game fucked up."

"Man, fuck you! Don't nobody need you 'round here! You ain't shit, but a bunch of muthafucking talk —"

Teddy shot across the room and knocked Taevon over like a football player in the middle of his sentence.

The TV went crashing to the floor.

"Noo!" Ma screamed, and ran toward the fight.

Krystal ran out the room.

I was too scared to move.

Furniture scraped the floor.

Picture frames and vases smashed into one another and glass flew everywhere.

Pop.

My heart jumped and then my head shook on its own. I put my hand on my belly as I watched blood gush over Taevon's hands.

"Arrrghh!" Ma screamed like her soul dried up, and then she pulled Taevon away from Teddy.

Krystal sobbed in the hallway.

"Why?!" Ma cried. "Why?"

Taevon dropped the gun and wiped his hands on his shirt. My body started shaking. Taevon stared at Teddy and then he looked at Ma, crying on her knees beside him. He stepped backward, and then he ran out the living room, past Krystal, and out the door.

This wasn't happening. It couldn't be. I'm dreaming. I know I'm dreaming. My head kept shaking. I sat down on the couch and listened to Ma cry into Teddy's chest until I blanked out.

■ ■ ■ ■

PART V

■ ■ ■ ■

CHAPTER 46
TINKA

The room was bright when I opened my eyes. I felt a warm body lying in the bed beside me. I looked over and saw Ms. Shelia knocked out with a purple scarf covering her hair. *Why was I at her house?* I sat up and climbed out of the bed, then headed to her bathroom. I ran hot water in the sink, until the mirror was cloudy with steam, then I used my hands to wet my face and wipe sleep from my eyes. I wiped the mirror with my hand to look at my face. My eyes was red, and it was dark under both of them. I combed my fingers through my hair and then turned the light off.

I stopped by Krystal's room and opened her half-cracked door. Kayla was sleeping cuddled up beside her like a teddy bear. I couldn't believe what happened last night. It was too much to think about.

Teddy dead.

Where was Ma? I walked around the quiet

house and checked all of Krystal's brothers' rooms. Duane's door was closed. Raynard and Sammy's door was open, but nobody was in it. Antonio's room was closed, too, but I could hear his voice talking on the phone. I went downstairs and saw Van sleeping on the couch. Ma definitely wasn't here, and there was no way she slept in our house last night. I crept in the kitchen and made a bowl of cereal. I had to wait until somebody woke up to find out what was going on.

Antonio came down the stairs a few minutes later, mumbling under his breath. "What's up?" he said, then he snatched open one of the cabinets and grabbed a Pop Tart.

"Where's Taevon?" I whispered.

"Man . . . ," he said, and then shook his head.

"Do you know?" I asked.

He paused for a second, and then said, "No."

I knew if he did, he wasn't gonna tell me. "Well, you know where my mother at?"

"She at the hospital."

I blinked hard. "For what?"

"I'll let my mother tell you."

"Tell me what happened, Antonio!" I snapped. "I can't take nothing else, for real."

"All I know is when the police got to your

house last night, she was lying beside Teddy with . . . no clothes on, trying to wrap his arms around her."

My eyes squinted as I tried to hear what he was saying. "I just don't think she was in her right mind, Tinka."

I froze as I let his words crawl over me.

"She was having some kind of breakdown or something."

I rubbed my eyelids. This was too much. My head pounded instantly. "You know which hospital?"

"I think she at Washington Hospital Center, but I'm not sure."

I pushed away from the table and marched upstairs. I woke Ms. Shelia up and she told me everything from the minute Krystal came and got her last night. She told me that I had fainted, and that Taevon disappeared, and that my mother was just like Antonio had said, lying naked beside Teddy, wrapped in his limp arms, covered in his blood. I ain't know what to think about that. Ms. Shelia said it gently, but it still ain't make sense to me. She said we could go see Ma at Washington Hospital Center. Something about a seventy-two-hour hold.

Krystal stayed in her room with Kayla for most of the morning. I went in her room to take my mind off of everything that hap-

381

pened. She looked drained, but forced a dry smile in my direction.

"Thanks for what you did for me yesterday."

I nodded. It was strange to talk about that, after everything else that had happened. But maybe if I didn't walk in when I did, Krystal could've been dead like Teddy.

"Go see what Grandma doing, Kayla," Krystal told her daughter.

"Okay," her sweet voice sang. I watched her climb off the bed and then run out the room. Krystal looked like she was dying to tell me something.

"Monte killed them."

I froze and tried to let her words sink in, before I sat down on her bed.

"Keion, LaSheika, Laila, Ms. Tracy," she whispered.

My neck snapped back. *No way.*

"I'm sorry, but I gotta tell somebody," she said with eyes that wanted me to believe. "Taevon knew about it. He tried to stop Monte, but he wouldn't listen."

My mouth hung open. My head shook slowly from left to right. I couldn't believe what she was saying. This was impossible. Not Monte.

"I swear to God," Krystal said.

"But why? Why?"

Krystal shook her head. "Just to prove Creature wrong. Creature chumped the shit out of Monte. Hell, he was embarrassing him like every single day. Niggas was starting to pick on him for dumb shit. Call him bitches to his face and everything. Creature carried him every chance he got. Made him run silly errands for him, shit like taking his clothes to the cleaners."

No. I couldn't believe it.

"One day Creature told Monte he wanted Keion dead, because he was snitching on them. Taevon said Monte wanted Creature to feel like Monte was liable to do anything. Talking 'bout how he ain't give a fuck about this or that and how he was sick of niggas disrespecting him . . . I shook my head, cuz none of this ain't sound real.

"Taevon started stressing. Him and Antonio walked around all uptight about Monte tripping out. Taevon started acting paranoid about everything. I mean he straight-up stopped trusting Monte. He said he ain't know him no more. I ain't blame Taevon. He was trying to distance himself from whatever dumb shit Monte stupid ass was up to. But then next thing you know, Tae gon' swear all up and down Monte liked me," she said, shaking her head. "He actually thought I was cheating on him with

383

Monte at one point."

My eyes grew so wide that I felt my face tightening up.

"He kept saying it over and over again, but me and Monte ain't never have shit going on. I tried to tell Tae that. But he ain't wanna believe me, though. He just been so paranoid about everything."

I had noticed that Taevon ain't seem like himself. He was drinking and smoking like crazy, and he was just letting himself go.

"He couldn't sleep after what Monte did to your friend's family. Taevon thought Monte was capable of doing anything after that. He ain't trust him."

The sides of my forehead throbbed. I rubbed them until they felt better.

"He stopped trusting everybody. Even me."

She breathed in deep and rubbed her hand across her hair. My eyes focused on a handle on Krystal's dresser as she talked. I couldn't believe what I was hearing. I shook my head. "Taevon was so paranoid, Tinka, it was driving *me* crazy. What happened to Teddy was an accident. Taevon ain't mean to do that. I hope your mother forgive him."

"I can't listen to no more."

I felt like Krystal was killing me with every word that came out of her mouth. Nothing was making sense. Was Monte after my brother now?

Nine picked me up from Anacostia Station. I didn't wanna tell him nothing about what had happened, but I couldn't help it. My head was going crazy. Teddy dead, Taevon on the run, Mommy going crazy. Monte a killer. I just wanted to scream every time I thought about it.

As soon as I got to his house, Nine had some Chinese food waiting for me.

"I don't know if you hungry, but it was the only thing I could think to do for you," he said, passing me a plate.

I tried to smile, but a tear slipped from one of my eyes. "What you get me?" I mumbled.

He wiped my tear away and said, "Chicken and broccoli."

I smiled for real this time. I liked the way he ain't sweat me about what happened. He just let me eat in peace.

When we was both done, he rolled up a blunt and passed it to me. It wasn't his first time smoking around me, but this *was* his first time offering me a hit. Nine thought weed couldn't be all that bad for the baby — he even asked the people at the birth center. The midwives said it wasn't enough studies out there to say for certain, so Nine took that to mean it ain't hurt.

"You sure?" I asked.

"Man, you been through it. Here," he said.

I reached for his lighter and lit up. It ain't take long for my headache to go away. I closed my eyes and let my mind drift up over Barry Farms, across the Anacostia River, past the Navy Yard, the new baseball stadium and the Capitol Building, and over to Sursum Cordas. Everything that happened the night before played over in my head. Taevon was scared. I knew he ain't really mean to kill his father. He loved Teddy, even when he was pissed off at him. I thought about what Krystal said and wondered how much of it was true. I thought about Monte and Creature and LaSheika. I puffed again and blew smoke clouds across the living room.

"You gonna share that?" Nine said, laughing.

I smiled and passed the blunt back to him.

"Na'eem, you got twenty dollars?" his mother said, floating into the room like a ghost. She was so frail looking. He rolled his eyes, then dug in his pocket and peeled off a dub.

"Thank you, baby. You always look out for Mommy. Mmwwaahh," she said, smacking her lips against his cheek. "Love ya."

He rolled his eyes again and then said to me, "You ready to go?"

I nodded, but couldn't help but wonder why he gave his mother money for something he knew she was doing to hurt herself. I had my own problems, so I ain't bother bringing it up. The ride on his bike was exactly what I needed to forget about every single one of them problems, at least for a few minutes.

CHAPTER 47
TINKA

Nine went with me to Washington Hospital Center.

He knew I ain't wanna go see my mother by myself, and I didn't want to be there with Ms. Shelia. I loved her to death, but I just wanted to get in and out. The pysch unit wasn't as big as I thought it was gonna be. I showed the people at the front desk my ID, and then they said only immediate family members, so Nine couldn't go to the back with me.

"It's okay. I'll be right here."

"Okay."

I walked down the bright hall to her room. She was sitting on the edge of the bed in a white smock covered with WHC letters that tied up loosely on her back. Her hair was combed straight back.

"Ma?"

She ain't budge.

"Mommy?"

Still nothing.

I walked around the bed, to the side where she was sitting.

"Mommy?"

She looked up and smiled. Her eyes bold and bright. "Hey, Tinka. You here to take me home?"

"No," I whispered.

"Teddy here?"

I looked at her for a long time and then she said, "Girl, what you staring at me for. Where Teddy?"

I reached over and gave her a hug, holding her close to my chest for a while, until I noticed we was rocking from side to side and I was crying.

"Why you crying, Tinka Tink?" she asked. "Aunt Renee gon' come back. She ain't dead, you know?"

Why was she thinking about Auntie?

"You can go see her next summer, if you want. I bet she already got plans for you in Italy."

"Mommy? What you talking about?"

"You. Pouting around here like you ain't never gonna see her again."

How was I supposed to remind her that Teddy was dead? That their son was the one who did it? That she was in a hospital being evaluated?

"I used to be so jealous of Renee. She always had it better than me. Mama treated her different. Like she was special. Just because she loved her father more than mine," Ma said with a tense jaw. "I always tried to treat all my kids the same, even though y'all had different fathers. I made sure y'all had *my* last name, because y'all was mine. All y'all was special to me. Maybe that was where I messed up with Marquan. Maybe he thought I treated him different. That I blamed him for Mark. I don't know. Teddy good to us, though. Don't you think so, Tinka? He did more for you than your own father."

"Ma, Teddy —"

"Huh?"

I couldn't do it. I ain't wanna ruin whatever was left for her, so I kept my mouth closed.

"What, baby? Teddy what? He on his way?"

"Yeah . . . he coming tomorrow."

She smiled wide and then rubbed her hair. "You gon' make me pretty first?"

"I . . . I'll do it later."

"Okay. Make sure you hurry up. I don't want him to see me looking like this," she said, raking her fingers through her hair. "My hair look all crazy."

"I will." I used her comb and gave her two French braids. I cried, but smiled as my fingers worked. I couldn't believe all of this was happening to my family. We was breaking apart. When I finished, I leaned down and kissed her before I eased out the door.

More tears slid down my face the minute I left her room. Nine wrapped his arms around me and I broke down.

"It's okay, Tinka. Let it out," he whispered in my ear and rubbed my back.

I stayed with Nine because I ain't wanna go back to my house for nothing. Wasn't nothing there for me. I couldn't go back to school either. Wasn't no way I was gonna be able to focus. Nine told me not to worry, that I could stay with him as long as I wanted and he'd take care of me.

The first few days, I stayed up through the night half-sleeping, just like Nine did. I had too much going through my head. I kept seeing Taevon wiping blood on his shirt, over and over again. All I wanted to know was where he was and how he was doing. If Krystal had been telling the truth, he was probably with Ced or Bear, just like Marquan was that time he was on the run. Wait . . . *Oh my God.* That's what Nine meant when he called Marquan Hit that time. Hit was short for Hitman.

"You knew Marquan killed people?" I asked Nine while he was taking his clothes off to get in bed. He was shocked I asked him. His eyes shifted around like he was seriously thinking about lying, but then they softened, and he nodded.

"I ain't know it was a *secret* secret. I thought you knew."

"No, I never knew."

Nine pushed his dreads out of his face and then laid down. "That's what his father used to do for Rayful. That's why he still locked up. He had all those bodies on him. Everybody used to call him Hit."

"I never knew that."

"Everybody knew that. I don't know when they started calling your brother Hitman Junior on the low, but . . ."

I shook my head.

". . . I thought everybody called him that."

I stared at the TV, even though the volume was on mute. I thought about Marquan's first charge for stealing the car involved in that shooting in Ivy City when I was young. Then I thought about that big shooting out Carter Terrace when that little boy got killed in his sleep, and how Marquan disappeared the next day, talking about how he fucked up. Everything was starting to come together and it made me sick. I felt nauseous. I had to sit down and catch my breath.

"You gon' be all right?"

I shrugged my shoulders.

"Look, Tinka, *you* gon' be all right. You got me, I got you," he said, reaching over and rubbing my stomach, "and we both got the baby."

A week later, I called Jillian to see if I could still go with her to see Marquan. She told me to meet over her house on Trinidad Avenue in the morning. Nine dropped me off.

Jordan was dressed so cute, in his little gray Solbiato sweatsuit.

"Why you got him looking so grown? He's just a baby," I teased her.

"He gotta look like his daddy," she said, smiling.

It took us forever to get through all the security checks at D.C. Jail. First off, the line was so long with girls and baby mamas trying to see their man. A couple of dudes was in line, too, but it was way more females all done up with makeup and fake lashes. The officers felt me up so hard I felt like I was getting raped. They emptied out my bag, then they checked Jordan's baby bag and made Jillian take off his diaper before they felt her up, too. I couldn't believe it. Did I commit a crime I ain't know about? Marquan was sitting behind a glass looking relieved to see me. Jillian told me she had already told him everything, so I was glad I ain't have to be the one to do it.

"How Ma doing?" he asked me through a phone.

"Not good. I think she's blocking everything out."

He looked down.

"When I saw her, I don't think she knew what was going on. I mean she knew she was in a hospital, but she never asked me why she was there."

He bit his bottom lip and stared at the table for a minute. "You seen Taevon?"

I shook my head, then said, "You know where he at?"

"I think so. You do, too . . . think about where I would be." We both knew our conversations was being listened to.

I nodded, cuz Taevon was with Ced around Trinidad like I thought.

"But give him some time. I know he probably fucked up right now."

I nodded again. He was right. Taevon was too twisted that night. Regardless of whatever he might've been into, I know he ain't mean to kill his father when he squeezed that trigger.

"You doing okay?" he asked.

I gave him the strongest smile I could, but even I could tell it was weak.

"Come on, Tink. Be strong, man. I know shit crazy right now, but you can handle it. You ain't a dumb girl, so I know you goin' be all right. Where you staying? With Ms. Shelia?"

I shook my head. "My friend Nine's."

Marquan looked at me sideways. "You know I don't like that shit, Tinka."

"What am I supposed to do, Marquan, huh? Be by myself? I ain't got nobody now, thanks to y'all!"

Marquan's eyes grew large. He wanted to snatch me up and shake me. "Let me talk to Jillian."

I gave her the phone. Marquan might be mad at me for what I said, but it was true. All I had was Nine now.

CHAPTER 48
TINKA

Mommy was too messed up to leave the hospital for Teddy's funeral. I mean I ain't have no plans to go to the church Ms. Shelia said Teddy's mother was having it at, either. Ms. Shelia also told me the psychiatrist was thinking about sending Ma to either PIW or St. E's, since she still ain't remember what happened that night. I couldn't believe Ma was gonna be up in that crazy house with people like that dude who tried to kill President Reagan just to prove how much he loved that actress. Not my mother. She wasn't crazy. She was just hurting right now.

Reaction Band blared from the tall black speakers leaning against Nine's bedroom wall. The hallow but sharp-sounding congas and heavy drumbeats pounded the walls. He puffed on a J while he counted out a trash bag full of cash in neat rows on the bed. Ever since the day he took me for that little bike ride to pull that gas station stunt in Alexandria, Nine had gotten real comfortable letting me see his stash. Him and Clint robbed liquor stores mostly, but sometimes they hit up gas stations or corner stores . . . depending on the situation. He said banks was way too risky, even though it was more money in them. They robbed a store at least once a week.

They kept the stolen bikes in the black trailer Reggie drove that time I went with them to Budds Creek. They used U-Haul trucks to back up in neighborhoods in the middle of the night, to make people think they was moving into the neighborhood, then scoped out the bikes they wanted, cut the chains with a gigantic pair of cutters and rolled them up in the truck. Somebody rolled the bike up a ramp while the other person looked out. Sometimes they kept the bikes, but they sold the majority of them to some Panamanian dudes at a dealership in Northeast off of Kenilworth Avenue. I couldn't believe Nine and his little crew.

I ain't know how I felt about him no more. I saw him differently. He still treated me special and with respect, but I couldn't get past what he did for money. The car-detailing business he said him and Clint had was all a lie. Who knew what else he was lying about to me? I ain't know him like I thought I did.

"Your mother told me about your brother Anwar. How come you ain't never tell me about him?" I asked him one day.

He looked at me like I said something wrong, then he flicked ashes from his J in his soda bottle. "Ain't nothing to tell."

"How can you say that? How old was you when he died?"

Nine took a deep breath and said, "Thirteen."

"Oh . . . How he die?"

He took a pull from his J and blew a spiral of smoke across the room. Nine raised one eyebrow and looked at me sideways. "You really wanna know?"

I nodded and took the blunt he passed me.

"He got shot in the back of his head right in front of me."

My eyes grew big. I covered my mouth with my hand.

"The worst day of my life," he said. "And I dream about it every time I go to sleep."

No wonder he couldn't sleep at night. "I'm so sorry, baby."

He nodded and then reached for the blunt. "It's okay. It is what it is . . ."

I walked over and hugged him. "Baby, I'm sorry." I ain't know what else to say. I couldn't imagine one of my brothers getting killed. "Was it an accident?"

Nine looked like he ain't wanna answer my question, but then I saw a light flash in his eyes. "No. I used to do a lot with my brother when I was young. He the one who showed me how to rob niggas in the first place." He puffed the blunt and blew smoke in the air. "We used to roll around and look for niggas to rob. My brother was cool as shit. You would've liked him. I remember how he used to always love Cheez-Doodles. My mother used to hate that shit, because he always left them nasty-ass cheese stains everywhere," Nine said, laughing.

I smiled.

"But, um, Anwar used to go right up in hoods we knew wasn't faking and just clip niggas off at their knees. I'm talking straight getting niggas for whatever they had and shit. Gangsta."

My heart skipped as he talked.

"My brother used to ain't give a fuck. He took their shit so we could eat."

We was quiet for a while. I watched Nine relight the dwindling J and then puff big chunks of smoke.

"Somebody killed my brother just like

that. Like it wasn't nothing."

I reached over and rubbed his bare back while he puffed. He reached back and handed me the J. I puffed on it until it was too tiny to pinch anymore. Nine rolled me over on my stomach, knocking the money stacks over, then he pulled my panties down past my ankles. He slid up inside me hard and forceful. Dollar bills stuck to my sweaty stomach as he stroked. I thought about all the fingers that touched each one of those dirty dollar bills that was now touching my body. I closed my eyes as Nine released his pain inside of me. He ain't even notice I wasn't throwing anything back because it was hurting so bad. After a few minutes, he flipped me over and wrapped my legs behind him. Maybe he ain't even care. He rocked against my body hard, before he shuddered and collapsed on top of me. I rubbed his back, even though my body was the one throbbing, until we both fell asleep.

I was flipping channels when I heard Jim Vance say on the news, "The notorious Temple Courts apartments are now completely empty. Demolition is scheduled to begin in the coming weeks as the next phase of the city's renewal plans for the North

Capitol and K Street corridor get under way."

What was I seeing? Floor after floor of empty apartments flashing across the TV screen. GTI had did just what they said they was gonna do, and this was really happening. Nine told me Clint's family had moved out Suitland, but I ain't think it had nothing to do with GTI. I had to call somebody. I called Ms. Shelia.

She answered after the first ring. "Tinka, what took your tail so long calling me?!" she said. "I've been worried about you."

She was?

"Girl . . . ," she said, sounding out of breath.

"Huh?"

"You know we tried to get everything out of your house a few weeks ago before Mr. Duncan and them threw everything out, but . . ."

"They got rid of our stuff?"

"A lot of it over here, but we had to let some stuff go, because you know ain't enough space over here. Hitler had to go to the pound."

I bit my lip. This was déjà vu.

"Where you living at?"

"With my boyfriend 'round Barry Farms."

"Oh, okay . . . Well, you know they done

401

moved your mother to St. E's like they said they was. Go see her soon. She been asking 'bout you. Me and Van try to see her a couple times a week."

St. Elizabeth's Hospital was right up the street from Nine's house, but I was scared to see my mother like that again. She wasn't herself.

Like Ms. Shelia was reading my mind, she said, "Tinka, she need to see you. The same person who loved you all your life is still the person she is."

"I know," I mumbled so low I ain't know if I actually said it aloud until Ms. Shelia said, "Good. Oh, and I got your journals, but I hate I couldn't save all your books."

I ain't think about my journals in forever. "Thanks, Ms. Shelia . . . for everything."

"It's no problem, sweetie. I do what I can to help. Oh, and I got all y'all mail being forwarded over here. So it's a couple things over here for you. You need to come see me soon."

"I will."

"Tinka, make sure you visit your mother soon. I know you can't tell, but she knows it's you."

At least she admitted Ma really wasn't all together. "I will," I mumbled.

"Listen, things gon' get better, Tinka. You

just can't let your mother forget you care about her. You hear me?"

"Yeah."

"Wait one second, Krystal wanna talk to you."

I heard Ms. Shelia's muffled voice saying something. It sounded like she was covering up the mouthpiece of the phone arguing, then Krystal got on the phone.

"Um, hey, Tinka."

"Hey."

"Antonio . . . ah, told me he saw Taevon on Minnesota Avenue the day before yesterday."

"He did?! Where at? What he say?!"

She let a deep breath out and then she said, "Antonio said he ain't look too good. Like he ain't take a bath or eat in a minute . . . He said Taevon acted just like he ain't know who he was."

I heard her talking, but I couldn't understand her. "You think he still around there?"

"I don't know. Antonio said he looked like he been smoking dippers. He was wandering around like he ain't care where he was going and just looked trifling."

"So y'all just left him out there like that?!"

"What Antonio was supposed to do?!"

"What?!" I said confused. "What you mean 'what Antonio was supposed to do'?!"

"Look, Tinka. I don't want nothing to do with him. I gotta worry about me and my daughter."

I always knew she was a bitch. I could taste her bitter words in my mouth. I couldn't believe her. "Okay, Krystal . . . I gotta go. Tell your mother bye for me."

It took me a minute to calm down after I hung up. She acted like she never loved Taevon. Hell, maybe she didn't. I just wanted my brother to know *I* still had his back. I stared at the phone for a while, thinking about my brother sleeping in the streets somewhere, cold and alone, with nowhere to go. Antonio should've made him come with him. After all these years, they was supposed to be tight. How could he let Taevon just go on his own somewhere, clearly out of his mind?

I turned the TV off and closed my eyes tight for the night, but I couldn't go to sleep when my world was upside down. Taevon was suffering, Mommy was losing her mind, and Marquan was sitting up in jail having no idea just how messed up everything really is out here. I wished Aunt Renee was here so bad. I bet she didn't even know what had happened.

"Hey, wake up," Nine whispered. "I need

your help."

I rubbed my eyes and blinked a couple times.

"Hurry up, Tinka, I'm bleeding." Something fell out of his mouth and landed near my face.

I sat up and squinted to see what it was in the pitch-black room. "What you talking 'bout?"

"I got grazed," he said, holding his arm.

"What?! Oh my God."

Nine was bleeding so much, his black T-shirt looked shiny. Red streams ran down his arm.

"Put that on me," he said, nodding toward the white tape and gauze beside me. "I can't do it by myself."

My hands shook when I reached for it.

"Hurry up, Tinka, for real."

I pressed the netted material against his arm and then covered it with cotton pads that had been soaking in peroxide. He winced as soon as it touched him, but he stopped long enough for me to tape him up. My fingertips was stained with Nine's blood. I couldn't believe what I was doing right now. This wasn't supposed to be my life.

"What's wrong with you? You act like you the one who got shot," he asked.

"Nothing."

"Yes, something is. I know you, Tinka. What's up?"

I let a deep breath flow across my lips, but I still couldn't bring myself to say what I was thinking. How would Nine ever understand this wasn't how it was supposed to be? Just a few months ago, I was in school writing essays and reading my favorite books. Answering my teacher's questions like it wasn't nothing. Trying to do whatever I could to graduate this year. And now my life was upside down. Everybody I ever knew and cared about was gone, except for him. I was three and a half months pregnant, and basically a high school dropout. Now, he's sitting here bleeding in my hands.

"What's wrong, boo?" he asked again.

"Nothing."

"You mad at me?"

I shook my head.

"I'm not gonna be doing this shit forever. So don't worry about me."

That wasn't even the point, but if he ain't know that now, he wasn't ever gonna know.

CHAPTER 49
TINKA

Ma looked pretty when I walked in the room. She had long, golden brown micro-mini braids. I knew Ms. Shelia did it for her, because she always did them way too big. That's why I used to let Niecey do mine. Ma had on a light gray sweatsuit and pink T-shirt under the hoodie. She had color in her cheeks, and her lips looked soft and shiny like she rubbed Vaseline across them. Ma was sitting in an armchair watching TV with a few other women in her age group. She almost looked herself, except for the glassy look in her eyes. The hair on my arms stood up when she looked at me. I could tell she ain't know who I was when I smiled at her.

"Hey, Mommy," I said.

She smiled back. "Tinka? That you?"

I nodded.

"Come here and give me a hug, girl. Stop playing with me. Alicia, Deenna, Benita . . .

this my daughter Teyona."

I hugged Ma and smiled at the women sitting on the flowery-printed 1970s-looking couch. One had thick eyeglasses with wide brown rims. She kept pushing her fake teeth in and out of her mouth with her tongue. The other two looked normal, I guess. But I knew something was wrong with them if they was up in St. E's.

"What you been up to girl?" She pushed my thigh gently.

I looked at Ma sideways. She seemed normal to me. It had been two months since the last time I came to see her . . . and then she ain't say nothing. She just cried and smiled over and over again. Maybe she was doing much better now. Maybe she was ready to come home. I smiled just thinking about us living together again.

"I been good. Real good."

"That's good. You look nice."

I smiled again. "You do, too."

She smiled. "I got a letter from Marquan this week."

"You did?"

She nodded. "He said he doing good, too."

"Oh yeah?"

She nodded. "He said, they might be sending him to Colorado, just like Mark. Maybe they gon' be near each other," she said, smiling. "He need to be close to his father."

I bit my lip and then looked down at my fingers.

"How come Taevon don't come to see me?"

My eyes beamed. Maybe Mommy remembered what happened that day. I opened my mouth to tell her that I ain't never catch up with him, but then she said, "Him and Teddy act like they don't love me no more. They don't never come see me." A tear slipped from the corner of her eye, and then she wiped it away with the back of her hand. "I get pretty for them every day and they still don't come. I don't know what else to do."

My heart broke. Mommy was still the same. I took her hand and covered it with both of mine and then I put it against my cheek. I held it close for a long time, then I kissed her hand and placed it back in her lap.

"I love you, Mommy."

She looked at me, like she was normal again, and then she said, "Tinka, I love you, too. Stop talking crazy."

I looked deep in her eyes. My mother was there. Somewhere deep inside. I looked until her eyes went back to being glassy again. Mommy wasn't the same. And she probably was never gonna be the same person who lived in that house around Sursum Cordas. It was so hard for me to see her be this new unrecognizable person. She was like a cracked picture frame. Of course, I knew it was her, but Ma was nowhere near the perfect picture I remembered. I stood up to leave. I smiled at Ma one more time before I left the room.

My plan was to go around Ms. Shelia's house later today. She had been begging me to come get some of my stuff from her house for weeks now. She said it was too crowded over there, and she needed some extra space. I knew she was telling the truth. So many people lived there. New grandkids kept popping up every time I talked to her. I don't know how she saved anything that was for me or anybody in my family.

I been putting it off for a long time. I just ain't want nothing to do with Sursum Cordas no more. There was too many memories. Good and bad. But Nine said it wasn't gonna be nothing for him to take a U-Haul around there to see what I wanted.

"It ain't like you ain't got nowhere to put your stuff anyway," he kept saying.

But it wasn't that easy. This stuff *was* my family. It was gonna hurt to see it and remember who's stuff was whose and the story that matched up with whatever it was I had to decide whether to keep or throw away. Nine told me I ain't have to throw nothing away, that he could rent me a storage, but I ain't want to keep every single memory alive. I was gonna have to be strong and pick through it, and throw stuff in the trash that wasn't pressing.

When me and Nine turned off of New Jersey Avenue down K Street, my eyes almost fell out of my head.

"Dayum . . . you see this shit?" he asked.

"Oh my God," I mumbled.

A gigantic pile of broken brown bricks filled the spot where Temple Courts used to be. A wire fence with a big white sign that said GTI in large blue letters separated the bricks from Sursum Cordas and from what used to be a building that housed so many people I knew.

"I can't believe this . . . they did it, huh?" I said.

"Damn," Nine said. "Sursum Cordas is next."

"Where all them people move to?" I asked.

Nine shook his head.

"I feel like crying."

"Me too, a little bit. I'm not even gonna fake."

411

We sat quiet in the parking lot near LaSheika's house. As I looked at her empty house with the boarded-up windows and then over at the pile of bricks in front of me, I wondered if maybe tearing it all down wasn't such a bad idea after all. There was so many sad memories I had about this block. Maybe paving over it all made more sense than I first thought.

Nine drove around the circular parking lot and then he made a right back out on to K Street. He made another right on First Street, then a right on M Street. I saw a blue trailer with GTI on front of it, parked beside Ms. Carmen's old house.

The neighborhood seemed different. I couldn't tell what it was. I ain't see nobody outside. Maybe that was it. Sursum Cordas seemed like it was dying or like it was getting dressed for a funeral. Hushed into a humble peace. It was like everybody had given up already. No more fighting with GTI, I guess.

Nine turned down First Place and stopped the U-Haul truck in front of Ms. Shelia's house. I looked over at my old house and saw the first-floor windows boarded up. It looked cold boarded up. Death was written all over it just like Teresa's burned-out house. Nothing had changed. I shook my head. Our stuff got thrown out so fast, like GTI couldn't wait to get rid of us.

We climbed out the truck and knocked on Ms. Shelia's door. I looked around the neighborhood. I smiled when I saw Ms. David's curtains swing back and forth. *Same old Ms. David being nosy like always.* I saw Teresa's kids playing with a skateboard in their front yard. As soon as the door flew open, I could smell fried fish and hear the TV blaring in the living room. A little girl laughed loud like somebody's tickling was way too much. *Same old Ms. Shelia's house, too.*

"Hey, Tinka," she said, smiling hard. " 'Bout time you brought your tail around here. Give me a hug."

I smiled and wrapped my arms around her.

"It's so good to see you. How the baby doing?" she said, squeezing me.

I squeezed her back. "It's good to see you, too, Ms. Shelia."

"Hi. How you doing?" Nine said, stepping inside.

"I'm doing fine. You taking care of my girl?" Ms. Shelia asked.

"Yes ma'am," he said.

"Good. Come on and get some food. I cooked for y'all."

"You ain't have to do that," I said.

"Girl, you got two mouths to feed."

Kayla came running from around the corner with Antonio right behind her.

"Hey, what's up?" he said.

"Hey," we both said.

I wanted to tell him how fucked up it was that he ain't make my brother come with him that day he saw him on Minnesota Avenue. That I hated him for probably getting my brother smoking them dippers in the first place. I seen the bottles of water in his room once and I knew that was the chemical stuff they dipped the cigarettes in that made people lose their minds. But I ain't say nothing. I kept my mouth shut. Antonio already knew I was pissed.

"I made macaroni and cheese and some greens, too," Ms. Shelia said from the kitchen.

Nine looked like he was starving and headed right to the kitchen. I followed him and watched Ms. Shelia stack our plates high with steaming, delicious-smelling food. Krystal, Kayla, and Van walked in and said hi not too long after we started eating. Duane, Raynard, and Sammy came running down the steps like bulls and I said what's up to everybody. They passed plates, hot sauce, and cans of soda around before everybody went to separate corners of the house.

After we ate, Ms. Shelia handed me a bag of mail.

"I've been saving this stuff for you for months. It's a lot, ain't it?" she asked, raising her eyebrows and smiling. She always seemed so jolly to me. I nodded and looked at everything in the Giant Food grocery bag.

"At first I was going through it, and letting people know your mother was sick and everything or that Teddy was deceased, but now I just let it pile up. I mean I throw out all the junk mail, but it's stuff in there I know you might want."

"Thanks, Ms. Shelia. I think I'ma open this stuff up later. Sort it out and everything."

"Oh, trust me. I understand," she said, smiling.

We spent the next couple of hours going through closets where she had Mommy's stuff stored. Important papers like our records, birth certificates, Social Security cards, and all of Marquan's court papers and everything. Then Ms. Shelia showed me a bag of my clothes she kept, even though I knew Krystal probably been digging through it already, snatching pieces she wanted.

"Krystal, you want this stuff?" I yelled up the stairs.

"Nah, not really," she said.

Exactly. Because she already took what she wanted.

Duane and Raynard helped Nine take some furniture I really ain't care to keep over to the big trash bin out back. Sammy carried a couple boxes of Marquan's and Taevon's stuff to the truck.

"I sent everything I thought was Teddy's over to his mother's. I know you ain't want to see none of that," said Ms. Shelia.

"I don't know what I would do without you, Ms. Shelia."

"Girl, y'all family. Ain't nothing else to it . . . and I'ma tell you something. If you ever feel like that little nigga you with ain't treating you right, you can come stay with me, you hear me?"

I smiled and gave her a hug. Ms. Shelia ain't have no idea that I would never sleep around Sursum Cordas again . . . not even if somebody paid me. I'm not gonna lie, there was good memories, too. The block parties, the house parties, and some of my neighbors and friends, but right now, it just hurt too much to think about being here.

"I love you, okay," she said, walking me to the door.

"I love you, too."

"Keep reading them books, and writing," she said as I walked toward the U-Haul. "Don't forget to tell me when you having your baby shower, either."

"I won't," I called over my shoulder. I climbed inside the truck and waited for Nine to close the back door and get in, too. I looked around my neighborhood one last time, at the quiet streets, and then I waved bye to Ms. Shelia.

When Nine pulled away from the curb, I saw Monte come out of his mother's house. He looked frail, like he ain't been eating or like he was on something or sick. Even though he ain't see me, I thought about telling Nine to stop the truck just so Monte could look me in my eyes for what he did to my friends. But I didn't. I watched him slip into an alley and disappear.

CHAPTER 50
TINKA

I wasn't so surprised about the two letters from Marquan stuffed inside the grocery bag filled with mail Ms. Shelia saved for me. But it was the postcards and envelope with Renee Hampton-Straus's name on it that made my heart leap in my throat. A winding, gray stone-covered street was on the front of one postcard. The other one had a stunning, stark-white church that seemed to stretch for blocks. Both was signed, "With lots of love. XOXO," with no name underneath. I guess Aunt Renee figured wasn't no way in the world we was gonna be getting postcards from somebody else in Europe.

I opened the envelope and froze when a Travelocity airline confirmation page fell out. I looked at the June 22 date printed on it before I read the letter.

Dear favorite niece,

Now she know I'm her only niece, but whatever.

Is the phone disconnected again? Nobody paying the bills, Tinka? I know you'll tell me the truth. Teddy know he need to find a job or something and help your mother out. I've been calling y'all almost every day. Hell, don't nobody miss me? Well, I miss you guys. How you know Uncle Matt ain't did something crazy to me over here? Nobody's called me in weeks.

I wiped away tears that ran down my cheeks.

I'm just teasing. Uncle Matt is doing fine. I'm fine, too. We have a gorgeous house on the base, but I try not to spend too much time in it. I'm in Italy, for God's sake! The base is just like being in America and I get sick and tired of these military wives complaining about their husbands cheating on them with these willowy, model-looking Italian women. Matt better not even think about it! But for real, I'm telling you, Tinka. If you never learn anything else in life, you have to take advantage of opportunities that you know will better your life.

I smiled. That's Aunt Renee again, always trying to tell me what the right thing was to do. I missed Mommy doing that.

Italy is so beautiful. You should see all the hills and winding roads and the buildings are so amazing, especially the churches. Seems like it's one at the end of every corner and they stretch so high to the sky, they block the sun in some places. It's remarkable.

I like to ride my bike everywhere I go. Buy fresh baked bread, pasta, and flowers, visit the museums. Oh, Tinka, they are so breathtaking. Italians really do take their art seriously here. Everywhere you go, you see chubby babies with wings painted on the walls, on the ceilings, carved into stone, in the smallest of places. It's unbelievably incredible. And they know how to enjoy life, Tinka. They eat great food. They take long naps in the middle of the day. They drink rich wine. I love it!

Uncle Matt and I are planning to visit Rome next week. I absolutely must see the Basilica. I can't wait. Europe is so different from America, sweetie. It's hard to explain it. Everything here has a fascinating story, or a war behind it. We're not used to so much history. America's a young country, so things still look new there, or the history is so recent that it don't really hit home the same way. Here . . . everything is centuries old, but strong and grand . . . Just think about it. Castles and fortresses, where Kings and Queens once ruled the land, places where great battles were fought! Tinka — you've got to see it for yourself to truly appreciate such mind-blowing grandeur.

And that's exactly why I sent you a plane ticket. Italy's a place I know will make you open your eyes and dream beyond your backyard. I don't want to hear nothing about you not being able to make it, either.

You better be doing your best in school. I'm sure you are though, because I would never do this if I thought anything less.

She was gonna kill me when she found out I had quit going.

Imagine how much this could help you with writing. You have so much raw talent, you have to come and develop your skills. Speaking of which, you need to send me some of your work. I've met a wonderful young woman named Andrea from the local university who teaches me tennis on the weekends. Anyway, she told me about a writing program that you can apply to at her school for aspiring writers. Let me slow down. There's so much to tell you. But I need to talk to you first, so call me. 013-237-991-4432. I miss my family. I miss America. Tell everybody I said hi and that I love them. I love you, too.

With lots of love,
Aunt Renee

P.S. You'll love shopping here, too. I can't wait for you to come. Make sure you don't talk yourself out of it.

A tear rolled down my cheek. She had no clue about all that had happened since she left.

Nine walked in just as I folded the letter back up.

"Here, you want some of this?" he asked, handing me his carryout plate of shrimp fried rice.

I shook my head.

"What's wrong? You crying?"

422

"Nothing."

"Tinka, man, when you gon' realize I know you like the back of my hand. What's wrong, girl?"

"It's just . . . my aunt wrote me and I miss her." I folded the letter back up to put in the envelope.

"She did? That's cool. Ain't nothing wrong with that. We can go see her if you want to. That might be what you need."

I stared at the flight confirmation ticket in my hand and nodded. "You really mean that?"

"Of course."

"She lives in Italy now and she already sent me a ticket."

"What?" he said, frowning up his face. "Italy?"

I nodded.

"She *sent* you a ticket?"

"Yeah." I showed it to him.

"Damn," he mumbled, as he read the confirmation sheet.

Nine's mood completely changed. He ate the rest of his food without saying a single word.

"Why you so quiet?" I asked after a few minutes passed.

"Ain't nothing."

"Yes, it is, Nine."

He stayed quiet and watched TV for a little while. I had more than enough to worry about in my life instead of pulling Nine's teeth for information. I reached over to the nightstand and opened up one of my journals. A long time had passed since I really wrote something from my heart down.

I scribbled a few lines before I crossed it out. I tried to write again, but nothing made sense. I scratched it out again. Maybe I can't do it no more. Maybe I lost the little bit of talent everybody thought I had, because I stopped using it. I bit my lip and closed my journal.

Nine lit up a blunt and puffed.

"Na'eem, you got twenty dollars?" his mother asked, peeking her head in the bedroom doorway.

He dug in his pocket and handed it to her. I watched her eyes light up when she reached for the money. How could he keep nursing her habit like it wasn't nothing?

"Why y'all so quiet in here?" Roxanne asked. "Look like somebody died or something."

We both stayed quiet.

"Hmmmm, whatever. I'll be back."

"So you gon' leave me?" he asked, as soon as the door closed.

"What you mean? I'm just gonna visit her."

"And what am I supposed to do here by myself?"

I was confused. What he mean, *here by hisself.* "Baby, of course, I'll be back. It ain't 'til June anyway."

He puffed quietly in the corner, then said, "How long you gon' be there?"

"I don't know, maybe a couple weeks. Why you acting like we're breaking up or something?"

Nine stayed silent while I looked through the bag of mail. There was some old bills, some papers from Ma's last job, and a letter from the District Youth Poetry Association.

"You can't be flying while you pregnant, Tinka."

I looked at him like he was crazy. "Yes I can. You sound crazy."

"Don't call me crazy, Tinka. For real."

Whatever. He was sounding crazy.

"What if I ain't want you to go?"

Why he gotta be like this? I thought as I rolled my eyes to the back of my head. "Nine, why you can't understand she's the only family I got? I haven't seen her in forever. I need to see her."

He looked like I had done something to hurt his feelings. He nodded and then took out a bag of weed. Nine was quiet while he slit the cigar skin and emptied the guts of the blunt. I went back to checking the mail while he smoked.

Junk mail, junk mail. More bills. I looked again at the large, yellow, square envelope from the District Youth Poetry Association. I had never gotten an envelope from them before that was this big. I opened it and read the letter.

Congratulations! Your poem "Forgetting" placed third in the Annual District Youth Poetry Association competition for the High School Division. You will receive a $1,000 prize and your poem will be published in our annual anthology. You are invited to come share your winning poem during our . . .

No lie. But how? I never sent them nothing. Then I smiled. It could only have been Ma.

CHAPTER 51
TINKA

A few days later, I woke up in the middle of the night feeling like somebody was standing over top of me. When my eyes focused, I saw Nine staring at me. He had been watching me sleep. Nine only slept in bits and pieces, so this wasn't the first time I woke up and he was wide awake. But he never spent his time awake watching me sleep. At least not like now. A blue glow reflected off his dark skin from the TV. He had a bottle in his hand, and Nine wasn't one to drink like that, so I was even more confused. The rich smell of weed filled the room. I reached over and grabbed my cell phone off the charger. The time said 1:53 a.m.

"Hey," I said, wiping my face with my hand. His face was completely erased of any kind of emotion. He scared me. "What's wrong?" I whispered.

He swallowed the rest of whatever was in

the bottle and said, "I don't want you to go."

I sat up on one arm. Nine held his blunt toward me.

"Nah," I said, blocking it out of my face.

He put the blunt out and sat quietly for a few minutes, then he turned toward the foot of the bed where different parts of his gun lay. I wiped sleep completely out of my eyes with my thumbs. Why did he have to clean it at this time of night for?

"Tink?"

"Huh?"

"I got this . . . sick feeling . . . in the pit of my stomach that when you leave me, you not coming back. Not here. Not to me."

I watched him as he put the gun back together.

"Na'eem, whatever. You know I'm coming back. Why you acting so paranoid about a silly trip out the country?"

"I don't want you to go. It's that simple. Promise you gonna stay with me," he said, turning toward me.

I rolled my eyes, sat up, and scooted backward so my back was pressed against the wall. I couldn't believe he was acting like this. I wished he could hear how ridiculous he sounded. "Yes, Nine! Okay! Is that what you wanna hear me say? Yes! God!"

428

"Why you got a attitude, Tinka? You the one gon' just up and take my baby all the way the fuck over there. I should be the one with the attitude! I can't take care of you all the way over there."

I sucked the back of my teeth. "Baby, you ain't gonna lose me just because I'ma go see my aunt. That's just . . . ignorant. Come on, now."

"Whatever." He stood up and walked around the bed. I couldn't believe how stressed out he looked. He walked back to me and blew out a deep breath. "You gon' get over there and realize we live in the projects and shit. That this is all we got, this rundown house and me robbing niggas to take care of us. This ain't gon' be good enough for you no more."

My heart ached for him. I loved Nine so much. I reached over and wrapped my arms around his neck and kissed him. "I'm not leaving you, Na'eem. You understand me? You been the only person in my life since all this craziness. I love you too much to just forget about what we got. You think I'm gonna take your child away from you? Move to another country and forget about what you mean to me? I'm not leaving you."

He kissed my lips and sucked them so hard that it hurt. The taste of liquor, still fresh on his breath. "You promise?"

"I promise," I said. "I'm coming back."

A doubtful look appeared in Nine's eyes I had never seen before and my chest got tight. "So you still going, huh?"

"Huh?" I said, confused. "Yeah, I'm going. Of course. Aunt Renee's the only family I got left."

His jaw clenched up like I said something wrong, but he ain't say nothing. He just nodded. I looked at him sideways. *What was his problem?* He was really being stupid right now. *Whatever.* I laid back down. He could sit there staring into space all he wanted, making up any storyline that would keep him pissed. *Don't let my snoring stop you.*

Nine was the first thing I saw when I woke up the next day. The room was unusually bright and quiet. Besides Nine's soft snoring and the eerie sound of white noise, there was complete silence. No laughter from kids playing outside, no cars driving by, no TV on from upstairs. Nine was sitting on the floor beside the bed, his head leaned against the wall, his eyes finally closed, his gun in his hand. *Was he there all night?* No, he had his shoes on.

I threw the covers off me and sat up. I

saw a pile of crumpled bills, and not one but two empty bottles of Svedka on the dresser that wasn't there before. I stepped out the bed just as Nine cleared his throat and opened his eyes.

"Where you going?" his hoarse voice asked.

"What?" I said, rolling my eyes. "To the bathroom. Why?"

"I'm going with you," he said, standing up.

"What you mean you going with me?"

"You heard me?" he said, nodding toward the door. "Go 'head if you going."

Pssst. This dude is really acting simple right now. I pulled my panties out my butt and moved around him. He was two steps behind me. "You really gonna follow me in the *bathroom,* Na'eem?"

"Just leave the door open."

"You really overdoing it right now!"

"Leave the door open."

"All this because of a stupid fucking letter!" I said, sitting on the toilet. "This is retarded!"

"Yeah, whatever."

"I can't believe this," I said, rolling my eyes. I flushed the toilet, washed my hands, washed my face, brushed my teeth — the whole time with Nine standing in the doorway watching me. He stood there with his arms across his chest.

"As much as this baby making me run back and forth to the bathroom? How long you gon' do this?"

He ain't say nothing.

I shook my head and walked to the kitchen. "I'ma make some cereal. Is that okay with you?"

He followed me into the kitchen, too.

"You want some?"

"Nah, I'm not hungry."

I shook my head and took out a bowl. "Well, I am."

Suddenly, Nine sprinted to the bathroom. *Eerrup, errup. Eeeeerrruupp!* He spent the next two minutes hurling up whatever he had been drinking before I went to sleep.

"Babe, you okay?"

"Get me some water," he mumbled.

I rushed to the kitchen, grabbed a cup, and shoved it in his hand. "This ain't even like you to drink, Nine." I rubbed his back as he swallowed.

"I made a run last night. It ain't go too good."

My eyebrows shot up. I watched him wash his face and brush his teeth wondering what he meant by that. He stared at his face in the mirror for what seemed like an hour, and then he said, "I killed somebody."

My hand flew up to my mouth.

For the next few days, Na'eem stayed up under me. Following me from one room of the house to the next. He hardly ate anything, he barely slept, and he ain't say much to me or his mother, especially after the news showed him in the gas station on Landover Road. You couldn't see Nine's face, but we knew it was him. I finally realized he had turned his cell phone completely off when Roxanne came in yelling, "Why your phone keep going straight to voice mail?!"

Nine was even more paranoid than usual. Watching me like an owl when I slept. He was making me sick to my stomach.

"You wanna leave me now, don't you?" he kept asking every time he felt like I wasn't showing him enough attention. I was getting sick of it.

He didn't tell me what happened that night, just that he needed to stay low for a while, but on the news they said a clerk was killed and his son had been shot twice during the robbery. Nine was really fucked up about it. He was acting paranoid just like how Taevon was right before that fight with Krystal and Creature after what happened to LaSheika. Every time he heard police sirens outside, he froze for a few minutes, closed his eyes, and listened to see if they were coming for him. He'd grab his gun, then peek out the window. He had me on the edge, like I was wanted, too. I felt weird knowing I knew the person who actually was responsible for the death of somebody else. I thought about what my mother must've done for Marquan's father or what Jillian did about Marquan. *Nothing.*

The few times Nine finally closed his eyes to get some rest, he woke up sweating and shaking. His cousin Clint came by the house one day to see what was up with Nine's phone. Said he had been trying to reach him for a minute. I watched from the kitchen as Nine rubbed his forehead, like he was tired of fighting the sleep he knew he needed. He looked so drained and worried. I knew there was nothing I could do to help him. Maybe Clint could put him at ease. I tried to do what I could, and all it did was create a disturbed monster around here.

The only part of their conversation I could hear was Nine say, "My money running out, son."

He was right about that. We needed some groceries bad. Carryout food was getting old, quick. He ain't give his mother money when she asked for it either. He was too suspicious of everything to leave the house. It was driving all of us insane, especially him.

"Here," Clint said, handing him some money from his pocket.

"Tinka," Nine said, "go in the room for a minute and let me talk to Clint real quick."

I took my time walking to the bedroom, hoping I'd find out more about what happened, but they waited for me to leave before they talked. I wondered if Clint had anything to do with what happened that night. Probably not, since he was out and about and not looking over his shoulder. He stayed late, smoking and drinking with Nine. I fell asleep before he left.

A couple days later, out of the clear blue sky, Nine asked me for the ticket my aunt sent me.

"Why?" I asked him.

"Just give it to me!" he snapped. "What's the big damn deal?"

Did he think he could use it or something? "Why you want it for?"

"I just wanna see it."

Psst. I reached for the letter that was in the nightstand and took out the confirmation pages for the flight. "Here."

All of sudden, Nine ripped the pages in half.

"Stop!" I yelled, trying to snatch it back from him, but he had already torn it into tiny pieces.

"You not going no-motherfucking-where!"

"Why would you do that?!" I begged to know. "Why?!"

"You not leaving this house and you not calling nobody either. I already smashed your damn phone up. All I need is for your ass to get some fucked up ideas about turning me in."

Turn him in? "You talking real foolish right now," I said, looking for something to put my clothes in. It was time for me to get the fuck up out of here. Ms. Shelia would make a place for me. I ain't have time for this shit.

"I don't trust you no more, Tinka. You ain't leaving this house."

"Nigga, you're fucking out of your mind, if you think you can make me stay in this house!" I said, jumping up.

"Sit your ass down," he said, pushing me back on the bed.

"No! Get off of me!" I shouted.

"Tinka, calm the fuck down and shut the fuck up! I'm not playing with your ass!" He slammed me on the bed. His red eyes pierced into mine. He reminded me of how

Taevon looked that night he was yelling at Krystal. I wasn't gonna let him get a chance to strangle me. I tried my hardest to sit up again, but Nine held me down tighter. "I said, calm down," he yelled.

Whatever demons he had been fighting all these nights was inside of him now. He was a different person. He had never hurt me before. I thought about my baby. He wasn't gonna hurt my baby, no matter how furious, confused, or skeptical he was. I squirmed and twisted until I finally got out of his grip. When I was free, I dashed to the living room, headed for the front door. Roxanne was walking in the house, just as I got close. Nine was right behind me.

"What is going on in here?" she asked, looking between the two of us. "Why she crying?!"

"Mind your business, Ma."

"Boy, you better remember who you talking to! Why you got that *gun?*" Her voice cracked with fear when she said *gun.*

My heart pounded a hundred beats per second. "Help me, Ms. Roxanne," I pleaded.

"She can't leave me, Ma. She can't."

My body shook as he talked. My mind scrambled. He was talking outrageous. I had to get out of here. Tears poured down my face.

"Na'eem," she said in a cool, sweet way. "Put that gun down, now. You're talking like a fool." She took a step toward him. I stood behind Ms. Roxanne. She was the only thing between me and the door.

"She mine, Ma," Nine said. "She all I got."

"Na'eem, baby, you need some fresh air. You been in this house too damn long. You talking crazy as hell. Come on. Me and you, we can go outside. Smoke a jack and calm down. Okay? You too hyped up right now."

"Nah. Me and Tinka gotta stay together."

"Na'eem?" Roxanne said, confused.

"I can't just let you leave me . . . What am I gon' do without you? You the one who keep me sane. The one who make me think about the day after tomorrow. What about me? Huh?"

I stared at him in disbelief. Who was he?

"You scaring me, Na'eem." My voice quivered when I spoke.

"I don't want us to be apart. How the fuck you gon' take my baby out of this country?" he said, just as tears filled his eyes.

"Is that what this is about?" Roxanne asked. "You leaving the country?" she asked me as she turned around.

I nodded. "Just to visit my aunt."

"She not gon' come back, Ma. I already know she not. I have no life without you.

438

Don't you see that?" he said, looking down at the gun in his hand. "I can't help it that everything around you done changed. I been trying to do the best I can to take care of us. I'm trying to be a man. Take care of my family, the way I'm supposed to. But . . . if you leave, I lose control."

"You can't hold a butterfly, Na'eem, don't you know that?" Roxanne said. "You hold it too long, you suffocate it. You hold it too tight, you crush its wings. If Tinka say she gon' come back, you gotta believe her. This girl love you."

"Nah, Ma," he said, shaking his head. "I don't believe her."

"Na'eem, you scaring me," I cried.

Roxanne blew a long breath out, before she said, "Look, son, you need to just smoke a joint and chill the hell out. You fucking with my nerves now. Matter of fact, I'ma roll one up for you."

I looked at Crazy's Crazy Mother leaving me in the room alone with her son.

"Come here, Tinka," Nine said. "I don't want you to be scared of me. I just got a lot of shit on my mind right now. Shit is hectic. Niggas looking for me. You talking about leaving me. I feel like I'm losing my mind."

He wrapped his arms around me. I sobbed on his shoulder, even though I didn't want to touch him. I felt the heavy weight of the gun against my back. I was too petrified to move.

Nine whispered in my ear, "All I need is you, man."

I sniffed back tears. Even though I was mad as hell, I wanted to forgive him and forget any of this had even happened. Maybe I could be strong for him.

Nine slept like a baby later. Something he hardly ever did. He was holding me so close, it was hard to breathe. I was afraid to get up and use the bathroom. Was he gonna kirk out all over again? I laid there staring at the shadows from the TV dancing on the wall for a while, but I had to go. I peeled his fingers off of me and wrapped them around my pillow, before I crawled out the bed.

In the hallway, Roxanne bumped into me. She was high and giddy acting. She was using the wall to keep her balance, but she was halfway down to the floor. "That was some scary-ass shit, wasn't it? My son not normal."

I helped her to the living room and sat her on the sofa.

"If I was you, I'd get the fuck up out of here, ASAP! You hear me? You need to get out of here before he wakes up. Fuck that. I know *my* son."

I looked at her, like for the first time, and realized that she knew more about Nine than I did, or maybe more than I'd ever know. She drifted off into Never Never Land and closed her eyes. What was I supposed to do? I knew he had a lot of shit with him. Night terrors, trust issues, and a dangerous way to keep money in his pocket. But I ain't never think he would threaten me or *my* life. I was different. I was about to be the mother of his first child. Nine *loved* me.

I walked in the room and watched him as he slept. His long eyelashes laid against his cheeks. His beautiful skin smooth as chaise leather. His locks fanned out across the pillow. He looked so peaceful. I knew Roxanne was right. I had to leave. I couldn't wait to see if Nine was really capable of hurting me, too. I needed to leave. If not for me, then my baby. I took a deep breath and did what I knew I had to do. I quietly packed up some of my things. I tugged open the nightstand that sometimes jammed to get my aunt's letter. It had her phone number in it so I had to grab it. She could always print off another confirmation ticket and send it to me. I stuffed it inside my bag, then I sat on the edge of the bed to put my shoes on.

A pop sound pierced the air and exploded against the wall in front of me. I jumped and ducked down to the floor. Another gunshot exploded on the other side of me. I swallowed the scream that was stuck in my throat. My heart pumped faster than I ever felt it before. I crouched between the dresser and the baby bassinet.

"Bitch, I told you, you can't leave me, and your ass in here packing your shit!"

"Please, Na'eem!" I screamed.

Short, hard breaths poured out my mouth. He climbed out the bed and stood right over top of me. My body was shaking. Tears crawled down my cheeks. *Why didn't I listen?*

"You was really gonna fucking leave me, huh?"

My mouth was cotton. I couldn't say a word. He sat on the floor next to me. Sweat drops dripped down his face.

"Why you making me do this?" he asked.

I glanced at his nine millimeter and knew for the first time that Na'eem was really willing to take my life before he ever let me go out of his sight. That thought frightened me more than everything else. And this was a man I loved.

We sat there for a long, quiet moment, before he took my chin with his free hand

and kissed me forcefully. "I love you, Teyona. I ain't never loved nobody as much as I love you."

"What about the baby?" I whispered.

"I'ma take care of all of us."

He wiped my tears with the nose of his gun. The searing heat singed my cheeks and I flinched away from him. I closed my eyes and waited for whatever was gonna happen next.

"You ain't gotta cry, Tinka Bell. I'll do you first, then . . . I'ma do me. We'll all be together."

"No, Na'eem! No! Please, God. No!" I screamed loud enough to wake up the whole neighborhood. A soul-piercing cry that uncaged a spirit in me I never knew existed. I wrestled with Nine, fighting with all my might. Thoughts of my family raced in my head. I thought about everything I been through, and all the chaos at every turn. I couldn't let go. I couldn't give up. I couldn't let him end what was only just beginning. Suddenly, Na'eem stopped fighting and looked at me with a deep sadness in his eyes. A sadness I knew would never disappear, no matter how much I loved him.

"I thought being with you would make me be different. Better even. But I am . . . who I am. You are who you are. And you ain't supposed to be with a nigga like me. Ma's right. I'm holding you back."

I sniffled and wiped away tears. He wiped away my tears with his free hand.

"I'm sorry, Tinka," he said, before pointing the gun under his chin and squeezing the trigger.

EPILOGUE:
TINKA

I stared out the little window at the bright, puffy white clouds floating in the sky and wondered if those exact same clouds had drifted across the ocean from America first. I wondered if Mommy saw those clouds when she looked out her window this morning, or if Ms. Shelia saw them in Sursum Cordas. I wondered if Marquan saw them when he looked out his window in Colorado. Maybe Taevon was looking up at the clouds, wherever he was and thinking about one of us. I thought about the day in Hains Point park, when me and Nine watched planes take off from the airport. Way back in the beginning. Back when everything was still sweet and easy and romantic. I never imagined I would be on one and he wouldn't be here with me.

"We will be departing the plane in approximately two minutes," the flight attendant said with a thick Italian accent, breaking my thoughts. I reread the letter Mommy gave me all those years ago for my birthday:

Tinka, I may not be able to give you the world like your Aunt tries to, and the way your father should be doing, but as long as you keep your head in them books you'll be able to see the world for yourself one day. Take plenty of pictures for me when you do. Happy Birthday!

Love,
Mommy & Teddy

"Do you need help with your overhead bags?" the flight attendant asked.

I shook my head as she went to the next person behind me.

I had that old letter tucked inside the letter I recently got from Marquan. I reread the last lines of his letter again as I waited to get off the plane.

I am so proud of you for doing what I couldn't. You had the courage to do something new and nothing like what nobody else around you was doing. I don't know why I'm acting so surprised, because you always been that kind of girl, even when you was reading all them books and everybody else was out in the streets fucking around with their life. I always admired that about you. I know Mommy proud, too. She just got a new way of showing it now. I miss you, Tinka. Make sure you send me some pictures and postcards from Italy and the next chapter of that book you writing.

Love,
Marquan

I still needed to finish school. After all the drama in my life, wasn't no way I could focus on school work. Aunt Renee gonna have a fit when I climb off the plane with my five-month-old baby bump and no high school diploma, but she's always been there for me when I needed her. She'll help me get my life together. I know she'll understand, somehow. I still had to tell her the whole story about Ma, Taevon, and Teddy.

I folded Marquan's letter up and tucked it back inside my journal. He was doing life in Colorado. We took turns trying to keep each other's heads up. So much had happened in such a short time. Too many people around me was dying or getting locked up left and right. I had to leave. I needed a new start. Na'eem was special to me. For the life of me, I wished it didn't end the way it did.

There are nights I wake up three or four times just to stop the nightmare of what he did from playing in my head. I tell myself it's not my fault. I know in my heart, it's not. I couldn't control him or nothing around me. He wanted to control me and that's not who I am. I control me and my destiny. I also control the things I can change. The things I can't, well . . . I'd just have to learn to let it go. The things that wracked Na'eem's mind drove him crazy. I rubbed my small belly and thought about what I was gonna have to teach our daughter, Phoenix, about life. Ever since I found out I was having a girl, I knew I was gonna name her that. I'd never forget that myth I read, about the bird that rose from ashes. There would be so much to teach her, like what her name meant and why she should never give up or stand still. Hopefully, the cycle that I was trying to break will stop with her.

I took the cap off of my ink pen and wrote: *Italy today. Tomorrow Paris!*

READING GROUP GUIDE
DISCUSSION QUESTIONS

1. Single mothers are often faced with the difficult challenge of making tough decisions for the stability and the endurance of their families. What choices do you think Nicola made that both hurt and helped her family the most? What choices should she have made to solve some of the problems she faced?
2. Why do you think Nicola initially allowed Teddy back into her life, knowing his history and his checkered past? Should she have considered Tinka's feelings?
3. Is it common for women to compromise their relationships with their children for the men they date?
4. Did Teddy's presence negatively affect Tinka? If so, how?
5. Do you agree with Tinka that her mother showed favoritism toward her brothers Marquan and Taevon? If so, was it justified? Why or why not?

6. Are women generally harder on their daughters than on their sons, or is this disparity seen more with single mothers? Do you think single fathers are tougher on their sons than married fathers?
7. How much of a difference would it have made if Marquan's father, Mark, was around in his life? What about Tinka's father?
8. Should Renee have been more involved with helping her sister, Nicola, since she had more? Compare and contrast Nicola's best friend Shelia to Renee.
9. Low-income housing neighborhoods are rapidly being eliminated in urban centers across the country in exchange for expensive town houses and condos, breaking up communities, leaving impoverished people with nowhere to live, and even separating entire families. Do you agree that these changes are necessary?
10. Why did Tinka fall for Nine? In what ways did he add to Tinka's life? Did she make the right choice concerning her future?